Beloved Mother, Queen of the Night

by the same author:

Flute

Shona Ramaya
Beloved Mother,
Queen of the Night

First published in Great Britain in 1993 by
Martin Secker & Warburg Limited,
an imprint of Reed Consumer Books Limited,
Michelin House, 81 Fulham Road, London SW3 6RB
and Auckland, Melbourne, Singapore and Toronto

Copyright © 1993 by Shona Ramaya
The author has asserted her moral rights

A CIP catalogue record for this book
is available from the British Library
ISBN 0 436 40408 7✓

Typeset in 12/15 Perpetua
by Deltatype Ltd, Ellesmere Port, Wirral
Printed and bound in Great Britain by
Mackays of Chatham PLC

Acknowledgements

For their generous help and support, I'd like to thank Raghu, Tula, Dympna and Becky; for their invaluable critiques, Michael Martone, Antonio DiRenzo, Bob Gates, Susan Thornton, Safiya Henderson-Holmes, Mary Elsie Robertson and Sally Daniels. I'd also like to thank my editor, Dan Franklin, who has been most understanding; and Vicki Harris, the copy editor, was a pleasure to work with.

But most of all, I want to thank Toby Eady, my agent, who materialised six years back quite like the mythic genie, and ever since has been, simply, wonderful.

What concerns me is not the way things are, but rather the way people *think* they are.

Epicetus

Contents

Gopal's Kitchen

I sat at the table and blinked a few times. Eggs, orange juice, my mother, my brother, the servants, the smell of warm, thick date syrup over toast, all shimmered like apparitions. 'Eat something . . .' My mother's voice was far, far away, weakly penetrating the dense fog squeezing my head. 'You can go back to sleep . . . sleep your jet lag off . . . this is what happens when you make seventeen-hour flights once in six years . . .' Scrambled eggs. A delicate hint of coconut and almonds, silken against my tongue. 'Rajiv Gandhi assassinated . . . Tamil Tigers . . . God knows what kind of riots will start . . . Floods, prices going up . . . Who's to take over . . .' Eggs melt in my mouth with that blend of secret spices only he knew – I dropped the fork and stood up startled, the grogginess vanishing for a few seconds, swept away by a roaring storm of light.

'Who made the eggs?'

'Don't scream so.' My mother pushed me back into the chair.

'Namaste, didi,' I heard from the kitchen door.

'Gyan,' said my mother. 'Taken over, two years now.'

He stood against the doorframe, bowing his head slightly, clasping his hands against his chest. His white kurta had a few turmeric stains. He shifted his weight from one foot to the other, smiled, touched his forehead. I nodded. He nodded back, swinging his lank, straight hair that fell across his eyes. There was something very gentle and calm in his face and about his slight form.

'Who's he?' I muttered under my breath.

'He's the one,' my mother answered, touching my shoulder. She let out a nervous giggle. 'He's the one – the one – he got the kidney.'

The fog coiled around my head, making me gasp. At the centre of its steely haze, I saw a fresh green coconut.

Gopal's kidney. I lay on my bed and looked around the room I had abandoned eight years earlier. Rajiv blown up the night I landed in Delhi. 'India is finished,' my brother said. 'There's a strange calm all around, like a lull before a storm.' Just like that day, years back, coming back from school I heard my mother's shocked voice, 'How could you?' And Gopal, bowing his head, asking her to keep it down, not to tell the children. That long scar across his back. But his face calm, a tired calm, in spite of it all.

My room had a petrified calmness about it this afternoon. Eight years ago it used to look like a hurricane had ripped through it. Clothes, books, shoes, cassettes scattered in heaps all around. Posters of twisted agonised faces and bodies screaming silent messages of chaos. Plants, half-collapsed from lack of water, lying limp in pots as if ready to give up the ghost any second.

The books, the posters, the plants were all still there. The bed was in the same old place by the windows. My desk next to it, then the dressers. The rug had been cleaned and the reds and blues glowed bright. The paisleys on the rug turned into little kidneys from time to time as I stared at them. They turned green for a second, altered shape, became green coconuts. I wiped the coconuts off with one strong blink. Paisleys, kidneys.

4

So he had it now. Gopal's kidney. Gyan, then, was the murderer. And here he was, how, why, bringing forth those exquisite, Gopal's special, scrambled eggs.

For the next few days, lunches and dinners were raging storms of food. Gyan overwhelmed the table with Gopal's special lamb chops, chicken korma, biryani, all the different vegetable and fish concoctions, and the fabulous desserts that Gopal had been famous for. I chewed and swallowed cautiously, every mouthful a cyclone of flavours. Curling shrimp quivered at the end of my fork as if ready to explode. We ate, smiling, cracking jokes, bursting out laughing. '*Tatva-gyan*,' my brother said to Gyan, 'hey, Enlightenment, get more rice, *yaar*.' Gyan, quiet, shy, withdrawing, smiled and vanished into the kitchen. He didn't have Gopal's garrulous charm, his effusiveness. 'I don't understand,' I said to my mother and father. They smiled, shrugged.

'Well, it's sort of this way,' my mother said. 'He appeared just after Holi two years back. Said he could cook and wanted to work. Of course, I was wary at first. You know, he had never worked anywhere before, he said. There was no one I could call to enquire about him. And he refused, just flatly refused, to tell us where he was from. He begged for a trial run. So I let him cook for a day. Well, that was that. When we sat down to eat, we nearly passed out with amazement. Gopal's egg korma! Gopal's shrimp curry!'

'We found out about the kidney business almost a year later,' my father said.

'The *mali* found out and told me,' my mother added.

'How is it you didn't choke on the kormas and curries,' I asked, 'knowing that Gopal died of kidney failure four years ago?'

'But the food, sis,' my brother rolled his eyes, 'made us lose it – just swoon. Hey, A-gyan, rice!' 'Unconscious', my brother called him, heaping rice on to his plate.

5

'What are we eating here?' I asked weakly, in spite of wanting to scream.

'Just delicious,' my brother drawled, a snarl of a smile expanding across his face. 'Let the taste seduce you.'

The persisting jet lag ushered me clumsily back to my room half an hour after lunch on the fourth day at home. 'Sleep it off,' my mother said, poking her head into my room.

'Close the door,' I snapped.

'Don't go raiding the kitchen in a couple of hours, now that your jet lag is wearing off and you seem to be getting into your old routine. Ring that bell next to the bed if you want a snack.' Her head withdrew and the door closed. I regarded the gleaming white button above the headboard with surprise. Hadn't noticed it before. My room wasn't the same then. They had interfered with its internal mess. Establishing civilised communication. Or was it concern? I hadn't entered the kitchen yet, since I'd been back. The kitchen used to be my favourite haunt – when Gopal was there.

How to re-enter that kitchen now? To sit in that familiar spot in front of the windows, three yards from the stove.

Gopal in his starched white *kurta* and white cotton trousers, tossing glittering spices into pots and pans which sizzled and smoked like magic cauldrons. His slender hands flying around, snatching a pinch of this, a dash of that, and the smells changing from one delicious aroma to another.

The hot kitchen would become an enchanted cave, full of curling smoke rising from shining vessels, startling your eyes with sparkling cascades of spices, oils, herbs, fascinating your nose with a thousand aromas. You breathed in deeply, coughing, choking, laughing as if breathing in new life, awakening to a higher consciousness. Gopal looked at you quizzically through the

6

glistening haze of smoke and steam as nature metamorphosed to art in a saucepan. Flames texturised flesh.

And through that kitchen window, through the mingling sounds and smells of food, spices, clothes and dishes being washed, detergent, mangoes, sandalwood incense, crows and sparrows fighting over spilt garbage, through the glittering magenta bougainvillaea, the flame-hot turquoise dazzle of the Delhi sky became a stunning, hurting, mystifying brightness. Gyan – what about Gyan? What kind of enlightenment from a kidney?

'I will run away, if you don't tell my why,' I had screamed at Gopal.

'You can run away,' Gopal had said, 'but it runs along with you.' That long, wry smile. 'Come sit,' he'd say, as my mother and father left for work. 'Come sit here on this stool and let me tell you . . .'

But all of a sudden, I couldn't remember a thing. So many stories – I knew them all. They refused to surface. My mind was disobeying in the most hateful manner, swimming and blurring, my eyes closing in spite of my need to see, hear, remember. My body was not mine any more, it seemed. Something else was interfering, making it give in, give in, lose –

'For you.'

A smell of chicken and spice and lemon. I rubbed my eyes and rolled over towards the smell. A plate of sandwiches on a tray. Six wafer-thin two-inch triangles of white bread. The very special – 'Masala chicken sandwiches. I know you get hungry at this time – three-thirty.' The sandwiches had spoken.

I shook my head and looked up. Gyan, smiling shyly.

'What the hell are you doing in my room?'

'I knocked,' Gyan said, his eyes apologetic. 'I didn't want you to wake up hungry and then not feel good about going to the kitchen.'

I blinked at the sandwiches. Damn it, I was hungry. I always got hungry around this time. But these sandwiches? 'Who told you about these?' I asked, anger spiking my voice higher. 'How dare you come here, to work here, you're the cause of his death –'

'Gopal would have never said that.' Gyan cut me off, his voice calm, soft.

'Why not? How do you know?'

'I have to go make tea now.'

I separated the compressed pieces of bread and stared at the meat. Lifting one open triangle of bread, I bit into it cautiously. That same flavour. I ate the sandwiches slowly, chewing carefully so that nothing escaped down my throat, missing my teeth and tongue. I ate each piece reverently, with eyes closed, with the acute concentration of a yogi meditating, as if each of those neat triangles contained some hermetically sealed knowledge that could only be transfused through internal membranes, osmosis, blood.

The kitchen waited.

The corridors, rooms, stairs, all so quiet, darkened and cooled with thick drapes, unobtrusive air-conditioning, and everyone lulled to sleep with its low, languorous hum. The kitchen has remained frozen. That same stool under the counter, that same stunning light through the window. I pulled the stool to the window and sat down.

Gyan enters through the back door. 'Tea?' he asks, a smiling enquiry in his sharp dark eyes, 'coffee?' I shake my head. 'Idiots,' he says softly, 'asking Sonia Gandhi to take over. Of course she refused. Don't know which way we're heading any more. Tea?' I want to ask him about himself. I want to know, desperately, how

8

and where he learnt to cook like Gopal. From Gopal, he said. I bite my lips in frustration. What words will I use? My curiosity metamorphoses to angst.

'I won't be here long.' Gyan turns from the stove.

'Oh?'

'I'm not really a servant. Wasn't born one.'

'I see.' I look at him in utter bewilderment. So some are born servants, then.

'Gopal wasn't born a servant,' Gyan adds.

'How does it feel, then?' I asked, 'to cook here when you're not one of them?'

'Good.' He nods his head vigorously. 'But now it's nearly time to leave. Make some money, marry.'

'Win a lottery or something?' How else do you make sudden money? Inheritance, bank robbery . . .

'Oh, no.' Gyan waves a knowing hand. 'All that's wishful thinking. Will it happen, will it happen? Not that. I'm getting eighty thousand rupees. I'm going to donate a cornea.'

He pronounced it slowly since it was an English word and a very alien one: c-o-r-n-e-a.

Why, why, why? I had railed at Gopal. Why did you do it?

He's given, donated, oh, God, sold a kidney! My mother gasping in the living room.

Why? I had asked, sitting right over here. Gopal had smiled at me, shaking his head to say Don't worry, I'm fine. 'Why did you?' I persisted.

'Sometimes, you have to do certain things,' Gopal said, a tired look coming over his face.

'What things?'

'Tch – tch.' He poured the eggs into a frying pan on the stove and began to add his mysterious ingredients. 'Want to see my scar?' He lifted his white shirt and turned his side to me. A dark jagged line – more than a foot long – ran diagonally from the middle of his back and disappeared under his trouser waist. Someone had tried to slice Gopal in half with a huge battleaxe, I felt, with one massive crescent sweep. I could see that he had lost weight. His ribs showed, and his shoulders had lost their bulk. He had developed a slight stoop, which deepened the look of tiredness about him.

'You shouldn't have,' I said. 'It's wrong. Whoever asked you for your kidney should be shot. What'll you do if something happens to your other –' I started to cry. 'How will you ever buy it back?'

'You can't buy it back twice,' Gopal said, a faraway look coming into his eyes while he scooped the eggs on to a plate, added sautéed tomatoes and pieces of toast, and gave it to me. 'I feel like I've paid back.'

'Paid back what?' I set the plate down on the floor. 'You tell me now, or I'll run away.' He put the plate back in my hand.

'Go to the table and eat.'

Gopal was not going to talk. As the eggs and toast slid down to my stomach, a dull, desolate, wrenching curiosity squeezed upwards to my throat. 'I won't eat,' I said, pushing the plate away. 'If you don't tell me, I won't eat ever, anything you make.'

Gopal came out of the kitchen. He had that long wry smile on his face again. 'When you're hungry enough, you'll eat,' he said. 'Then you'll eat all right.'

'Neither tea or coffee? Yet I know you like both.'

'Where is that kidney exactly?' I ask, staring at Gyan's middle.

'Oh, right here.' Gyan lifts his shirt, lowers his trousers slightly to reveal a four-inch scar near his left hipbone. 'Right in here.' He pats the scar. I look at the scar, narrowing my eyes. Gopal's kidney – right there. A pelvic kidney. Dislocated so completely – could it turn into an ovary through this relocation?

Gyan fills the kettle, puts it on the stove. He slices a rum cake, makes delicate cucumber sandwiches. 'I understand,' he says, concentrating on the bread, butter and cucumber slices, 'how you must feel. Gopal told me a lot about you, all of you.'

'You knew Gopal!' I clench my fists slowly and try to contain something that wants to implode inside me.

'He told me not to tell anyone but you.'

'What –' A storm of blinding light breaks inside my head.

'I was going to die,' Gyan said. 'I was resigned to my fate. But my father wasn't. I was the only son, you see, and he wanted me to take over his business. My father searched all over Murshidabad and around for a kidney donor, and after several months Gopal came forward.'

'Did you meet him, before – ?'

'No. But I felt this need to meet him later. My father wouldn't tell me who it was. So I bribed the doctor who had performed the operation, and got the information. I met Gopal three years after he returned to his village. I was drawn to him in a way I can't explain. I forgot everything.' Gyan paused, turned from the sandwiches. His eyes became unfocused, haunted. 'I told my father I didn't want anything to do with his business, that I didn't want to stay with him, or my mother. They were like monsters all of a sudden, disgusting, greedy, unscrupulous monsters. Poison.' He stopped again, shut his eyes tightly for a few seconds. 'I found Gopal in his paddy-field. I worked with him, lived with him. I felt happy, happy like I had never been before.'

'Where were you when Gopal died?'

'Why, right beside him.'

'And you didn't –'

'He wouldn't let me take him to Calcutta, to a hospital. I

11

pleaded, yelled. He was adamant. He kept saying It's time, it's time, something about scorching ash. I didn't know what to do except cook for him, take care of him. It was terrible – being there, unable to do anything, not allowed to help –' Gyan covered his face. 'It was my hell –'

It had surely broken loose on that afternoon – yes, that dazzling afternoon, returning now with its crystal clarity. I was sixteen then, and Gopal had gone to his village on his yearly leave. But that year he went home for three months instead of one. He said he needed the extra time, but wouldn't tell us why. I returned from school in the most joyous spirit the day he was supposed to come back. I knew he'd open the door as I ran down the drive. Our ayah opened the door and I heard agitated voices inside.

'How could you have done this?' my mother was saying to Gopal. She struck her forehead with her hand. 'How could you? What are we going to do?'

Gopal raised his hand and shushed her as I entered. He looked tired. I'd never seen him look so tired before, or so dejected. 'What's wrong?' I asked.

'Don't –' he said to my mother.

'Don't what?' my mother said, in an angry whining voice as if she was at the point of tears. 'It's you who shouldn't have. Oh, God, he's given away a kidney, given, sold, why, you idiot?'

'What kidney?' I asked, blinking rapidly as if a star was going supernova against my face.

Was he going to die? Was he then not the same any more, one kidney less? Gopal not the same any more. Not special any more?

'He told me about all of you,' Gyan continues. 'He loved you people like his own family. You *were* his family. He whispered recipes to me, recipes he created for you, and I sat near him with

12

my eyes closed, a disciple before his guru, absorbing mantras. I know what Gopal meant to all of you, especially you. I felt I took him away from your lives, even destroyed his. Gopal was special; God, I know Gopal was special.'

'Do you? I wonder.' I turned to face the window.

Gopal started working at our house long before my brother and I were born. Gopal was eighteen then. An old *khansama* had brought him to my mother because she had been looking for a cook. Gopal was with us for more than thirty-five years.

Gopal made sure we got to school on time, all fed and dressed, scolding our ayahs, my mother, checking our schoolbags to see if we had all our books, notebooks, pens and pencils, sandwiches. Had our shoes been polished till we could see our faces? Was my hair braided just right? Was my brother's tie quite straight, his laces tied . . . Our ayahs never lasted more than one or two years under Gopal's taxing reign. 'They are not good enough,' he'd snap at my mother, lifting his chin.

His imperiousness always made me squeal with laughter. Gopal looked so odd when he lifted his chin that way. He was somewhat awkwardly put together. He was of medium height; judging by the size of his head and his face, he should have been a small person. But he had big shoulders and a barrel-shaped torso. His arms and legs were strong, muscular, but his hands and feet were small, slender. He had a narrow face with a long aquiline nose, and a trim moustache. He wore his wavy black hair short and swept back from his domed forehead. His long thin throat seemed at odds with his powerful shoulders. So when he threw his head back, lifting his chin in contempt, the rest of his body didn't seem to comply. But in spite of this slight ungainliness, there was something incredibly regal about Gopal, and all the servants from the neighbouring houses, the *malis*, the dhobis, all treated Gopal with a certain reverence, as if he was someone special. I even saw our dhobi touch Gopal's feet once. 'Why did he do that?' I asked our present ayah. 'For a blessing,' she said to me. 'Gopal has a special life.' I asked her what she meant, but she wouldn't explain. She shook her head vigorously, and touched her own forehead.

So there was something special about Gopal, I realised. Something secret, unknowable, imperious, mysterious, that made all others pay attention, obey, including my mother. My father never raised his voice before Gopal or repeated a request. But then Gopal was quite irreproachable. He ran the house like clockwork so that my parents could lead their own lives, forget about us, and not worry about the menu or the state of the house when corporate hot-shots came to dinner. My aunt decided to bring up my brother the right way; she whisked him away to her house two or three days a week. That left me on a stool in the kitchen while Gopal worked.

He was special, all the servants said. He had never married. My aunt said he was continuously having affairs with our friends' ayahs. Murderous husbands would appear with axes, she told my mother. But no rolling-eyed, foaming-mouthed husbands ever turned up flailing axes. Instead, I saw some of them bow their heads as they passed Gopal on the street. That small fine head and the barrel body, and the contemptuous lift of the chin.

He told me how weavers worked their looms, how they wove into their cloth stories of angry river gods sweeping away villages; resolute parents dragging their children back from the underworld; men and women leaping into pyres to burn away their weak flesh, to be reborn as invulnerable beings with glittering eyes. I learnt how cocooned silkworms were gathered from mulberry bushes, boiled, the silk unravelled, spun. Climbing up date palms, slashing the trunks, tying buckets under the cut to

14

gather the juice, and so sweet the stolen juice, so sweet with bread, so sweet off sticky fingers. Gopal's eyes glistened as he talked, as he unveiled the thrill of sneaking out of windows of mansions, scrambling over walls, up mango trees. Oh, to become orange-yellow with mango-juice, stained purple from *jamun*. Then the thrashings would follow, and defiant laughter. 'Your childhood?' I asked him, wonder making me whisper. Gopal smiled, looked out at the burning June sky. 'Has she eaten?' my mother asked from somewhere. 'She ought to get out of her school clothes.'

'You don't have to tell me,' he said to her, turning from the window.

'Gopal-da', we called him. 'Da' for older brother. But I meant father, I think. When he took his yearly leave – a month – to visit his village near Murshidabad, a small town north of Calcutta, I used to roll on the floor and howl. 'Take me with you, don't go, take me with you.' I was a kid then. After I was twelve, I simply stayed at a friend's while he packed his bags and took his leave.

'So I will make this money and leave, and I will have a happy life.' Gyan looks defiantly at the sandwiches.

'A happy life?'

'Yes. I found out the secret to it at the blood bank. I was waiting with a friend who was there to donate blood, and this man came up to us . . .'

Nightmare – I rub my eyes. Were we returning again to the beginning of the farce?

'One of his kidneys!' My father ripped his tie off and struck the bed with it. He made frantic phone calls to doctors and urologists that evening. 'They're all doing it,' he said to my mother, looking aghast. 'For money, for happier lives! The whole damn country.'

15

'Call my brother,' my mother said to him. So our uncle, the surgeon, was called after midnight.

'Why do they all say it's OK?' my father yelled at his brother-in-law. 'It's not OK, thirty thousand or not, it's definitely not OK, and it wasn't a relative either, some damn contractor's son!'

'Why didn't you give Gopal-da the money if he needed it?' I screamed at my father. He held the receiver away and turned to me with a scowl.

'Where do you get the idea that I can make donations of thirty thousand at the snap of your fingers?'

'You should have tried – if Gopal-da can give away a kidney, why can't –' My father stopped me with a glare.

'Is Gopal capable of any housework on one kidney?' he asked our uncle, just as he had asked all the other doctors that night. 'Can he lift bags, cook, take care of things as before?' Apparently, my uncle informed us, Gopal was fully functional. 'This should be completely illegal,' my father was saying, 'why isn't it?'

It was all voluntary, my uncle confirmed. Dialysis is expensive, uncomfortable, and if someone is willing to donate a kidney and there are so many who need, really need kidneys, and have the precious money to buy, could a doctor say no, he or she wouldn't do this?

'But there is an international ban on selling organs from live donors.'

Not in India, we learnt. People come from all over the world to certain hospitals to get kidneys. Alas, my uncle himself had done such transfers, fifty-seven to date, and prescribed tons of immuno-suppressant drugs for the recipients so that their bodies didn't reject the shiny new thirty-thousand-rupee kidneys. 'You criminal!' my father shouted into the receiver.

He was over-reacting, my uncle said to my father. A kidney is

16

nothing. People are selling corneas, skin, even one eye sometimes, if both are perfect. People in the villages need money, and a lot of people in the cities will die without kidney transplants.

At two in the morning Dad called the Deputy Commissioner of Police – an old schoolfriend of his. We found out that organ-selling was going on like any other trade, selling potatoes, say, or like donating blood. Indeed, blood donors were often proposi-tioned by middle-men regarding further, more lucrative dona-tions. The police were never able to make any arrests, because nobody complained or reported or testified. 'Well, I'll testify,' my father said. 'I'm going to go donate blood, and if anybody propositions me, I'm going to drag him to the police station – no, to your office.'

'Can you guys shut up,' my brother was groaning from his room, 'I can't sleep.'

'But can Gopal still cook those wonderful meals?' my mother sighed. 'Can he still take care of the house, move furniture, lift heavy things?'

'How can you be worrying if he can manage *your* life?' I yelled, bursting into tears. 'He's had a major operation. We don't even know if he'll live or die – what if his other kidney fails? – Why can't you kill the surgeon who removed Gopal-da's kidney?'

'I will, too,' my father said firmly. 'And the damn contractor and his son who got the kidney.'

Next morning – thank God, we didn't have school because one of our teachers had been crushed by a school bus – my father put aside his ad campaigns, although my mother left for her Rotary Club meeting, and announced he was ready for the bastards at the blood bank, that he had a master-plan. He would go to a clinic to donate blood; if anyone solicited him, he would throw a half-nelson and grab the scoundrel, and drag him off to his police

17

commissioner friend's office. My brother and I accompanied him for this adventure, not because we thought anything was going to come of it, but simply because we wanted to see how our willowy father in his silk suit would get anyone in a half-nelson. I needn't add that he was terrified of needles. A journalist friend of his told him about a certain clinic in south Delhi which had a shady reputation – many people had been propositioned there and had made small fortunes in the bargain. On the way to the clinic we repeated about a thousand times that the nurses usually manage to get a needle into a vein after ten to fifteen jabs. The drive over was jerky. The car stalled five times.

The line of blood donors stretched a quarter-mile outside the clinic. Farmers from villages just outside Delhi, office clerks, college students, government officials, all stood in the hazy, humid September heat, wiping thier faces, spitting out chewed *paan*, smoking, chatting, cursing government policies. Looking at the irritated, sweaty faces all around, I ran Gopal's words inside my head: If you're hungry enough, you'll eat all right. Why were all these people really here? Did they all want to make small fortunes through a simple, horrifying trade? To make ends meet – No, I don't think that's what Gopal meant. We ushered Dad to the end of the queue. 'I hate standing in lines,' he said, making a face. 'Why are they staring at me?' People were staring at him. Nobody went to a clinic to donate blood dressed in a silk suit. And people who wore silk suits and managed ad campaigns didn't bother donating blood.

We reached the clinic entrance after an hour and a half. Dad had removed his jacket and tie, handed them to us, and rolled up his shirtsleeves. Shortly, we entered the lobby and a nurse handed us some forms. We helped Dad fill out his, and turned the forms in to the man sitting at a counter marked REGISTRATION. Then

18

we stood in another line outside a large room in which people lay on beds hooked to bottles. Dad turned pale at the sight of the redness filling up the bottles. 'Why hasn't anyone propositioned me yet?' he asked, his voice shaking a little.

'You haven't donated blood yet,' we said. 'The organ brokers usually hang out at the back, like your journalist said. They find out the blood types and all that and then they choose their guys.'

'Then I've been waiting in the wrong line!'

'No. You'll be in that line soon, on the way out, after you've donated blood.'

'But I don't really – I mean, I came here so that – I mean, I want to go – let's go out that way. If I hang around at the back of the clinic long enough someone is sure to come up to me. I look quite clean and healthy.'

Since Dad's voice had cracked to falsetto and his silk shirt was drenched and sticking to him, we ushered him out. We stood in the back alley and watched people walk out slowly. 'Look!' my brother said suddenly, his voice excited. A man of about forty, dressed in drab brown clothes, had taken a man and a woman aside. The couple was definitely from a nearby village, judging from their clothes and dialect. The three were whispering under a tree. The man and the woman shook their heads negatively. 'Got him!' Dad said, and shot forward before we could stop him. He grabbed the man's arm and turned him around. 'What is it this time? A kidney? Two? An eye?' The man in brown freed his arm with a jerk, pushed Dad hard, toppling him to the ground, ran down the alley and vanished around the corner. My brother ran after the man, and I, to help Dad up, dust his clothes. The man and the woman huddled against the tree. 'What did that man say to you?' I asked them. They shook their heads.

'We don't know,' they said. 'We must go or we'll miss the bus.' They moved backwards, the woman pulling her sari over her face, the man half covering his face with one hand. 'We must go.' They shuffled backwards down the alley, looking furtively at us, a slow desperation filling their eyes.

My brother returned, panting. 'He got into a taxi and –' He shrugged and turned his palms upwards. 'I tried.' Dad was still gasping from shock. 'I don't understand,' he said twice. 'Something's changed beyond – beyond –' He smoothed his hair gingerly.

We drove back home, taking the most secluded of roads. 'I'm speechless,' Dad said, sitting down heavily on a couch, and asked Gopal for a double Scotch.

'Life changed then, completely, beyond my – beyond my –' Gyan lets out a sigh. 'But this time I'll change things. Life will be in my hands.' He places a frying pan full of cocktail sausages on the stove. 'Life can be happy. You have to know what to do. Know the right secret.'

To know the secret. Years passed, I got out of high school, got into college, my brother made it to tenth grade without failing any exams, our parents continued to throw their dazzling parties, and Gopal-da managed everything as before, imperiously lifting his chin as and when required. But his hands moved more slowly, his eyes seemed weary, and his shoulders stooped. Everything was pretty much as before, except for one difference: Gopal didn't take his home leave for two years. I spent less time in the kitchen and more afternoons with new-found college friends. But that dull, twisting curiosity about Gopal's kidney refused to subside.

Summer holidays brought me back to my stool in the kitchen, to Gopal's stories about his village. I asked him if his staying away from his village had anything to do with his kidney, but he refused to talk about that. 'Was it just the money? Just tell me that,' I implored. 'Please, please. I won't tell, keep it a secret till I die, I swear.'

'No,' he said gently. 'Not just that.'

I lay in bed at night, my mind wild, racing two hundred miles a second, painting various scenarios in my head: Gopal wanted to save a long-lost love; some woman he could never have; now united through this kidney. Perhaps it was for an illegitimate child somewhere; perhaps he had left this woman, and now, guilt-ridden, he returned to save their child. Why did he not visit his village any more? Questions whirled hurricane-like, crashed, scattered. Dad tried to track down the doctor who had performed the operation; but without any information about where it had taken place – Gopal wouldn't say – he got nowhere. He gave up.

The summer following my BA exams, Gopal announced that he wanted to visit his village. After five years! Two days before he left I sat in the kitchen and watched him prepare dinner. Once more in this cave of marvellous transformations. Wrapped again in the seductive smoke of this different planet. Here, anything could happen, here, in this world of continual metamorphosis. Here, goats that destroyed spinach fields lay sizzling in strips with chopped spinach in incredible, delicious harmony. A shower of grated almonds blessed their perfect union. All boundaries collapsed in this world, as predator and fodder fell under the same shining blade in Gopal's slender hand. Catalysed by the last rites of hot oil, cumin, coriander, bay leaves, cloves, cinnamon, a new entity was resurrected. It steamed, rich green and brown on blue china.

'My grades will be out soon,' I said, breathing in deeply this heady smell of reincarnation. 'Dad wants me to apply to American universities.'

'You must go,' Gopal-da said. 'You must make sure your future

21

is bright, wonderful, successful. You can't sit in this kitchen for ever.'

'What about your future?' I asked. 'Why are you going to your village after staying away for five years?'

'Future,' he murmured, 'future . . . For me there is only the past . . .' his voice trailed away.

'I'm going to ask you one last time,' I said. 'The secret.'

He gave me a one-sided smile. 'Sometimes it's best not to know certain things. Secrets must remain secrets.'

'If I guess, will you tell me?'

'Guess?' Gopal laughed. 'Will it be your story, eh, or mine?'

Voices, voices, delicious smoke, a very hazy world, and I think I heard –

Many years ago, in a village hidden between a forest and a hillside sliced by silver torrents, was a large mansion. It had marble columns, a gleaming stone courtyard, and was sheltered by broken walls and mango and *jamun* trees all around. Inside this mansion lived a middle-aged zamindar, impoverished by high taxes and low-yielding crops, and his dying son, his only child. His wife had died of tuberculosis years back. He sat by his son's bedside every morning and touched the pale, limp hand near the pillow. He felt the pulse and exhaled slowly. The village doctor had given up hope. He didn't even know what ailed the fourteen-year-old boy. A city doctor had been called in. He, too, had shaken his head gravely.

The boy lay on the bed and stared out of the windows at the play of shadow and sunshine on the brick wall and mango leaves, and on the gleaming skin of the weaver's son, who spent afternoons sneaking up those mango trees and stealing the ripest mangoes. The weaver's son – the same age as he – caught his eye many

22

times, and winked and laughed. He appeared like a woodland deity, sometimes all yellow-orange with mango juice, sometimes stained purple with *jamun*, his eyes glittering among mango leaves, his dark body almost a part of that dark glossy tree. The zamindar's boy heard him shriek with laughter when the zamindar's men caught him and thrashed him for stealing the fruit. He flew kites outside the walls, and the zamindar's son tried to raise himself to see him, hearing his reckless laughter. He heard his father's men curse that weaver's son. He heard his father moan to the village priest, 'It breaks my heart to see that healthy strong weaver's son run around so, while my son lies dying.'

'I wish I could be like that weaver's boy,' the zamindar's son said to the burning turquoise sky. 'I wish my body would stop aching. I wish this awful tiredness would leave my limbs.' The world outside trembled hot and bright.

'So many doctors,' Gyan says, 'and all shook their heads the wrong way. "Only another kidney can save him," they said. So awful, all those months, hooked up to that machine. A tube through my wrist every third day. All my blood going out into something then coming back in. Just wanted to die. Wanted them to let me be. Wanted my father to give up. Not that tube through my wrist. But he just wouldn't give up. Kept searching and searching for kidneys. My friends looked in once in a while, telling me about football matches. I would touch the ball they sometimes brought with them – that wondrous planet I would never have access to.' Gyan sighs again. 'Maybe I didn't want my father to give up – I don't know.'

The zamindar continued to strike his head against the temple altar. He fasted and lay before the altar for three days. He performed innumerable rituals, called on every god and goddess he could think of, whispering, sobbing, 'Don't take my son away, please, my only hope.' He even carried the sweets he had offered to Vishnu to the Muslim sector of the village, and offered them to the mullah. Some of his men, worried by such an act of desperation, fearing insanity, told him to go and find the *tantrik* who lived in the heart of the forest in the forbidden Kali temple. Perhaps he could give him a magic herb. But then, he might also cut off the zamindar's head on Kali's altar. You have to take risks if you want to save a life, they told him. So the zamindar went into the forest, shaking, desperate, sweating, muttering Hari's name for protection.

His men waited outside the forest for four days. The zamindar's head is rolling at Kali's feet, they said to themselves, and returned to the mansion. The zamindar's son looked so corpse-like that the men decided to prepare a pyre of sandal-wood. It's a matter of hours now, they thought. While they were busy piling wood on wood, and collecting baskets of white flowers, the zamindar stumbled in through the enormous iron gates of the mansion, followed by a tall, thin man in a red loincloth, grasping a seven-foot trident.

The *tantrik* had arrived! The zamindar was alive – whole! The men gaped at the lean old man with fiery eyes. 'Where?' asked the *tantrik* in a rasping voice, striking the ground with his trident.

The boy who had lain still as a corpse for four days opened his eyes when the *tantrik* touched his pale forehead with his trident. 'There is only one way,' the *tantrik* said. 'Is there another boy, strong, healthy? And are you willing to accept whatever the consequences might be?'

'Anything,' the zamindar whispered, 'everything.'

'We will wait for a moonless night,' the *tantrik* said, and left.

Three days later the *tantrik* reappeared, and lit a fire in the courtyard after dark. The glow of the fire was the only light in the darkness, as the sky was moonless and overcast. He poured butter and incense and flowers into the flames. Then he took a fresh green coconut and sliced off its top. 'This will be the vessel,' he said, holding out the coconut, and placed the sliced-off portion on it like a lid.

Through that dark night rumbling faintly with thunder and frog-calls, when all the huts were dark, and not even a dog or a cat could be found on the dirt roads, the *tantrik* walked towards the weaver's hut with the coconut. He held the coconut in one hand and the sliced portion in the other. The zamindar's men leant out of windows to see him. They saw only the darkness. 'It's Kali's darkness,' they muttered, 'and the *tantrik* has become part of it. Let's go to bed, close our eyes. We are not supposed to see or know what lies ahead. We cannot know. It's better not to know; then whatever the curse – for there will be a curse – will not be on our heads.'

The *tantrik* walked like a black shadow towards the weaver's hut. Whispering mantras into the coconut, he walked on, almost floated, for his feet didn't touch the ground. He blew over the water inside the fruit three times as he reached the weaver's hut. Closing his eyes, breathing deeply, he waited till that uncertain hour of hazy darkness between night and dawn. And then he called out.

The weaver's son, sleeping peacefully on a mat near the door, heard a strange sound. The voice of his beloved aunt who lived in the next village. She had taken care of him till she had been married off. His own mother was too weak and frail to take care of the children. He opened his eyes and sat up. She was calling, 'Come out, child, I haven't seen you for so long. Come out and see what I've brought for you. Your favourite sweets.' His parents and sisters were sound asleep. Hadn't they heard? Again, 'Come out child. Can you hear?' So plaintive that voice.

'Yes, I hear you,' he cried out, 'I hear you.' He felt a burning ball of light leap out with his voice and vanish in the darkness.

His mother and father woke up with a start to see their only son clutch his throat, writhe, then lie still.

The *tantrik* clapped the top of the coconut back on the fruit as soon as the weaver's son answered, covering it, resealing it almost. 'Now the soul is in here,' he said to the fading night. 'Once more my art has proved to be perfect. The call of Nishi never fails to seduce life from the living.' He returned smiling to the mansion. The zamindar's son was woken up gently. 'Drink this completely.' The *tantrik* held the coconut before his lips. 'Drink up. Not a drop should be spilt.' The zamindar's son drank all of the coconut water and collapsed on his bed. The zamindar howled and fell to his knees.

'You've killed him too!'

'If he wakes up in ten hours then he will live,' the *tantrik* said. 'I can make no promises. My work is done. Give me the ten goats you promised, and the fifty gold coins.'

After seven hours the zamindar's son made a moaning sound. He asked for water. Within the hour he sat up, asked for food. The zamindar ran to the kitchen himself, too amazed to yell for his servants, and brought back some warm milk. His son asked for meat, fish, rice, honey, mangoes . . .

It was as if the world had stopped and restarted, spinning the other way. It was as if the sun was rising in the west and setting in the east. The zamindar's son started to walk around his room, out into the courtyard, even step outside the gates, throw his arms up, smile at the sky, the mango trees.

The weaver and his wife and daughters carried their boy to the edge of the forest and set him on the pyre the zamindar's men had prepared for the zamindar's son. 'Lucky we don't have to buy wood,' the weaver muttered to his wife. The villagers gathered to

26

watch the flames leap and curl round the limp form on the pyre. The zamindar sent more sandalwood, flowers, butter, oil to the weaver. 'It is a sad thing,' he said to the weaver, 'to lose the only son. But who can prevent fate, who knows who Hari will keep, who He will take? It's all a grand illusion. A sleight of hand, you could say. A trick of something dark, uncontrollable. Take comfort in your daughters. I will provide you with their dowry. Don't lose heart.'

Meanwhile, the zamindar's son ran around the courtyard, singing, laughing.

'You must resume your studies,' the zamindar told his son. 'I will send for your tutor again. It's been a year and a half, and you have a lot of catching up to do. You will be a barrister when you grow up. And you have to be educated, trained, you have to go to the university. We'll be rich again, once you're established.' So the old tutor was brought back from Calcutta, and he greeted his pupil with tears in his eyes.

'How much better you look. I haven't forgotten how clever you were – are – how refined your manners, how princely your bearing. You will make a fine barrister.'

But the zamindar's son puzzled his tutor and his father as days went by. He seemed to have lost interest in the classics, in mathematics, in philosophy, in science; in books, in short. He looked at the mango trees while his tutor lectured. His hesitant walk changed to a lazy, heavy-footed stride. His frail, slight body developed muscles, became broader, tougher, while his face, throat, hands and feet remained thin, small, delicate. His gestures lost their gentleness and became bold, aggressive, even coarse. He began to eat with both hands, stuffing food into his mouth eagerly, hungrily, dropping part of it on his clothes, part of it around his plate. He licked his fingers after eating while his father and tutor stared with their mouths open. The servants couldn't stop whispering when the boy was seen stealing sweets from the pantry. One morning the zamindar's son couldn't be found anywhere on the premises. The tutor spotted him suddenly, and screamed in shock.

There he was, swinging from the mango tree, hands and feet hooked around a thick branch. He swung violently for a few minutes, shaking ripe and unripe mangoes off the tree, then leapt down and landed on the ground on all fours. He looked up at his father and the rest of the household with a wide, imbecilic grin on his face. He scratched his armpits and his bare chest vigorously, spat on the ground and clambered up the tree again. The zamindar let out a moan and passed out.

'I never understood it – the madness that took over. After the operation, the new kidney put in right here,' Gyan pats his left hipbone, 'I got desperate to meet this man who had given me back my life. Don't know why. Wanted to know him, know what he knew, learn his life. My father refused to locate the person. Learn the trade, he said. Need someone to work with me, take over. But I was going mad from the smell of paddy-fields swirling around me constantly. It came from nowhere, everywhere, brick walls, flowers, my hands, windowsills, clothes, cement blocks. I dreamt of living in mud huts, wading knee-deep in paddy-fields. I smelt food, all kinds, fabulous smells, fantastic images of kormas, cutlets, pulaos, couldn't understand, wanted to touch cloves, cinnamon, explored kitchens, ours, other people's, secretly, when no one was around, smelling, touching, tasting, even mustard oil, salt, turmeric, spinach. It was as if I was rediscovering another life, like reincarnation, remembering who I might have been, becoming that other all over again.

'And there was this searing pain all the time in the middle of my palms, as if something was burning into my flesh, constantly. Water, lotions, ice, nothing would get rid of it.

'So, grasping this burning pain tightly in my fists, I asked the engineers about their lunches – to see them, feel the chapatis, the dal, the rice, try to figure out if the dal was the right texture – instead of enquiring about the structure of buildings, or testing the quality of cement, or checking out how reinforced the concrete really was. My father sent me reeling with a blow to my head one day, when he caught me checking out a bewildered labourer's *rotis*. I had completely forgotten about the shipment of bricks, forgotten to make the payment. When my father asked about the bricks, I asked him to look at the *rotis*. He went crazy. After flooring me with the blow, he began to bang his head against the half-constructed foundation of the building.'

For a few days, the zamindar's son refused to come indoors. He stayed in the treetops, slept under trees. The villagers came to watch. Possessed, they muttered under their breath, or mad, or both. What's happened to my son? the zamindar wondered. 'Perhaps he's just exercising,' some of his men said, offering helpful shrugs. 'Newly developed muscles, sudden revival.' The zamindar stood under the mango tree and begged his son to come down and into the house. 'My golden boy, hope of my life, come and sit with me, come share these sweets with me. I'll give you anything you want, only come down here.' The boy grinned at him and made odd squealing noises. The zamindar beat his chest, slapped his head, and appealed to all the gods and goddesses.

A few days later, the zamindar's son left the trees and ran down the red dirt road that led to the weaver's hut. The door was ajar, so he went in. Two girls sat in a corner playing with shells. They screamed, seeing him, and huddled together. He made whimpering noises at first, and went towards them. They shrank against

29

the mud wall. 'Why do you look at me with fear, my sisters?' he asked. 'Where are my mother and father?' The girls screamed and threw pots and pans at him. He ran out with a bleeding forehead, straight into a group of villagers who had gathered before the hut, hearing the screams and the din of crashing pots and pans. 'Where is the weaver and his wife?' the zamindar's son demanded, wiping his forehead with the back of his hand.

'Why do you care?' they asked him sullenly. 'Rich zamindar's son, healthy and strong all of a sudden – what do you care?'

'The weaver's wife, my sister – so weak she was – do you know?' The village potter came up to him, shaking his fist. 'The moment her son gasped and went limp before her eyes, she, too, gasped, choked and fell on his body. Dead. Just like that. Shock, grief, call it what you will. And then the weaver gets drunk and wanders into the forest. We found him this morning, his body swollen, black from a cobra's bite. So what are you going to do about it, eh, rich man's suddenly healthy son? A miracle, eh? Why are you here all of a sudden? Why have you been climbing trees like my nephew?'

'We spit on the zamindar,' the dhobi said, and spat at the boy's feet. 'These two girls left here in this hut with no food, no money. Rich people think they can do what they like, yes? Poor people's lives, yes?'

The villagers spat at the zamindar's son, kicked him, threw stones at him. He ran into the hut for shelter, only to be beaten out by the girls. 'I'll take care of the girls,' he yelled at the villagers.

'Oh? And will you perform the last rites for the weaver and his wife, too?'

The boy ran back to the mansion and asked his father's men to get sandalwood. He had the men carry the logs to the edge of the forest. There they built a pyre just like the one they had built before, right next to the ashes of the weaver's son. The zamindar's son carried the swollen bodies of the weaver and his wife to the pyre and laid them on it, side by side. The brahmin from the temple sprinkled holy water, flowers, incense, said the necessary mantras, and the zamindar's son lit a torch and circled the pyre.

He touched the bodies three times with the torch, the eyes, the mouth, very lightly, then lit the pyre. The dry logs exploded into flames. The zamindar's son had to jump back, for the flames leapt viciously at him as if they wanted to brand him for some terrible mysterious crime. In the roaring pyre, he heard voices crying out – Why, why, why? He covered his face and fell to his knees, screaming in fear and confusion. He felt a distilled melting pain, felt his own flesh scorch and burn, shrivel, melt off his bones, then his bones burn with a white heat down to white ash. He was nothing, nothing, just a handful of ash, and he stood there before the screaming flames holding in his cupped hands the hot white ash of himself.

After five hours of tending the flames, making sure every particle was reduced to ashes, the boy gathered the ashes in a clay pot and went to the mountain stream two miles outside the village. He dropped the ashes in the running water, bathed, then returned to the village without looking back. He shaved his head, as a son is supposed to after the death of his parents. For twelve days he ate fruit and boiled rice, and slept outside the weaver's hut in the dusty yard.

The girls watched him cautiously for four days. Their aunt arrived to take care of them, the same aunt who had taken care of the three children until the day she got married. She cried when she saw the zamindar's son, telling the girls their brother had returned from the dead and they should welcome him back. Hari had played a strange game with them, but they should be thankful all the same. They allowed him to enter their hut and eat with them.

31

The zamindar, who by this time was practically losing his mind with confusion and anguish, sent baskets of fruit and rice to the weaver's hut for his son. So they all ate well. On the thirteenth day, the zamindar's son invited the brahmins for the final ritual. The brahmins, thrilled with the feast after the rituals and the gifts of clothes and money, blessed the boy, assured the villagers that a miracle had taken place, and that they should all try to accept fate and live in peace.

The zamindar fell at his son's feet and implored him to return with him to the mansion now that all rites had been observed. He swore to provide for the girls. 'But you seem like a stranger to me,' his son said to him. 'I don't know what has happened. But I want to live here with them. Go away, now, old man.' The zamindar went back to his house shaking. He sat quietly for a long time by his son's empty bed. Then he ran into the forest to find that *tantrik* again. But instead he found a shattered, empty temple whose stones echoed his desperate footfalls.

Back in his house, he lay in his bed for days, refusing food and water. His men went to the weaver's house and pleaded with his son to come back home or his father would die. He came back with them to see his father. 'I'll spend time here, too,' he said to the zamindar. 'But I cannot be everything you want me to be. I'll be what I am now.' So the boy divided his time between the mud hut and the mansion, clumsily working the loom half the day, and falling asleep while the tutor droned on about tax laws. He regained some of his old imperious gestures, a toss of the head, a shrug, and lost some of the coarseness he had developed. He went to bed at night, overwhelmed by a fatigue that made him cry silently into his pillow.

'I couldn't live with this any more. My father banging his head against that wall, screaming hoarsely. And this madness that was draining me – oh, the tiredness! Couldn't sleep. Just dreamt endlessly. From one pain to another – a strange journey.

'It would have to end if I was to live on. I told my father I was leaving, didn't want any part of his business, didn't want to be their son. I bribed the doctor who had done the transplant, and got Gopal's name and the name of his village.

'My other life took over after that. Gopal understood.'

It was the zamindar's *khansama* who realised the boy's dilemma. He is not going to be a lawyer, nor is he going to get anywhere with the weaving. And the boy's used to a soft life. 'Come here,' he called the boy one day, and took him into the kitchen. 'I'll fix it for you,' he said to the boy. 'You listen, and you watch. You are, after all, a zamindar's son, almost a prince, an aristocrat by birth. Strange things have happened – evil things have happened. Now you are paying for your father's misguided actions. You may have changed somewhat, but it is impossible for you to become a weaver's son – you do not possess a weaver's hands. Weaving is not for you, and alas, due to other people's evil actions, the law courts are not for you either. I have seen you grow up, made your favourite dishes for fourteen years. I have eaten your father's salt for twenty-five years. Now I see you cry at the loom and fall asleep before your tutor. Tears come to my eyes. Life is hard. I want to help you so that life is not too hard for you, so that you find a place in a rich man's house, so that you're treated kindly, with respect. Therefore I will teach you all my secrets, teach you to be the prince of cooks.'

So began his new life. Surprisingly, he turned out to be a magnificent cook. '*Hai Allah!*' the *khansama* would gasp from time to time. 'You were born for this. Perhaps all that has happened was meant to happen so that you would become what you were meant to be – the prince of cooks! Who can tell how destiny unfolds.'

Slowly, the weaver's daughters grew fond of him. The two girls, one eight, the other twelve, liked him in spite of all the vicious talk about the zamindar. The boy was sweet, gentle, soft-spoken. He didn't pull their hair, push them or torment them the way their late brother used to. He listened attentively to everything they said, did whatever they asked him to do, including climbing down the dark well to retrieve balls the two girls tossed in for fun and just to test if this new brother was as compliant as he seemed. Stoically, he allowed them to sit frogs on his head, to slap dung cakes against his face. The girls relished the new experience of tormenting this boy the way their brother had tormented them. The younger sister, more outspoken than the timid older one, declared she preferred this brother to the last one. The older girl looked down demurely at her toes, but nodded hesitantly all the same.

Their aunt began to spoil him like she used to spoil her late nephew. Since she had been widowed recently, by cholera, and her only daughter had died a few days after birth, she settled into her old family with a vengeance. Twisting her long dark hair into a coil on top of her head, 'What?' she'd hiss, coming up behind him while he reached up towards the baskets hanging from the ceiling to steal the sweets. Her false sternness would vanish at the sight of fear sweeping across his face. 'Here,' she'd say, bringing the sweets down, 'here,' and feed him, ruffle his hair, hug him as if he really was the boy she had cared for for eleven years, and loved fiercely.

The villagers – after much discourse with the brahmins – regarded him with a mixture of disbelief and awe, as if he wasn't quite real, quite flesh and blood. They touched their foreheads when they passed him in the streets, wondering if he were a curse or a blessing.

Accepted, even loved, the boy wasn't allowed to escape guilt.

'Not really your fault,' the doting aunt said to him. 'But things have happened. And there's no man in this family to take care of the girls. They have to be married off, their dowries provided. They must feel assured that there is always someone, a brother, really, that they can turn to in times of despair. Husbands, these days, are not quite reliable. Can you promise to be there, to help, really help, if there is ever a need?' The boy nodded vigorously, of course, of course, of course. He felt his palms burn with that white ash again. When the cool spring water didn't wash the burning away, he clenched his fists and held tightly to that melting pain. Never to lose it, now, never, this desperate hot ash that fused him with a misery he couldn't understand.

The zamindar grew thin and weak year by year. Drought ruined the crops, and famine drove the villagers to beg in the city streets. They cursed the zamindar for their misery. The zamindar commissioned a priest to stay at his house and read the Upanishads and the Gita to him morning and evening. 'Did I sin?' he would mutter to himself constantly. 'Did my desperate action bring about this famine? Are we cursed? Is there no forgiveness?'

One night he passed away in his sleep. His son performed the same rites as he had done for the weaver and his wife, and fed the brahmins one more time. He sold the mansion and all the zamindar's property to the government and received very little money. He distributed the money among the zamindar's servants and the weaver's two girls and their aunt. The villagers threw stones at him, asked him to sacrifice himself to Kali and get rid of the famine.

The *khansama* took him by the hand. 'Come with me to the city,' he said. 'I'll place you with a good family, and then I'll return to my village in the south.' The *khansama* was very particular about where the boy should work. For five months they explored many households until the *khansama* found the right one. The boy, eighteen then, became part of a wonderful family and worked for them for over thirty years. He visited his village once a year. He sent the girls money, even got them married.

Then one day, he got a letter from his aunt. 'I have found husbands for your sisters' daughters,' she had written, 'but we don't have the money for the dowry.' When he went to his village and sat with his aunt, she laid it down quite plainly. 'We need thirty thousand to marry off my two grand-nieces. Their fathers were poor farmers, their prospective husbands are poor merchants' sons. The girls will be climbing up socially – and that's a good thing, considering everything. Now, their fathers didn't make any provisions – how could they? One fellow trod on a cobra in the dark; the other wanted to get rich by growing opium, and the government has spies everywhere. Won't get out of jail for the next ten years, that one.' She caught his hands and pleaded, 'We have to get the girls married – thirty thousand for dowries and other expenses – they don't have a pair of gold earrings between them – floods, famine, had to sell, you know – I've given my word – we'll never live down the shame – their lives will be ruined. What to do, tell me?' She struck her forehead twice. 'Fate, fate . . . but perhaps fate is in our favour, nephew. Right now,' she said, an excited gleam entering her old, foggy eyes, 'a contractor is looking for a kidney for his son. Some men came to our village and propositioned us for kidneys. Thirty thousand they said. So I wrote to you at once. You have lived on the life of my nephew. You can sacrifice a kidney for the second life you received. I wouldn't have asked this of you – but then we have quietly accepted everything that has happened. We have never asked you for anything. Whatever you gave us, you did out of your own free will. We are all grateful. But now there is a need. Who else can we turn to?'

He looked at his hands. Every day of his life, of his new life, he had felt hot ash in his hands. To burn away that ash – to perform, finally, the very last rites, and be free at last.

I could believe anything in this kitchen. The smells and smoke lured me to a different planet where mystery was the essence of living, and that hot white ash the core of life.

I saw Gopal lying on a mat on the floor, in pain, thin, frail, just like that boy had once been –

'Are you here then out of some odd sense of gratitude, obligation, guilt?' I ask. I see myself face to face with Gopal, shaking him, screaming, Why, why, why?

'At first, that's how I felt.' Gyan inclines his head, pauses. 'But not any more. That hideous feeling just drained away after a year. I feel no connection to the past any more, to myself in that hospital bed, to my family, to Gopal, to those days in his hut. That's all gone, like cut-off hair. Don't know why. I like being here. I enjoy cooking. I do love living here with your family.'

I see Gopal again, tired, looking older day by day, as if the thin stream of the water of life that boy had drunk had been drained out with his kidney. He left two days later, and after three weeks sent Dad a letter saying he wouldn't be coming back: he was getting old and tired; he wanted to grow rice, live in his village. I left for the US two months later. Five years after I left, my father called to tell me about Gopal's death. Poor health, typhoid, bad doctors, finally kidney failure. I stayed away for eight years, unable to return, to face a Gopal-less home.

'So you said you would marry? Raise a family? Go back to your family?'

'My father disowned me when I left for Gopal's village. He won't take me back, and I don't want to go back. But I think I will marry. After I make some money. I want to build a house, a very

37

small house –' Gyan stops, smiles, draws a house in the air with his hands. 'Then only will the woman I want to marry marry me.'

'And where will you build this house?'

'Oh, not very far away from here. In a small village in Haryana. Next year I will make the money I need for this house.'

'I see.'

'I met a doctor, through that man at the blood bank, an eye-doctor who's going to arrange for this money. I'll be admitted to a hospital for an eye problem. Nobody'll know anything. They'll give me eighty thousand – cash. They'll take my left cornea.'

I took a deep breath, then another to fight the reeling sensation in my head. 'If you donate a cornea,' I said slowly, as slowly as he had pronounced 'cornea', 'you will go blind in one eye.'

'I can live with one eye. They both see the same thing anyway.' He waved his hand, flicked back his hair.

'You absolutely must not do this,' I said, my voice hard. 'It is wrong, illegal. You will not donate your eye while you live. Do you understand?' He looked at me, puzzled. 'You are not starving, Gyan, you are not on the streets. Why do you have to do this?'

'My wife-to-be's uncle has sold a cornea. Eighty thousand rupees! He now owns a TV, a scooter and a refrigerator. The gentleman who bought the cornea for his daughter was very generous. He even gave them two gold watches. My wife-to-be's friend's cousin and his wife have both given a kidney each, and their –'

'What's the big deal about a –' I stopped. I understood perfectly. I didn't have a clue. 'You said yourself that you felt you had taken Gopal away from us by taking his kidney. How can you talk about corneas and kidneys so blithely now?'

'But this is different. I'm fine now. Gopal, and all that, that's in the past. I don't even feel that burning in my hands any more, except just once, the day you arrived. But it's gone now. So.'

38

There was anger in his voice, and scorn. 'I've burnt the past away in this kitchen, you could say, performed the last rites to end one life. I'm going to start a new life now, truly free this time. Marry someone I want to marry, like I see them do in the movies.'

'Don't do this, Gyan.'

'Tea? Coffee? Sandwich? Cake?' he enquired with a weak smile. I got up and left the kitchen.

The elections are over. Changes will sweep the country, I hear, like the cyclones sweep Bangladesh, Orissa. Gyan continues to take his daily dose of immuno-suppressants and steroids. I think of that boy in that village climbing mango trees one summer afternoon. 'Your story or mine?' I hear Gopal's laughing voice clearly. Who's to tell? And does it matter?'

I wonder where Gyan's left eye will go. I wonder how it will perceive the order of things. Will it see the world the way the zamindar saw it when his son lay dying? Will it see an eye for a house, TV, scooters, a kidney for a daughter's dowry? Will it envision a new and wondrous world where specially healthy people are kept in exclusive communes and bred for dazzling eyes, glowing skins and shining kidneys? That stormy ball of light burns through my head. I feel hot white ash melting my palms. I see Gyan walking towards a river holding smoking ash in his cupped hands. A very different ash – or a very different Gyan, I don't know. He doesn't feel the scorching pain. He walks on, smiling, towards golden rice fields and roaring muddy rivers rising up to swallow the land. The ash in his hands implodes, particles rush closer and closer, density increasing, mass reducing to a small white ball with a dark spot that contracts with light.

I'm afraid to look out of this kitchen window, all of a sudden. A nauseating, gnawing fear of seeing a tall, lean shadow, and a hand holding out a green coconut metamorphosing to a steel scalpel.

Beloved Mother, Queen of the Night

'Old woman,' screams Shanta, 'hag,' tugging at the gunny cloth that screens my shack, 'oy, up, out, come take care of the kids for tonight.' She looks so alluring in her red sari, with her hair piled up on her head, a gardenia tucked behind her ear, her eyes sparkling like the fireworks lighting up the sky. And, ah, as she leans against the doorpost, one arm raising the sack, her body taut like a drawn bow, 'Hag,' she says, 'make sure the kids go to bed by midnight or else Memsaab will fire me. So scare them good. Tell them about your ugly face and that scar of yours, the curse of Kali!' She throws back her head and laughs, her body curving like a leaping wave. 'Tell those spoilt wretches about the curse of Kali – perfect for tonight. Go on, now. The *arati*'s about to start in a few minutes, and Kamal is going to dance all night again.'

To seduce that young rascal has been Shanta's goal for her twenty-fifth year. I was twenty-five once, I think, two hundred years ago perhaps, or was it a hundred? Shanta walks ahead swiftly, her bare waist like two crescent moons crossed. A sahib said that of my waist once. I follow in her starlit wake, coughing, spitting blood, limping a little because of my knees, my shrivelled-up self, shrivelled to this one long scar that runs from the corner of my left eye to my chin, a curved, crescent scar, like

43

the crescent blade in Kali's hand. They say my scar glows on moonless nights such as this one, an arc of fire, burning, burning, burning.

The slum assaults your nose with every gust of wind. Drains regurgitating putrefying filth from the mansions. They are all lit up tonight, those mansions, and our slum, too, with candles and oil lamps. No one turns on electric lights tonight, for tonight is the festival of lamps, the festival of Kali, the night we get rid of all demons with fire. So the sky is continually slashed with rockets shooting up and thundering and cascading arrows of fire.

'Get in,' Shanta says, opening the back door, pushing me in, 'upstairs, come on.' The children run back from the lamp-studded balcony rails as a rocket flies up too close and explodes. 'Chitra,' Shanta calls the oldest, who is sixteen with hair swinging loose to her waist, 'Chitra, you four can sit here for a couple of hours. That's all. Pass your brother over to her. She'll put him to bed.' She tosses the one-year-old to me. 'A pest,' Shanta says. 'Spank him lightly if he gets too much, but make sure his bottom doesn't turn red.'

'Where are you going, Shanta-di?' Chitra asks.

'To the *puja*.' Shanta's smile is sugary. 'We've almost got rid of all demons, haven't we? Our own flag went up three months back – do I have to remind you? This time *Kali puja* has new meaning for us. OK, hag, all yours. Pull her rat's-tail hair, kids, if she falls asleep out here, and shove a feather up her nose.'

And she's off like an arrow.

'Whose ayah are you?' Chitra asks me.

'No one's.'

'Oh, my!' The two boys come up, six and nine, and touch my scar gingerly with their forefingers.

'It slices,' I say, 'like a sword.' The baby yawns and settles in my lap, his eyes closing.

Chitra comes forward. 'I know – you're the scarred one Shanta talks about. You live in a black hole, she says, and you speak to no one, but you mind kids once in a while, when ayahs want to take nights off.'

'Well, sit down,' I say, 'and let's watch the fireworks and listen to the priest's chant. Do you know what the priest is saying?'

'Go away demons, go away demons, go away demons!' The two boys laugh and roll on the polished red floor of the balcony. 'He's trying to get rid of the riots breaking out all over the place.'

'No, you sillies. The priest isn't concerned about riots. Even if the city burns to ashes, even if rioting mobs surround his altar, the priest will carry on as if possessed by the spirit of the great mother.'

'Riots,' Chitra murmurs, 'riots in spite of him.'

Yes, in spite of the Mahatma's pleas, his fasting, the riots still rage. 'Violence is addictive, children.' Ah, what have we freed ourselves from, I don't know any more. Knowledge seems irrelevant tonight. Tonight is filled with sounds, with words, magical, heady.

'Shh, listen,' I say to them. The priest's voice comes through clearly from the speaker fastened on top of the mango tree. 'He is invoking her, children, the terrifying mother, the merciless, beloved mother, queen of the night. But first, he prays for purity. I'll translate for you. You must know, and remember what is spoken tonight. Tonight can change you for ever. Some words can change you for ever.'

Leaning towards the rails, I listen to the rhythmic voice. Ah, how familiar the words are. I don't even have to wait for him to finish the *shlokas*. The first word unfurls my memory. I see the words spring like sharp waves of flames.

'Listen, children: Impure we are, our acts, our words, our thoughts. But at this very moment, when we close our eyes and

45

call on you, we are pure, for we pray for purity. So come into us now. Allow me to invoke you in the only way possible: let me imagine you, let me create you in my mind as I imagine you. Come among us through this darkness with your sword and your fury. I see you as you are here on this altar, clothed with severed arms and legs, with your garland of heads, bathed in blood. Your eyes startle us like the sun at dawn; your hair, a black swirling storm. Your skin is dark as the darkest raincloud. You look at me with a mother's terrifying rage. You raise your crescent blade with one hand, hold a severed head in the other. I fall to my knees, trembling. But then you fill me with courage and love with your third raised hand, the palm open towards me. And with your fourth hand opening like a lotus just blooming, you bless me, grant my wishes, allow me my secret desires.'

'And then they'll chop off the goat's head.'

'Later, later, after the *arati*, the dance, the offerings of flowers, milk, honey.' Their eyes shine as they lean over the rails again and try to discern what's going on in the park in the distance where the altar has been set up. They were there earlier on. Parents nowadays don't like their children to witness sacrifices. When I was their age, I remember thrusting my hands into the frothing pool of blood between the goat and its head.

Chitra turns from the darkness and comes towards me. She touches my scar lightly. 'Do you have a husband?' she asks.

'Who would marry a woman with a scar, child? But you will be married, beautiful. Next year, I heard.'

'So they tell me.' She looks away at the darkness again and blinks as rockets explode too close to us. This Calcutta night is blazing with sound and light and chanting all around us. The riots going on in the northern parts don't affect the festive lust out here. 'Tell us something,' Chitra says, 'a story or something. How did you get this scar?'

46

'Kali struck her,' the nine-year-old says, turning, a wicked grin on his face.

'Shut up.' Chitra glares at her brother.

'You shut up,' the boys snap back together. 'You'll be married and gone next year. You won't be able to boss us around. We'll do as we please, so there, so there.' They stick their tongues out, stamp their feet.

'Maybe I won't marry,' Chitra says softly, 'maybe I'll run away, or die, or be rescued by – by Kali.'

A sigh escapes me. The wondrous radiance of a face that is wistful and desperate and resolute all at once. Sometimes there is strength in innocence and purity when one is as young as Chitra, when one's body is untouched and sacrosanct. I clasp my hands and close my eyes. Passion, passion. Kamal must be dancing, losing himself to the night, the drumbeats, the fragrant smoke that wraps him. They say the dance is in his blood. They say he burns with it. Ah, the burning. Burning away the self. What else is any act of worship? Annihilation. The chanting carries on relentlessly.

'Forgive us, Mother, for we will act and speak impurely, imperfectly, our motives are tainted. But we will try for one moment of truth in our flawed way. So forgive us, now, knowing that we will commit unpardonable acts trying to adore you, trying to survive, trying to lose ourselves in you, trying to be ourselves truly.'

To be oneself truly . . . one might have to be, in the definition of the world, bad . . . Someone said that once. I remember.

'Come,' I say, 'come, children. Let's get into a palanquin and travel through a dark forest.' I carry the baby indoors, and place him in his crib. He sleeps with his thumb in his mouth.

'Fight with robbers,' the younger boy says, his voice rising with excitement.

47

'No. Fight the sahibs, be a band of robbers, dacoits, hack off heads, leap into caskets of gold coins and rubies and emeralds!'

'What about the scar?'

A hacking cough makes me double up. I stumble to the rails and cough and spit thick phlegm. Blood again. Maybe death is near. Must be time. Though time hasn't moved for centuries. Time froze when I was twenty-five. Chitra helps me back to the cushions on the floor. She brings me a glass of water. I lean my head against the wall after a few sips, and run my fingers along my scar.

'A forest, children, lit up gold in the mid-afternoon sun. A forest dancing with shadow and light, a forest where nothing is what it seems, where a single thought of yours can alter the shape of things, where a whispered word can catapult you to a different planet, a forest where one's life can change, utterly, between one bird-call and another. Change –' Bloody phlegm chokes me again. Perhaps this choking is a warning. Not for tonight this story – this story that I have told a hundred times before to children spellbound by my words, fascinated by the horror that is my face. But never on the night of Kali. Should I now do what I have never done? Let the words out on this night of nights? Something essential might change absolutely. And change can be terrifying. When meanings change – and what one has always believed to be true. The horror of that.

'Then what?' urges Chitra. 'Why are you quiet? Talk.'

Chitra's eyes compel so. And I want to satisfy, even surrender.

'A group of eleven men moving through it, following a thread of a path between bamboo groves and mango and banyan and tamarind trees. They carry guns and knives, for these woods are not safe at all. Dacoits often raid parties going through these parts. Leading the group, a sahib in a khaki uniform on a white horse and a young, handsome zamindar on a grey horse. They laugh and talk as they ride, occasionally turning their heads to glance at the other riders, and the palanquin following them, which is carried by four men.'

—Inside, the palanquin is lined with pale yellow satin. The two seats are made of the softest padding, and covered with the same satin. It is so cosy inside, so cushioned, that you would feel like staying in it for ever. A young woman, just a little older than you are, Chitra, nineteen, yes, sits on one of those seats with her head leaning back just a little, letting another one, who is older, and who sits behind her on the same seat, comb her long black hair. The younger woman wears a red and gold sari. She is dripping from head to foot with gold jewellery. On her forehead is a tiny spot of vermilion powder, a trifle smudged. Her face is adorned with lacy patterns done with sandalwood paste. 'Jamini – ouch!' she said. 'Don't tug so.'

'What can I do?' Her maid, Jamini, made a face. 'So many knots and tangles. Who asked you to get on the swing with your hair loose and swing about with the vengeance of a monkey before you had to leave your father's house? Had you walked to the palanquin slowly, you'd have got a good look at your husband.'

'But you said he's good-looking.' She struck the seat in exasperation.

'Yes, Pratima, I know he's good-looking, and he's pretty good at what he should be good at. So you'll be fine, don't worry.'

'Did you get to see him all three days?'

'See him – yes, I did, I told you so.' Jamini smiled to herself. The bridegroom had given her a pair of gold bracelets. The sahib had favoured her with a gold necklace. She had laughed all the way to Pratima's room after she left the two men, who had fallen on each other as soon as Jamini had got off the bed. It was amusing how men sometimes fell into each other's arms after sharing the same woman. 'It'll be OK,' she said. 'He'll leave you alone after a week. Then we'll be together again. Aren't you glad I'm here with you? I wouldn't be able to sleep without you.'

'Nor I without you, *shokhi*.'

'Companion', Pratima called Jamini, *shokhi*, companion, beloved.

'What about your sahib?' Pratima turned to look at Jamini. Jamini flicked off a speck of dry sandalwood paste from Pratima's eyelashes. She ran her forefinger lightly along the intricate designs painted all over Pratima's face. That morning, the old ayah, practically blind with cataracts, had come with a plate of sandalwood paste to Pratima's room. 'A bride can't go bare-faced to her husband's home,' she said. With a matchstick the old woman had drawn the most exquisite paisleys on Pratima's cheekbones. Dipping the matchstick in the paste, she had drawn a line of tiny, star-like flowers over Pratima's eyebrows. Her chin had received a single paisley. The designs glowed on Pratima's face because her skin was darker than the paste. Jamini drew in her breath sharply as she always did when she looked closely at Pratima.

Dark skin had never been considered a sign of beauty. And Pratima's father had always bemoaned the fact that his daughter was dark, like her grandmother, and not light-skinned like her late mother. But Pratima's dark skin glowed like moon-washed temple columns. Looking at her face you saw a burning torch, not dark skin. Fierce, blazing eyes struck you with their flame-lash. You did not think about beauty when you looked at Pratima. Because she looked at you with that restless smile that moved with arrow-swiftness from her eyes to mouth to eyes. That smile flashed like a crescent blade, made your knees buckle. You became enthralled by the radiance of night, moonlit, moonless, sparkling, or swept by clouds throbbing with lightning.

'Well?' Pratima raised her eyebrows. 'What about your sahib?'

'Oh, I'll find another one.' Jamini shrugged. She smiled, winked, moved the curtain and looked out of the window at the riders. 'You had better start thinking about children, Pratima, sons, yes, a hundred sons.'

'What'll I do with them?' Pratima pulled her hair away from Jamini.

'You'll sit them on your knees, sing, rock them –'

'Is that why you sold yours?'

Jamini pulled back Pratima's hair and began to comb it vigorously. 'Stop! Ouch.' Pratima caught Jamini's wrist.

'You took the sahib who got your husband hanged as your lover. You sold your three-month-old baby to the zamindar in the next village. Every time you get pregnant you go to the doctor for quinine. I have never asked you why.'

'I hated the man my father sold me to. I didn't want his child. That's all.'

'And what about the sahib? How could you? We're trying to get them out!'

'He was generous and treated me well.' Jamini let out an exasperated sigh. 'What good is a man if he can't buy you a gold necklace or a silk sari from time to time? What's he worth if he doesn't have a kind word for you, if he never tells you you're pretty or wonderful? Would your father marry you off to a pauper, Pratima? You have a rich husband now, and thank your stars for it. Your life will be wonderful, and happy. The man chosen for you is –'

'Wonderful, I'm sure.' Pratima tossed her head and laughed.

'What's wrong with you today? You've been dancing with joy for the last two months.'

'I didn't realise, not until I was sitting inside this palanquin and looking out at the road and the people, the cows, horses, rice

51

fields passing by. I thought I was getting out, getting away . . .' Pratima's voice trailed. She narrowed her eyes and looked at the satin curtain covering the small square window. Her fists clenched slowly, her nails digging into her palms, her knuckles turning white. 'Will I be left dreaming impossible dreams? I hope something happens to – something, anything, so that –' Pratima stopped. She turned and looked at Jamini. 'I want to trust you always, *shokhi*.'

'What's that supposed to mean?' Jamini threw the comb down. She rubbed her eyes with her fists, puckered her face, and sniffed loudly. 'Just what does that mean?'

For seven years she had combed and braided Pratima's hip-long hair. Dressed her, sung her to sleep, fed her, pushing food between her mistress's lips when she sulked and refused to eat. On stormy nights, Jamini held her and let Pratima fall asleep in her arms. She had shared the same bed with her mistress, loving the comfort of silk sheets and soft mattresses. They would lie with their arms round each other, gossiping, laughing, calling each other '*shoi*', '*shokhi*', beloved companion, sister, pledging eternal loyalty and love. 'Shh,' Jamini would say, placing a finger against her lips, 'listen to me, always, I'll take care of you, never let anyone hurt you, *shoi*. For ever and ever.' Pratima never questioned Jamini.

Jamini replaced the old ayah within months. She could tell amazing stories, sing, dance, play cards, throw dice like an expert. With Jamini as companion, Pratima could play hide-and-seek at last in the bamboo groves at the far end of the walled garden, climb trees without being reproached, make faces at the hawkers in the street from her window. Only Jamini was allowed to be near when Pratima got into one of her black moods. When Pratima sat on her bed with her head bowed, making deep lines on the bed with her thumbnail, Jamini would run her fingers through Pratima's hair and murmur, 'What, *shokhi*? Tell me, please. Why do you brood so?' Jamini would stroke her shoulders, back, arms, for hours. She held her close from the back, rubbed her face against Pratima's shoulderblades, wondering why Pratima sat so silent, and how to ease away this unknown gloom. 'What is it?' she would ask again and again. Pratima would shake her head and whisper, 'Nothing.'

'Such depression – why?'

'No – not depressed.' Pratima struck the bed with her fist. 'Just exasperated.'

'Why?'

'Rooms and rooms and rooms, doors and doors, leading to rooms, to corridors, unending corridors. My body aches. Hold me.'

'I don't understand,' Jamini muttered, holding her tightly. 'Try to sleep. It's so late. Why so sad?'

'Walls and gardens, rooms, corridors . . .' Pratima continued to whisper against Jamini's shoulder. 'Not sad, just desperate.' Then she laughed suddenly, got off her bed, saying, 'Come, let's go sit on the swing.' In the garden at the back of the house, Jamini watched Pratima swing so fast and so high that she had to catch her breath in fear that the swing might fly up and around the bar on top, that Pratima might spin off God knows where, into the clouds maybe, or come crashing down and scatter in broken pieces.

The *mali* had helped Jamini get a job at the zamindar's mansion soon after Jamini's father, a starving indigo farmer, had married her off to the highest bidder in the town, the local liquor dealer. But Jamini had discovered the power of the sahibs. She had seen them hang two of the local thugs for spitting on one of their horses. She had seen the gold necklaces the women at the bazaar flaunted. Those were not ordinary gold necklaces either. They

53

had been confiscated from royal houses. When the sahibs came to the zamindar's house for taxes, Jamini made sure she was the one who carried the trays of food and drink. She lined her eyes with kohl, put flowers in her hair, rubbed sandalwood oil on her skin and wore red saris when attending on sahibs. And invariably she was left with a necklace or two, rings and bracelets, even loose change, and a few bruises.

Then she ran into the district magistrate. Twenty-nine, blond, and having shipped his wife back to England, he welcomed Jamini into his bedroom with not just gold, but pearls and rubies and silk. He even introduced her to whisky, and she, in turn, showed him the stuff massages were made of. The problem of her husband was solved swiftly. Jamini stuck out her lower lip and pointed out to the district magistrate that her husband was a drunken lout who thrashed her occasionally. The liquor dealer was hanged within the week on charges of conspiracy. Her son, three months old, she sold to a rich landowner in the next village. The baby was definitely the liquor dealer's and not the DM's, as his skin colour testified. Besides, Jamini didn't want to be anchored to a baby. Everyone knew the truth about Jamini, but no one dared say a word about the district magistrate's woman. Jamini was powerful, yes, in those days. If anyone needed a favour from the DM they approached Jamini; and if they handed her a decent-sized bundle of notes, she usually got him to do the needful.

Pratima's father was not too pleased about the situation. But his daughter adored Jamini, and then there was the DM. Besides, he didn't want to deal with bringing up a daughter. He got hold of an English governess for two years, hoping this Miss Ellis would displace Jamini by the colour of her skin and the force of a memsahib's personality. Well, people have illusions. Miss Ellis managed to make Pratima fluent in English, but could not change her feelings towards her maid. Pratima insisted that Jamini be taught some English too, and be with them all the time. Miss Ellis's presence began to create other complications. The local population began to spit on the gates and walls of the mansion. Some even called the zamindar the memsahib's whore, when he had ridden to the bazaar to inspect a new well. So Miss Ellis was given notice.

To recover his honour, Pratima's father asked the priest from the temple to give his daughter a few lessons in Sanskrit. The brahmin, however, was obsessed with Pali texts. Although he conducted all the rituals at the Shiv temple dutifully, he was a Buddhist at heart. He was also an incredible story teller. He fascinated Pratima with tales of bodhisattvas, the fragrance of *sal* trees, the magical garden of Lumbini. Pratima, infected by the old brahmin's passion, eagerly learnt to read Pali, and looked forward to afternoons of fabulous stories. She learnt about banished Buddhist monks who made caves their monasteries, and carved the teachings of Gautama on cave walls. 'Where are these secret caves?' she asked him. 'No one really knows,' he said. 'Somewhere in south Bihar, I think. Now they are the home of brigands, dacoits, of all those who had to run away. Survival,' the brahmin told her, 'just survival, and dreams. And the sense of power that courses through you when you know – ah,' he made a fist slowly and raised it to his face, 'that you've got away and you're still carrying out the dream. You burn and you burn.' Pratima looked into the mirror after that, and raised her fist, murmuring, 'The dream, the power, the burning.' After about seven months, this glorious time came to an end rather abruptly. The brahmin slipped on wet flowers and fell down the temple steps and broke his neck.

The zamindar, taken aback by the bad news, decided to marry off his daughter. She had turned nineteen, and, as his counsellors told him, he should have married her off five years ago. Soon Pratima's marriage was fixed, and the old ayah was sent to convey the news to Pratima. 'Oh,' Pratima said, looking a little puzzled. 'I must tell Jamini.' Jamini did get a little worried over the news. She didn't want to be left behind. But it was easy to convince the zamindar through Pratima. How could Pratima leave her maid behind, her loyal, beloved companion of seven years? Who would look out for her in a stranger's house? Who would shield her from the jealousy of older, ugly and spiteful sisters-in-law?

The district magistrate had wept at Jamini's feet, she told Pratima. 'He said he'll die if I leave. Isn't that thrilling? Look at this bracelet, look at the emeralds and rubies and sapphires! I hope he dies. I want men to pine away and die for me.' Pratima had stared at her blankly. Pratima didn't quite know the thrill of such things.

And now, mid-way between her father's house and her husband's, swaying with the rhythm of the moving palanquin, the low, humming chant of the bearers wrapping around them, Pratima was narrowing her eyes and saying bitter things, cutting Jamini to the quick. No matter what people said of her, what lies were whispered, what truths spat out, one fact was irrefutable: Jamini loved Pratima. She had never loved anyone or anything else. The laughter in Pratima's eyes made Jamini's day more than any gold necklace could. If Pratima frowned at her, Jamini was shattered. The day they met near the swing in the garden, the *mali* introducing her to Pratima and Pratima saying, with an imperious lift of her chin, Come play with me, Jamini entered a world she had envied from afar.

Jamini looked into Pratima's eyes and recognised the image. That's what she wanted to be. Born into this position of power, and not have to fight tooth and claw, seduce, serve, wile your way towards that elusive spot. Can you imagine Jamini's ecstasy when

56

Pratima would throw her arms round her and whisper, 'If you leave me, I will die, *shokhi*'? In spite of that imperious toss of the chin or head, that firm call, 'Come,' 'Get me that,' 'Now,' 'I want,' when Pratima turned and looked at her with that smile of hers flashing like a crescent blade, Jamini felt a little wave inside.

'*Shokhi*', she called Jamini, beloved companion, friend and lover.

The word was like a mantra to Jamini's ears. It elevated her to a coveted status and relationship: friend and confidante, lady-in-waiting and chief counsellor. Jamini had had a father, a husband and lovers. But never an adoring friend. She had never known the thrill of shared secrets. When she told Pratima about the district magistrate's abject adoration, about all the men who laid their broken hearts at her feet, Pratima listened with widening eyes. 'Come with me,' she said to Pratima one day, 'I'll show you something exciting.' She took Pratima beyond the women's quarters, to a screened balcony overlooking the zamindar's *baithak-khana*, the special drawing room where the zamindar sat with his friends and sycophants after dinner to play cards, or draw on the hookah, or listen to new poems from the young man he had welcomed into that special room recently. From this balcony, Pratima and Jamini could watch the goings-on without being seen. So Pratima watched, rapt, the young poet sing his lyrics of love and rebellion, tossing his hair out of his eyes from time to time, in rhythm with the beat of his song.

Pratima ran to her window when Jamini told her the poet was walking towards the house. Through the slats of the wooden shutters, Pratima scrutinised the young man's sullen face. She stood on the balcony outside her room one evening when Jamini alerted her to his approach. When he looked up and caught her stare, Pratima ran indoors shaking with fear and excitement. The very next day, the poet sent a poem through the local bangle seller to Jamini. 'A poem for you!' Jamini danced around Pratima with the sheet of paper. ' "I have searched through Ayodhya nights for your eyes," ' Pratima read, ' "I have searched over a corpse-strewn Kurukshetra for your face . . ." What should I do?' Pratima asked Jamini, striking her with her fists. 'What do I do?'

'My dear, you must simply ignore him. Look at him scornfully from your balcony. More poems will come. He will offer you his shattered heart. You will smile, even laugh, and pass him by. Lesson number one.'

'Shouldn't I meet him?'

'Nonsense. And out of the question. Your father would chop off my head. But wait till you're married. I'll work it out for you then.' Yes, Jamini said to herself, when you're married, and your rich husband has abandoned you after one or two children for his women at the bazaar, I will find you lovers, so that you too will know the pleasure and excitement. I will make sure you don't pine away like most zamindars' wives. I will take you to a world of constant excitement, where there is no stasis of loneliness. 'I'll always be with you, *shokhi*,' she said to Pratima. 'We'll be together, never alone. For ever and ever.'

Pratima lost interest in the poet's sullen face and gushing language after a few weeks – but whether it was due to the repetitive nature of the poems or Jamini's lessons on attitude, it's hard to say. She resorted once more to the games she used to play with Jamini.

Jamini raced around inside the old, crumbling mansion, playing hide-and-seek with Pratima, teasing and tormenting the old ayah, pulling her hair, pinching her, tripping her, throwing banana skins in her path. It was a mercy the bent old woman didn't fall and dislocate her hip or crack her skull. Grumbling, cursing, the old woman would shuffle through the long corridors, while Pratima ran up and down wide flights of stairs, screaming wildly, 'Want to dress up, want to dance!' She and Jamini would hold hands and spin and leap and sing. 'Get me garlands,' she would say to Jamini, 'get me a sword, a spear.' Jamini, laughing, would wrap a sari tightly round Pratima's tall, strong body. Pratima would leap up on the enormous mahogany four-poster, raise the bamboo pole that served as a spear, and freeze in that pose. Jamini would fall to her knees laughing, lift her hands and cry, 'Hail, Mother. Save us all.' The old ayah would cough and wheeze, her wizened body recoiling with shock, and when she got her breath back, say sternly in a raspy voice, 'You'll bring down a curse on your head, child. Playing at being such goddesses!' Turning to Jamini, the old woman spat out, 'You slut – you're the curse.' Her eyes filling with tears, she'd say to Pratima, 'You're the Lakshmi of this house, that's what you are. Not this. Like your name, Pratima – idol, golden idol, Lakshmi-pratima – you should know.'

But Pratima would stamp her feet, yelling, 'Bring me a sword,' and race around waving a stick wildly as if cutting off heads. Jamini would roll on the floor and laugh.

'Why this madness?' the old ayah would ask. 'Why can't you play at being a bride, a mother with a new-born baby?'

'A bride! Why, a bride can't even lift her head, or raise the veil. She just sits there, tears rolling down her face. I want –' Pratima would bite her lips and turn away.

'I don't understand,' the old woman would mutter, shaking her head.

'It's the feeling – the feeling, being Her, Her whom no one can check, before whom all kneel, yes, kneel, spellbound. You wouldn't understand.' Pratima would walk away, pushing the old woman aside.

One day, Pratima peered into the mirror after a bout of racing around their section of the house. The old ayah came up behind, grumbling as usual. Pratima picked up the silver, eye-shaped container of kohl, and smeared the tip of her little finger with the black paste. Looking into the mirror, moving back her hair from her forehead with one hand, she drew an eye on her forehead with the kohl. Then she whirled around and faced Jamini and the old ayah. Jamini gasped with laughter.

'You look just like her,' she said. 'You're tall and dark, and now with your hair loose and your sari falling off, you are the spitting image. All you need is that curved blade in one hand and a head in the other, and your foot on someone. Bite your tongue, go on, just like her.'

The ayah reeled backwards. 'Shame on you,' she said weakly. 'To draw the third eye on your face – you've stamped destruction on your head, for sure.'

'I need blood,' Pratima hissed through her teeth, smiling evilly.

'You wretched girl, you should know better than to invoke the Mother's bloodthirsty aspect so frivolously. You'll have to pay with blood for such disrespect some day.'

'Give me blood then,' Pratima said, laughing.

'To the temple,' Jamini said excitedly. 'They'll do the goat soon. It's almost time. Let's go.'

Holding Pratima's hand, Jamini ran to the crumbling Kali temple near the burning *ghat*. 'My father's men may see us,' Pratima gasped. 'He'll have me locked up, and throw you out.'

'Too dark. Don't worry. You've never seen this before.'

Jamini made Pratima cover her head as they neared the temple courtyard. She pulled the sari low over Pratima's face. The sun had gone down an hour before, and the sky was a glazed copper. The courtyard was empty, but they could hear the priest's chant within the temple, and voices of people repeating the *shlokas*. Through a pair of chipped, worn stone columns, Pratima looked at the altar.

60

The copper light fell on the black stone idol, giving it a red glow. Lamp flames made long quivering gashes against the dark stone. The crescent blade caught the swaying light and hit your eyes like sudden lightning. Two male dancers, holding a pair of clay braziers each, spun around before the altar to the frenzied rhythm of drums. Flaming incense and coal rolled off the braziers. The dancers danced over them, insensible to scorching flesh, swathed in thick whorls of smoke. Pratima covered her nose and mouth with her hand. The smell of burning flesh, incense, sweat, trampled wet flowers against mud. There was no air, it seemed, only this dense grey-brown fog. Voices rose in a crescendo. 'Jai Ma!'

A tall, well-muscled man appeared with a torch through the haze of smoke. He walked over to the left edge of the altar, lighting up the dark corner against the wall. Pratima saw a goat, its feet trussed up, its neck stretched painfully and wedged tightly between three posts – two on each side, one below. The goat struggled ineffectually, opened its mouth a few times as if bleating. The man inserted the torch into a holder in the wall behind the goat. He went to the centre of the altar, knelt, stretched out, touching the flowers, hibiscus and marigold, and the stone floor with his forehead. The priest sprinkled him with holy water and petals. When the man stood up, the priest smeared his forehead with sandalwood paste and vermilion powder and, removing the crescent blade from the idol's frozen grasp, handed it to the man.

Standing above the goat, the man raised the blade with both hands. 'Bless us, Mother.' Everyone picked up the cry. Pratima found herself whispering the words. 'Be satisfied, Mother.' Again the torrent of voices. Pratima, murmuring those words, looked at the dancers. Why were they slowing down? Long, slow circles, the two figures moving closer and closer, falling to their knees before the altar, swaying as if they were losing their balance, about to collapse, and in the corner, two hands gripping the blade, rising higher, higher, an arc of lightning slashing the darkness, a faint bleat, an agonised collective scream – 'Ma' and the dancers falling backwards, their bodies arching, the braziers tumbling to the floor scattering a flaming trail. A crimson river springing up, drowning your eyes, jubilant hands plunging into a frothing red pool –

Pratima turned around, almost choking. Where was the copper sky? As if the sky had drawn a veil of shining indigo silk across her face.

'*Shokhi.*' Jamini turned her around. 'For you. Her blessing.' Jamini's fingers were wet and warm against her forehead. Pratima shivered. 'Come, take the blessing.' Pushing through chanting bodies. 'Kneel, touch.' The stone was so warm. The strange smell made her head swim. Was she going to throw up? She breathed deeply to clear her head. Ah, the air was so sweet and fresh all of a sudden. Incense and crushed flowers, crushed against this warm red stone. The dancers still frozen in that backward arch, their bodies trembling. Pratima stroked the altar gingerly, touched the soaked flowers, lifted them close to her face. Hibiscus and this – this – So soft and warm against her skin.

'Get up. Let's go.' Jamini shook her, her voice urgent. Pratima stood up, let Jamini push her through the crowd towards the courtyard. Through the fine muslin that still veiled her face, Pratima looked with widening eyes at the people staring at her. 'You went mad or what?' Jamini was hissing. 'Trying to smear the blood like that, for so long, on your face, mad or what?'

'Beautiful,' Pratima whispered. 'Sweeter than the first rain.'

'Shut up. Never again. Should have known better. Let's wash in the well here. Come on, move, your feet are not glued to an altar.'

Pratima pulled Jamini off the narrow dirt road and towards the burning *ghat*. 'Not that way!' Jamini gasped in surprise. But Pratima seemed mesmerised by the three spots of glowing amber against the opaque indigo darkness.

'They're burning,' Pratima said.

'Corpses, silly, being cremated.'

Pratima slipped her hand out of Jamini's grasp and ran towards the pyres in the distance. Jamini ran after her, caught her. 'What's got into you?'

'Does blood burn?' Pratima asked. 'Blood that you hold in your cupped hands?'

'I don't know –' Jamini faltered. She had never heard such desperation in Pratima's voice before, as if the answer was the knowledge of some ultimate and unknowable truth. She couldn't understand why she, too, had stopped to wonder, all of a sudden, when she really should slap Pratima into her senses, drag her home, give her a hot bath, put her to – 'Why does that matter?' she asked in a whisper.

'I don't know.' Pratima looked around at the dark barren field and the pyres burning steadily. 'There are people who live here,' she said, 'people who light those fires. They would know, I think. It's possible to live anywhere, do anything, be anything, if She – the Mother – is with you, or –' she let out a short fierce sigh '– in you. Isn't that what the priest chants, "Come into us"? Does She then, to fill you with Her power, to make you free?'

'Enough.' Jamini clenched her teeth and gave Pratima a firm shake. 'You listen to me, girl.'

'They are Her people, those that live here, setting fire to dead flesh day and night. They believe in Her, these outcasts, and others like them who had to run away and hide, and they kill for Her, and the blood saves them –'

'You stop this nonsense right now.' Jamini gave Pratima a hard pinch above her elbow.

'I want to burn.' Pratima raised clenched fists to her face. 'Burn – like those dancers, burn myself away.'

'You just listen to me.' But Pratima's eyes remained frozen in their trance-like stare.

When they reached home, Jamini gave Pratima a hot bath, a hot glass of milk laced with opium, and put her to bed. 'Close your eyes,' she said sharply, several times. But Pratima stared unblinkingly at the moonless sky through the windows. Jamini shut the windows, then blindfolded Pratima with a silk scarf, saying, 'I'll close your eyes one way or another.' Pratima lay still, making no attempts to remove the scarf.

'I can still see what I want to see,' she muttered, and received a light annoyed slap from Jamini.

'What's got into you?'

'Nothing.' Pratima began to laugh softly. 'Come, sing me to sleep,' she said, nestling against Jamini.

Running her fingers through Pratima's hair, 'Come sleep-carrying ones, come sit on her eyes,' Jamini sang, until exhaustion made her sink down and curl up against Pratima's opium-stilled form.

The next day, the ayah railed at them for leaving the house at night. 'I know,' she screeched. 'I know. You foul creature, you'll be the death of us all.'

'Stop your stupid cackling.' Jamini slapped the ayah's shoulder. 'Stupid jealous hag. Cursing us because we are beautiful and young and can run around like wild deer.'

'You're the curse,' the old woman snapped at Jamini.

'She's my *shoi*, ayah.' Pratima ran to Jamini and hugged her fiercely. 'Don't speak to her that way.'

'Don't *you* sneak off to Kali temples this way, or else –'

'You'll tell father? Go ahead.' Pratima threw her head back and laughed. 'Nothing scares me. She's giving me her power, I think.'

'Here we go,' Jamini said, placing her hands on Pratima's head. 'I give you that power, I, Jamini, the night incarnate, the darkness of –' she broke off, giggling, and began to tickle Pratima. They struggled with each other, laughing hysterically, tears rolling down their faces, chanting the words they had made up for these games of theirs, while the old ayah watched aghast. 'Take this power –'

'It courses through me like flames!'

'You are darker than the darkest raincloud –'

'I'm not empty any more. I am me now, I am someone, one, me, I, I am, yes, not just Pratima, a clay idol, but that clay form come to life.' Laughing, fighting, they rolled on the floor.

'I invoke you, create your image in my mind –' Jamini caught Pratima's shoulders and tried to hold her down.

'I come to you as you imagine me,' Pratima was laughing, 'recreating myself, reinventing myself for your adoration.' Pratima squirmed, dug her nails into Jamini's hands to break her hold. 'I am alive with your imagination, your love. I am alive with my own desire to become myself –' Pratima twisted out of Jamini's grasp.

'Not so fast.' Jamini caught her waist.

'*Shoi, shoi,* maybe I love you, maybe I hate you, maybe I'd die without you,' Pratima said, spinning around and pinning Jamini to the floor with her hands and knees.

'Hope you don't die because of her,' the ayah muttered. 'Who knows what you are, what she is, I can barely see, and now the light is fading. I'm just a stupid old woman who sees strange shadows all around you, my child.'

'Come,' Pratima said, 'let's dance like temple dancers – come, let's cut off a goat's head, feel the spray of blood –'

'Sit down, you silly, let me comb out the knots from your hair.'

*

The arati *is going on! The boys cry. Can smell the myrrh, the incense, the ghee. Listen to the drums! They are trying to keep pace with the dancer's feet.*

Come Chitra, bring me your comb, come, sit. Let me comb and braid your hair. Lord, how tangled your hair is. Let me get these knots out. Must take care of your hair, child. When you marry and go off, take a girl with you to your in-laws. You must have someone to take care of your stuff, someone loyal only to you.

'You are mean,' Jamini said, wiping her eyes. 'You don't appreciate the quality of your life. Your husband was selected with care. He's on good terms with the sahibs. Who else will protect you from the dacoits who are slaughtering and robbing the zamindars and looting their properties these days?'

'What's that?' Pratima moved away and sat up straight. 'Hear that?' Pounding hoofs surrounded them suddenly. The palanquin fell on the ground with a thud, throwing the two women off their seats. People were running around. Someone screamed and crashed against the palanquin. A volley of gunshots drowned out screams and the sound of running feet for a few seconds. Metal scraped and clashed around the palanquin. Wood was splintering, snapping, cloth tearing, and, against the backdrop of running feet over fallen branches and leaves, Pratima and Jamini heard boxes tumble, and the tinkling cascade of coins. Then, just as suddenly it had all started, all sounds stopped. Inside the stifling silence of the palanquin sat Pratima and Jamini, hugging each other, waiting for the palanquin to be picked up and carried once more, waiting for that swinging rhythm to start, for the chant of the bearers to resume – Hein-ho, hein-ho, hein-ho.

A dry cough. Someone clearing his throat. Pratima disentangled herself from Jamini, and slowly pushed open the door. Her sari dishevelled, her hair falling over her shoulders down to her hips, the vermilion powder smudged across her forehead, she stepped out gingerly, keeping her eyes tightly closed. Her left foot fell on the warm dry grass. Her right foot felt under it something warm and wet that gave a little under the pressure of her weight. A warm spray came up and splashed her face and clothes. She opened her eyes.

The headless corpse under her feet spewed a fountain spray of blood for a few seconds. There were men all around. Their clothes were muddy and bloodstained. They held rifles and swords. Strips of red cloth were tied around their heads. They were all looking at the man who stood a few yards away from her. He was dark, bare to the waist. His long wavy hair rested on his massive shoulders, now glistening with sweat and blood. He was smiling at her as if he knew who she was, as if he had seen her before, many, many times. Pratima closed her eyes and swayed, feeling a strange lightness.

'Ma!' said the man in a hoarse, awe-filled whisper. 'Ma, you have come at last.' He fell to his knees and touched the ground with his head. All the men knelt and did the same. Pratima let out a gasp and collasped on the body under her feet.

Jamini drew in a deep breath and stepped out. She caught Pratima under the arms and tried to drag her back inside the palanquin. 'We're done for,' she said to Pratima's limp unrespons-ive form, and started to cry. 'We're finished. This is the end.' The man stood up and walked towards them. He knocked Jamini out cold with a backhand blow to the side of her head.

When Jamini opened her eyes, she saw nothing. It was black all around. Her head throbbed. She felt herself and found her clothes were intact, but her gold chain, bangles and earrings were gone. She sat up slowly, stifling a moan. Where was she? Where was Pratima? The hiss of a match made her start. A lantern before her face. 'Attend to your mistress.' The voice was deep, musical. He backed away with the lantern, towards a mattress on the bumpy stone floor. Pratima! He hung the lantern on a hook that had been driven into the rocky ceiling. 'I'll have some food and water sent over.'

He had the darkest face Jamini had ever seen. His long hair threw even darker shadows under his cheekbones. Jamini drew in her breath sharply. It was a face that was sometimes found on temple walls, carved with precision on stone or marble, perfect in its lines and unreal in its immortal and malevolent beauty. 'Babul-sirdar would like her to recover very quickly,' he said, glancing at Pratima's unmoving prostrate form. 'Sirdar wishes to speak.' He vanished slowly into the darkness, his slender body bare except for a piece of white cloth wrapped tightly round his hips and thighs. Jamini knelt on the mattress and stroked Pratima's hair. They had been spared – perhaps for later torments.

Pratima's body burned for four days. Jamini applied cold compresses on her forehead with water and a cloth brought in by a young man with a pointed impish face, who also brought in two meals a day, and lukewarm tea four times. He had even smiled at her. 'I'm Tilak,' he informed her. But he wouldn't let her out of that cave, except for a few minutes when he brought the food. He led her through narrow rock-walled passages to a hot spring. He would leave her there for about five minutes each time, then call, and appear. After washing, Jamini would look around wildly, but found no escape routes. Just rocks on rocks and dry scrub. So she would go back to the cave. He always rolled the boulder and closed its mouth when he left, leaving a crack at the top to let in some light.

Through that six-inch crack, Jamini felt the warm wind on her face, heard the tumult of bird-calls and bird wings among leaves and branches, smelt the dry, cracking earth, the fresh limey-bitter smell of *neem* leaves, watched an opalescent sky turn hot white, then bright yellow, to blazing copper, then suddenly glowing indigo. She never saw the moon. So she knew the cave faced either the south or the north.

She explored the dark, cool interior of the cave. The stone floor and ceiling and walls. The surface of the walls puzzled her. They were not smooth. They had etchings all over their surface. The lantern light revealed a strange pattern – uniform in shape and size, spread out in chains across the length of the walls. She measured the cave by walking across it. Sixteen steps long and ten steps wide. It was about twice as high as she was. Narrower near its mouth. Rounded on all sides. Even the ceiling had a bit of an arch to it. Two long narrow berths had been cut into the back wall. With the help of Tilak, she moved Pratima to the lower berth. 'She has never slept on the floor,' she said to Tilak, who shrugged. 'When will you, they, let us out?'

Tilak shrugged again. 'I'll ask Kanai,' he said.

'*Shaitan*,' she said under her breath.

'I'd never dare presume,' Tilak said with a laugh.

On the fourth day, Jamini found Pratima's sari and mattress spotted with blood. 'The damn curse, now of all times!' She struck her head with her hand. At sunset, the boulder was rolled aside. 'I must get out,' Jamini screamed at the dark form. 'I want fresh clothes for her, water, soap, oil.'

'Babul-sirdar wishes to speak to her.' Jamini closed her eyes at the sound of the voice. 'Tilak informed me you wanted to be let out.' He came forward and poured more oil into the lantern. So this was Kanai.

'She'll meet him a week later,' Jamini said. 'Get out.'

Tilak came the next morning and pulled Pratima outside. He

dragged her over dry brown rocks to that pool of bubbling hot springs. 'There,' he said. 'You have half an hour.' Tilak brought her five clean saris.

'Cotton!' Jamini sneered, feeling the rough, undyed cloth. The following day, a bar of crude soap arrived, coconut oil and Yardley's powder. A basket of fruits entered the cave the next day, and cooked goat meat and rice two days later. What a relief that was. For days she had eaten only lentils and *roti*. Pratima was sitting up, and eating as if she were a famine victim.

'I know where we are,' Pratima said, opening and closing her eyes.

'You've never even squinted through that crack over there.'

'This is a *gumpha*!' Pratima said with suppressed excitement.

'A what?'

'We're in Bihar, I'm sure, near the border, near Orissa and Bengal. See these berths, the way they were cut out? Buddhist monks, when they were outlawed by the Hindu kings, hid in caves like this one. There must be a whole chain of them here. These caves became like a secret monastery to them. They carved their doctrine on the walls. Check the walls.'

Jamini removed the lantern and held it near the side wall. 'Some kind of pattern,' she said. 'I discovered it earlier.' Pratima went to the wall and traced the etched script. 'In Pali! Bring the light closer.' Pratima felt the engraved words with her fingertips.

Under the lantern's glow the deeply etched words threw a strange weave-like shadow over them, and over the cave's stone floor. 'My god! This looks different. This doesn't start off with the usual "*Buddham saranam*". It isn't dated either, except for this sign – a half-moon! Look! More of these: crescents, circles, half-circles! "I", look, this means I,' Pratima touched the letters, ' "I have been here almost a month. Arunav still doesn't know. He looks at me and sees someone else. Perhaps I am someone else

70

now." Oh, Jamini, what on earth does that mean? I've got to read all of it! Does this continue on the other walls too?'

'Yes. But what difference does it make? We're prisoners, helpless –' Jamini put the lantern down and pressed her fingers against her temples.

Pratima picked up the lantern and ran from wall to wall, examining, feeling the surfaces. 'Yes! Yes! Oh, it'll take me weeks, maybe months, to read it all!'

'Sit down,' Jamini said angrily. 'Stop running around this way. You may not be strong enough. We have to make plans to escape. Months to read it – what a time for self-indulgence!'

'I've been dreaming,' Pratima said. 'You'd never believe any of it. I dreamt I was free as a god. I had kicked away, shattered the altar, and dived into the sea. A flaming sea.'

'We are prisoners, Pratima.' Jamini gave Pratima a shake. 'The dacoits have us. We're finished.'

'I think something magnificent is about to happen.'

'A slow death.'

'I feel like I'm on my swing again. Swinging –' She swung the lantern slowly from side to side. 'Dancing shadows.' Pratima smiled. 'Jamini, your face is covered with the shadows of these words. And my hands. Like patterns drawn with sandalwood paste on our faces, like henna on our hands and feet.' Pratima spun around slowly with the lantern, laughing. The shadow of the script wrapped around her, covering her entirely like dancing tattoos.

'Sit down, you idiot,' Jamini said sharply. 'You've been sick for a week. You'll lose your balance – you could faint. Sit down, and hang that lantern up.' She pulled the lantern from Pratima's hand. 'What's the matter with you? We've been kidnapped. Here we are in the hands of –'

A crunching, grating roar. Sunlight drowned the cave and dazzled their eyes.

Kanai stood against the light in a pair of well-fitting cream breeches. 'Do you think you could meet with Sirdar today?' he asked Pratima. He bowed his head slightly. Pratima, her eyes shocked with tears by the sudden brightness, nodded.

'Take me to the hot springs,' she said to Jamini. 'I want to bathe.' Kanai bowed his head again and left.

Pratima and Jamini jumped into the water with their one bar of dun-coloured soap and scrubbed themselves from head to foot. They got into fresh clothes and sat in the sun till their long thick hair was dry and shining. Pouring a few drops of coconut oil on their palms, they ran their fingers through their hair, and rubbed the excess on to their hands and feet and elbows. 'Ah,' Pratima sighed, 'I knew there was something waiting!'

'Hell,' said Jamini. 'We'll never get out.'

They walked back towards the cave. Kanai waited near the mouth. He escorted them past a series of caves to a much larger one lit with torches and lanterns. The man who had knelt before Pratima on that afternoon, smeared with blood, sat cross-legged on a heap of deer skins. Jamini counted twenty men sitting along the walls.

Babul-sirdar stood up as Pratima and Jamini entered with Kanai. 'Ma,' he said in a hoarse, whispery voice, 'I knew you would come one day, and you have. But I can't force you to stay. If you wish to go, I'll take you back to your father's house, or to your husband's.'

'They were slaughtered by you and your men,' Jamini said in a choked voice.

'Not at all. We killed only the sahib. The others ran away.'

'Where's our jewellery, and clothes?'

'Those, unfortunately, you will not see again.' Babul-sirdar smiled and winked at Jamini. 'Now, Ma, you tell me what you want to do. Choose.' Babul-sirdar's voice echoed in the cave.

'Get him to take us back to your father's house, tell him, go on.' Jamini clutched Pratima's arm and shrank closer. 'Your father, your in-laws – they must be sick with fear and anxiety.'

'Why would you want me to stay?' Pratima asked, her voice shaking a little. 'What will you do to us?'

Babul-sirdar laughed a thundering laugh. Yes, children, the entire cave rang with that laugh.

'What will we do to you? Eh, Kanai, what do we do? Come, Ma, sit down.'

'We're finished!' Jamini gasped. 'They'll – they'll –' Her voice trailed as she caught Babul-sirdar's eyes. Possessed – the word cut through her head. She saw temple dancers whirl in frenzied circles over burning incense and coal, the soles of their feet scorching, the air filling up swiftly with the smell of camphor and burning flesh. They said these dancers felt no pain because they were possessed by the Mother's spirit. Babul-sirdar, kneeling, his hands clasped, speaking in that hoarse whispery voice, his words swirling around them like the smoke that rises from altars.

'Mother, stay. You are the incarnation. The moment I saw you, I knew. She had come at last. You are not just Pratima, you are the clay *pratima* come to life with Her spirit.'

'I don't understand –' Pratima's voice faltered.

'You stood there before me, bathed in blood, your foot on a fallen form, one arm raised as if to strike. The *tantrik* told me a year back that you would come among us and make us conquerors.'

'And now he is here to collect his *dakshina*.' A voice came from the entrance.

They turned to see a tall, gaunt man in a red dhoti and shawl, holding a trident. His forehead was covered with vermilion powder and sandalwood paste. The glinting prongs of the seven-foot trident were marked with the same, and crowned with hibiscus. 'Give her to me,' he said.

Babul-sirdar stood up. 'She is here for us.' His voice was hard, the chant-like cadence gone, his eyes sharp, cautious, cleared of their ecstatic glaze.

'She is her shadow, and must be reunited with the Mother.'

'Take the other one.'

'Oh my God, he'll chop my head off!' Jamini howled and threw her arms round Pratima.

'I can't sacrifice a slut,' the *tantrik* said. 'Besides, you promised me, remember? If my prophecy came true, you swore you would do as I say.'

'Perhaps we should do as he says,' Kanai said to the sirdar. 'Perhaps it's best to get rid of them.'

'No.' Sirdar frowned at Kanai. 'Whose side are you on?'

'Are we divided already?' Kanai raised an eyebrow.

'She is ours,' Babul-sirdar said to the *tantrik*, ignoring Kanai's remark. 'I'll give you ten goats, if you like, or buffaloes, whatever you want.'

'You've seen the vision – that is enough. You can't hold on to it. You must not be taken in by *maya*, *mahamaya*. You must let the illusion pass, the spirit leave.' The *tantrik* paused and looked around at the men. 'Listen to me, all of you. Now is the time of sacrifice. If you don't offer her to the Mother, She will take her by force. She will not only take her but you as well, and you, and you, and you. What you consider your blessing will turn out to be your curse.'

'Why do I feel you're just trying to collect your hundred and eighth head to make your power complete, eh?' Babul-sirdar took a step forward towards the *tantrik*.

The *tantrik* looked down, smiled. 'Babul,' he said, 'why do we all use our mother so shamelessly, for our selfish purposes? Look at her, Babul. Is she Chamunda, the Mother's terrifying destructive form? She has appeared as Brahmi, the most beautiful; as Kumari, the pure. Will you distort this image to satisfy your need?' He shook his head slowly.

'She is the answer to our prayers,' Sirdar said. 'She is the blessing.'

'So certain, Babul?' The *tantrik* smiled grimly. 'We never know – you'll never know – curse or blessing. Deceiving ourselves with hope, belief, faith. We don't know very much, Babul. Don't have the ability to distinguish in the true sense, but ignorantly dividing, good, evil, either this or that – separations leading to confusion. There's only one truth ultimately, and that truth you never want to face. Because life would become meaningless then, living a worthless sham, a masquerade. We need to enjoy the masquerade, if we are to live. We need to believe fervently in the sham.' The *tantrik* struck the ground three times with his trident, turned around and left the cave.

Puzzled, questioning looks were directed at Babul-sirdar after the *tantrik*'s departure. 'What if he spoke the truth?' someone asked.

'Yes,' said a few others, 'what if?'

'The truth is,' Babul-sirdar said firmly, 'she is here, with us, to guide us, protect us. We must believe that, given the circumstances. If she stays –'

Babul-sirdar led them out of the cave to the savage brightness outside. They followed him up and down rocky inclines, through rock-walled passages, over patches of cracked earth. They seemed to be within a fortress of stone carved inside this plateau. Babul-sirdar brought them up on a flat boulder. They were at least fifty feet above the dry, barren fields in the distance. A few cows and goats, their hides stretched painfully over sharp bones, wandered aimlessly from tree stump to scorched scrub to shrivelled-up banana tree. Clusters of huts, ghostly, shadowy like shimmering dustclouds blended into a vaporising silver horizon. Jamini shifted from one foot to the other, unable to stand still on the heated surface. The heat seemed to drum against their eyes, ears, noses and mouths, beating against them with the force of a tidal wave, drowning them, filling their lungs. In spite of the eerie silence, the heat roared in their heads, making their senses swim. Even the shadows that fell glistened like molten lava streams.

'All gone,' said Babul-sirdar. 'Run away or dead. No rice will grow on this burnt earth unless we wash it with blood. Only blood can wash away that blue poison. My village was wiped out by it. Most of the men hanged or shot when they refused to destroy their land with it.'

He led them down through tunnels that echoed with the sound of bubbling springs. A strong sulphur smell swirled in on hot moist gusts of wind. The last tunnel opened up to sunlight again, banyan and pipal trees filled with birds' nests, and the ruins of a temple. Some of the columns around the small courtyard were broken. Drying creepers with wilting mauve flowers coiled around them. The altar steps were cracked. The high flat ceiling had beehives hanging from it. Bird droppings crusted the angles between walls and floors. At the far end of the altar, in an arched alcove, was a black stone statue of Kali. One foot on the prostrate Shiva, clothed with a skirt of arms and legs, a garland of heads, she stood there biting her tongue. One hand held a severed head, the second was extended as if to bless, the third was raised to offer courage and the fourth, raised like the third one, held a crescent-shaped, well-sharpened steel blade. The statue had been showered with petals, and red hibiscus lay all around, covering her feet and the fallen body on which she stood.

It was a few degrees cooler inside the temple, the breeze hot but moisture-laden from the springs. And all around them was a raging storm, it seemed – of whistling, rushing bird wings, piercing shrieks and cackle of bird-calls. Near the alcove, the altar floor was still red with dry sacrificial blood.

'Ma,' Babul-sirdar knelt before the altar and motioned Pratima to come forward. 'Look, Ma. There you are. And here,' he turned to look at her, 'you are. Brahmi, the *tantrik* called you, Kumari. Yes, so you are. How else would you come to us? If you had appeared before us with Chamuda's bloodthirsty eyes, we would be terrified. We can't behold that fierceness of yours with our frail spirits. So you have appeared as Shyama, the radiant dark one, the Queen of the Night, your fury arrested, as Maha-Kali, our beloved mother.'

Pratima paced the length and breadth of the cave. The boulder was no longer there. Jamini shook out the thin mattresses and coarse sheets and laid them out in the sun on the flat stretch outside.

'Tell them to take us back, right now. I won't stay here another minute. Your father must be going mad, your husband, your in-laws –'

'The Buddhist monks hid here, outlawed, condemned to death, but they carried on in the name of the enlightened one. Who do you think Arunav was, and who is the "I" of the story on the walls? I must read it all, must find out.'

'We are in the hands of assassins and thieves. We have spent more than a week out here with the vilest of men. I would rather sit with an untouchable. Have you any idea what kind of convincing it will take to make your husband take you back? Even Ram had problems with Sita. Your husband can think all kinds of things. Oh, lord!' Jamini struck her forehead. 'I always think it's a good thing for us to be together. But under these circumstances – they might think I corrupted you, made you like myself. "Like maid, like mistress," they might say. Oh lord, I never looked at things that way. I'd rather die than cause you such grief. How do we get out of here? Pratima, tell them now, tell that man to take us back. Go on. Your father will perish with worry.'

'Do you think they'll take me with them when they go on their raids?'

Jamini sat down and stared at Pratima. There was almost a glow on her face. She was looking straight into the sunlight without blinking. 'I never ever wanted to get off that swing,' Pratima said. 'Especially when the storms hit, when the rain came down like a million arrows, when the lightning almost sliced down to the ground.'

Jamini stood on a boulder and watched Kanai help Pratima on to a chestnut Arab mare, no doubt grabbed from a murdered sahib. No wonder they owned such good horses: a sahib's head had paid for each horse. Kanai, on a black horse, led Pratima's mare across the barren fields. Pratima, in a pair of beige breeches and a white cotton *kurta*, seemed to be adjusting to the horse quite well. 'Men's clothes!' Jamini had shrieked, when Tilak had brought the breeches to their cave.

'I asked for them,' Pratima had said.

'They've probably been ripped off some slaughtered sahib, and that *kurta* taken from some young, innocent zamindar.'

'So?' Pratima had raised her eyebrows.

'So? All you can say is "so"? Have you forgotten everything, who you are, what you are –'

What had happened to her? Jamini didn't have a clue. Pratima had lost consciousness, burned with fever, and at the end of five days, risen as someone else. Yes, that's it. She had turned into a

78

bhairavi. A dead person forced back to life by a restless spirit, a spirit unable to leave this world for the next, due to some curse. Now it possessed Pratima. It would make her do appalling things. Perhaps the *tantrik* knew what had happened, and wanted to sacrifice her to release the spirit, exorcise it for ever. Looking at Pratima on the cantering mare in the distance, Jamini gasped. It must be a male spirit then.

Kanai was urging the horses to a gallop now. His wavy black hair flying behind him, his slender body crouching over the horse's neck, one hand still holding on to the reins of Pratima's mount. Jamini drew in her breath sharply. She had never seen a man of such absolute beauty.

Two hours later Kanai brought Pratima back. Her face was red and sweaty from the heat. She pranced rather than walked. 'You'll be sore by tonight,' Kanai said. 'Get her to give you a massage.' Jamini pulled Pratima down on a fallen rock before the cave.

'Are you OK? Not feeling faint?' She brought water, and tried to wipe Pratima's face with a damp cloth. Pratima laughed, pushed her away. Kanai's mouth twisted to a sneer.

'Same time tomorrow,' he said, and left.

And so it went on, day after day. When Pratima was able to leap on to her running mare, ride without holding the reins, jump on and off even as the mare was going into a gallop, even ride bareback, then Kanai introduced her to the rifles. Against the sound of gunshots, bolts clicked into place, the snap and crack of cartridge packets being opened, Jamini cautiously explored life inside Babul-sirdar's hidden fortress, one thought turning in her mind restlessly: how to get out, together.

She wandered aimlessly over the plateau, thinking about oil-massages in the afternoons. Haggling with silk merchants, flirting with bangle sellers, the DM's blue eyes. What an alien world this was, where no man ever smiled at her. Sirdar's men passed by her often. But they hardly ever glanced at her. And even if they did look at her, their eyes never glowed like the eyes of the men at the bazaar, or the sahibs she had come across.

The only person who smiled and winked at her occasionally was Tilak. '*Arré, pyari*,' he'd wander casually up to her and say, 'how are you feeling these days?' Jamini would lift her chin and walk away. Tilak would follow. Then Jamini would sit down on one of the boulders and sigh heavily. Tilak would come and stand next to her, lean against a boulder, or put his foot up on one and rest one elbow on his raised knee. Slowly, stiffly, a conversation would start.

'I don't understand what you people are or what you do,' Jamini said to him archly. 'You expect us to believe that you slaughter the sahibs and the zamindars who have fallen in with them, rob them and distribute the money to the villages around? How do you men eat so well, and buy so many guns and swords, if you're giving all the wealth away?'

'Oh, we don't give anything away,' Tilak said with a laugh. 'What do you think – we're living in *satya yug* or what? Humans filled with divine compassion in a land flowing with milk and honey? *Kya, chutiya hai kya sub?* We only give to our families in the villages. We take care of ourselves and our own. That's all. We don't care who else lives or dies. We take care of us. They are out to get us, we, to survive.'

All the dacoits had wives and children in the three villages east of the plateau, Jamini learnt. The eastern and southern sides were pratically inaccessible to anyone who had no knowledge of the secret paths and underground tunnels. And between the plateau and the villages was a dense forest filled with tigers and snakes that very few dared to enter. Talking to Tilak, Jamini realised that most of the men were Bihari, two Bengali. Kanai was a Saontal from a tribal village near Jhargram. 'He's an odd one,' Tilak told her. 'Keeps to himself, you know. Babul-sirdar's right-hand man. Kanai sets up all the ambushes, organises the men. He's the best shot, and the best scout. He can smell sahibs a mile away. Indeed, he can even tell you, just by sniffing the air, how many sahibs and how many *desis*. And with a sword – why, I've seen him toss an apple up in the air, and then I just saw his sword flash up, and the apple fell to the ground in four pieces! Why else do you think Sirdar's having him train her? We were all trained by him and Sirdar. Without Kanai we'd be quite lost.'

'What about the sirdar?'

'He's the sirdar,' Tilak said. 'He gives us a reason to be and to fight, to survive.'

'Is he a terrible man?'

'Terrible? Maybe. He's kept us alive so far. What do you know? Coming from a zamindar's house, eating the best rice, sleeping on silk sheets? When our fields were ruined by indigo, when we could grow neither rice nor indigo, couldn't pay taxes, had to watch helplessly while our wives and children were sold off – then Babul came forward and brought us here. First, there were eight of us. Then Kanai arrived. His entire village had been butchered. They had revolted, chopped off a few white heads. Saontals are like that. But Kanai was softer, I think. Well, that was six years back.'

'What's he like now?'

'He can slice a throat just like slicing a fruit. His face never loses that coldness. We all have our women, you know, one wife, maybe two. But Kanai never keeps a woman for more than a few days. He even slit one woman's throat when she got to be tiresome. She would keep coming here, crying and wailing, saying she was carrying his child. Babul was afraid – so were we, actually – that out of desperation she might betray us to the zamindars and the regiment stationed near the villages. Babul suggested to Kanai that he keep her, you know, but one afternoon when she arrived again and began to howl, Kanai walked over, caught her by the hair and – well, that was that.'

Jamini saw Kanai help Pratima load a rifle, empty it, clean it, reload it, fire it.

'Kanai fills his cave with clay plates and pitchers,' Tilak told her. 'He paints on them.' He took her to his cave and showed her some pots that Kanai had given him. Jamini touched them hesitantly. The clay surfaces glowed with emerald and gold forests, turquoise and silver rivers, exquisitely drawn birds, fiery tigers, blood-red flowers. 'He doesn't sell them, though he might get a pretty good price for them. He was a potter before he came here.' Tilak turned a pitcher slowly, allowing the sunlight to pick up all the colours. 'He was the finest painter among his people.' Painter and killer. Jamini shook her head. Monster.

'Where do you men cook?' Jamini asked Tilak. 'I can help. I can cook well.' Maybe I can find a poisonous root around here, or *dhatura*, or something, she told herself.

Tilak roared with laughter. 'You must think us all *chutiyas*. Let you cook! Kanai warned us you might ask to do just that.'

Jamini pursed her lips. 'How is it no one's discovered this place? It's not exactly invisible.'

'No one has found the secret entrances. They've tried, believe me. No one comes this way these days, since those villages out there were abandoned and those fields ruined. Besides, with Madhu on the watch, we're quite safe from intruders who might get in. He was trained to be a scout by Kanai. Madhu knows all the secret trails. But come now, let me show you where we cook, eat, sleep, and even live.'

Tilak led her to a dark narrow cave. It was long, like an enclosed passageway which widened and brightened slowly, and all of a sudden, Jamini found herself at the edge of a stone courtyard, similar to the temple courtyard but much larger. It was framed by caves. Looking up, she saw another square framework of caves overlooking the courtyard. Steps had been carved from the caves above, leading down. Jamini ran to the middle of the courtyard. Above her was the high, rocky ceiling, which blended with the ceiling of the second tier of caves. And in the centre of that ceiling was a circular opening, about ten feet wide, shaded by the branches of a pipal tree, through which the sunlight filtered in. 'The heart of the plateau,' Tilak said.

'Has Pratima been here?' Jamini asked.

'Of course. Don't fall into the *chula*!' Tilak was laughing. Jamini looked down. A thick, soft carpet of ash. A foot away was a hole about two feet wide. Large pots sat on one side, some of them covered. A large basket of coal stood next to the hole, together with wood for kindling, and dung cakes. 'Come,' Tilak said, 'and do close your mouth – flies might go in.'

Some of the men were sleeping in the caves. Some were playing cards or with dice. They nodded at her as she passed the caves and looked in to see the interiors. She followed Tilak up narrow stone steps to the second level. One large cave had a potter's wheel and a kiln in it, and on the stone berths, rows of pots, some with a plain terracotta glaze, some of them painted. This particular cave did not have a ceiling. Bright sunlight streamed in through the rectangular space above. Bowls and cans of dyes stood on the stone shelves along with the pots, and brushes made from quills, feathers, twigs and horsehair. The adjoining cave had more painted pots, rifles, swords, knives, and a thin cotton mattress. Four unlit lanterns hung from the ceiling. At the back, a rope had been tied across the cave. A few clothes hung on it. Jamini breathed deeply. But no smell came to her except the smell of paints and dyes, and the acrid flavour of glazed terracotta.

She had imagined the fragrance of fresh sandalwood paste around Kanai. But there was only the cool scent of stone and clay and ash here. She wanted to go in, touch and smell the clothes. Tilak led her along the narrow stone ledge outside the caves.

Jamini saw glass bangles encasing bamboo poles in one cave. 'Hari's a bangle seller,' Tilak said. 'He goes to the villages, even now, with his bangles.' In another cave two men sat on the floor with gold and silver jewellery on a sheet before them. They were removing the set stones from all the necklaces, bracelets, rings, earrings. 'They're making the gold and silver market-ready,' Tilak said with a wink. 'The stones we sell separately.' Jamini was introduced to Chinmoy next, a skinny young man whom Tilak called 'the tailor'. There were heaps of clothes in Chinmoy's cave, and Chinmoy was swiftly sorting them out: breeches in one lot, trousers in another, shirts, *kurtas*, dhotis, scarves, saris, sheets, silk handkerchiefs, all tossed into separate heaps. 'I fit everyone,' he said, smiling, touching his head with two fingers. 'Anything you like?' Jamini smiled weakly and shook her head. As they walked past Kanai's cave, Jamini closed her eyes and breathed in that clay-and-ash smell again.

After weeks of shooting and riding lessons, Jamini saw Kanai and Madhu, a boy of seventeen almost as dark as Kanai, train Pratima to scale rock-faces. They taught her how to follow hidden trails, how to cover her tracks. All the time, Madhu was Kanai's shadow. Whenever they stopped to allow Pratima to catch her breath, rest, Madhu would nestle against Kanai, rub his head against Kanai's shoulder or chest. Jamini held her breath and waited with clenched fists for some show of extraordinary violence. When Kanai responded by ruffling Madhu's black curly hair or giving him a little shake by holding his neck, Jamini got weak at the knees. For a fleeting moment that cutting coldness vanished from

84

Kanai's eyes. His mouth curved into a smile instead of twisting to a sneer. Jamini sat and watched them all day.

Just seventeen, she thought, looking at Madhu. Just seventeen. He just might be easy.

When the swords began to flash in the distance, Jamini watched horrified. 'Just one blow,' Kanai was telling Pratima. 'The head must come off with one blow; therefore, at this angle. Remember you have to sever bone from bone. And you'll get just one chance.' Curved blades sliced through sheets of rawhide rolled up tightly around bamboo poles. Jamini chewed her nails and shut her eyes.

'Tired? Shall I give you a massage?' Jamini would run to her when she returned to the cave. Pratima merely shook her head. She hardly spoke to her any more. Yes, no, a nod or two. A lot of the time, she sat close to the wall with the lantern and read the engraved script silently. When her eyes were tired from reading in the dim light, Pratima would lie on her side on that stone berth and stare at the indigo darkness outside. Her face was becoming like Kanai's, Jamini felt. Jamini couldn't figure out her moods any more. Pratima without moods, without laughter or sullen tears. She neither smiled nor frowned. A terrible coldness had taken over her bright eyes, eyes that glowed with a strange fire only when she was on a horse, or running over slippery rock surfaces, or was lifting a rifle to aim, or slicing through thick rolls of rawhide. She lived in men's clothes. She even walked with Kanai's loping gait. One night, finally, Jamini sat down in a corner and began to cry.

'Why, what's the matter with you?' Pratima asked.

'The matter?' sobbed Jamini. 'The matter? What's the matter with *me*? What's the matter with *you*? You treat me like furniture. Your days are filled with all kinds of things, while I sit on a rock all day and wonder what you have become and why. When you return, you walk around me like I am a column in your way, you take food and water from me as if I were a table. And you ask me what is the matter?' Jamini struck her head against the wall. 'We used to talk, laugh, fall asleep together. Any time I come near you, you move away. I lie on a stone berth and watch you all night long, watch you stare into the night.'

'But I listen,' Pratima said, 'to Kanai and Madhu playing their flutes. They go far away from all of us to some abandoned village and play. One can barely hear them unless one concentrates. The sound is so far away from us.'

'Us! What's us! You and them. What about me?'

'Why, you're still the same, *shokhi*, the very same.'

Do you know how long it had been since Pratima had called her 'shokhi'?

'Tell me then, why, why this, why here? What's happened to you?'

'Why, nothing, nothing at all. I've merely learnt to breathe and walk. That's all. I love you still – how could I not love you?'

'What will become of us? Where are we heading?'

Pratima smiled, and for a moment Jamini saw a flicker of that girl whose hair she used to comb and braid – Pratima wore her hair in a tight coil high on her head these days. 'I can't wait to find out, *shoi*.'

Soon Babul-sirdar appeared, to watch Pratima's performance. He bowed before her, smiled, laughed, and walked with her arm-in-arm as if Pratima was one of his men. 'Think she's ready?' he asked Kanai, who shrugged, nodded. 'For the next raid – the first one, mind you, after the one in which we found you – you will come with us.' Jamini cursed that giant of a man when she heard that, when she saw Pratima's face light up as Sirdar spoke.

86

Sirdar's eyes disturbed her with their intense, possessed look, as if he had entered the world of his dreams, as if he had glimpsed the ultimate, and realised it. His face made you wonder, made you curious: what was this vision? When he looked at you with that straight, clear gaze, almost through you, at some distant light, you wanted to follow the direction of that gaze – to find that light. His men would gather round him, touched by this wonder; and Babul would turn to look at Pratima, bow, touch her feet. The men would drop to their knees, their hands clasped against their chests, and whisper, 'Ma, Ma,' their eyes closing.

'Mother, you give us validity,' Babul said to Pratima. 'Mother, you are the reality, our way. You are the darkness that shines brighter than the brightest light. Above all, you are ours, and we yours. Bless us. Make us come alive, just as we make you come alive with our words.'

The look that spread over Pratima's face then made Jamini shake. She had seen that look once before, at the burning *ghats*, after the goat sacrifice. A startling wonder. Babul's words seemed to open the doors for Pratima to some inaccessible world. 'I felt real,' Pratima said to Jamini, 'when he said that, when he knelt before me. I feel I am, at last. One day soon I'll find out if blood burns.' Bewildered, Jamini prayed to Kali, in fact prayed that Babul-sirdar might get his head chopped off, or receive a bullet in the right place. That man was taking Pratima far, far away. Jamini could barely touch her any more.

She sat mutely and watched Sirdar prepare Pratima for the night raid. An evening party was being held for the tax collectors at a zamindar's mansion twenty miles west. 'Kanai will lead,' Babul-sirdar said to Pratima. 'He becomes the darkness at night.' They dressed in black clothes and went to the temple after dark. They placed baskets of hibiscus before the alcove, lit lamps and incense and touched the altar with their heads. Like the rest of the men, Pratima took the lump of brown date sugar from Sirdar. Within seconds her blood seemed to pound in her head. She swayed, losing her balance, and sat down on her heels. Jamini forced her way through the men.

'Light,' Pratima said, 'blinding light.'

'*Dhatura*,' whispered Jamini, half crying, 'the sugar contains *dhatura*. You'll die. Spit it out quick.'

'Wait for me, *shokhi*,' Pratima said. 'Don't fall asleep.'

Shadowy waves crossed the barren fields and turned east and then south. Kanai, Sirdar, Pratima and the men vanished into the moonless night.

Jamini sat outside the cave with her chin on her knuckles. The scent of *bel* and *juin* touched her from time to time, and the dry dust with its quicklime-and-ashes flavour. Black as congealed blood, she thought, the night was. The only sound, the buzz of mosquitoes and the drone of cicadas. What had gone wrong, where? She rubbed her eyes. From the comfortable home of Pratima's father to the opulent and powerful home of her husband. What smoother transition could there have been? What better life? And for Jamini, a new, richer, better-looking sahib. Pratima could have got them out. Take us back, that's all she had to say. With that brute of a man on his knees before her, Pratima could have got anything, anything. There was a choice in the matter. But Pratima hadn't chosen. She had lapsed into a different being, allowed an awful otherness to take over. That man had seduced her with his lies, with his dream of an impossible state of being. Unbelievable, though. Pratima, who had no experience of men whatsoever, was so at ease with these men. Perfectly comfortable, as if she had known them all their lives, as if she was truly one of them. Perhaps it was the adoration. All of them on their knees before her. Would make you heady, make you forget a lot of things. Heady – what was that feeling like, really? She couldn't remember feeling exactly that. Jamini had occasionally got mildly drunk on the district magistrate's whisky. But heady – what was that?

Those dancers who dance before sacrifices, stepping on burning incense, feeling no pain, no fatigue, just falling to their knees, their bodies trembling, arching backwards when the blade swung down and severed the goat's head. Then they would drop, like a sari slipping down your body to your feet, cascading to the floor, their bodies easing, resting like a still pool of water before the altar. Heady – madness, madness.

She must get Pratima out, get them out, away, soon, before it was too late. Too late – but for what?

Too late for what, for what, for what . . . too late . . . The mosquitoes, the cicadas, the night drummed against her ears.

She fell asleep sitting as she was, the darkness wrapping around her, blurring vision, humming –

The drums are getting faster and faster, the boys whispered in excitement.

Shanta says that when Kamal dances with the clay braziers and lumps of burning incense roll off and fall to the ground together with pieces of hot coal, Kamal simply dances over them, swirling, swaying, his feet scorching, his eyes closed. He doesn't stop, or even gasp in pain. Did you know? Chitra asks, her eyes widening. He doesn't feel the pain, the burning.

They dance and they dance, the dancers, the thick perfumed smoke wrapping around them like Kali's darkness. And the priest is chanting, Come, come, overwhelm us, flood us. Yes, the drums are like pounding blood in our hearts. Listen –

'*Shokhi.*' Jamini woke up with a start. 'Come.' Pratima pulled her up. Half awake, Jamini stumbled over rocks, sliding, tripping, almost falling, unable to pull back, to stop Pratima, to ask why, where, to even look at her face. Pratima's wet, slippery hand grasping hers made Jamini's skin tingle uncomfortably.

In the temple courtyard lit by torches, Pratima stopped and faced Jamini. It was the look in Pratima's eyes that pushed Jamini's heart up to her throat, not the blood-smear on Pratima's left cheek or her blood-covered hands and clothes. Ecstasy or terror? Pratima's eyes were wide, shining, her whole body trembling. She was trying to say something, her lips moving, but no sound except the sound all around of laughing, cheering men, the shimmer and tinkle of coins, the hiss of torches. 'I was afraid,' Pratima said at last in a choked whisper. 'But then,' she added haltingly, 'right then, I wasn't.'

'*Jai Ma!*' Babul-sirdar's voice boomed across the courtyard. All others picked up the call, raising their fists. Babul-sirdar led Pratima to the altar. He knelt before her and covered her feet with handfuls of hibiscus, murmuring, '*Jai Ma, Jai Ma*, bless us, Mother.' The men came forward and showered her with the crimson flowers, touched her feet. They placed their weapons around her in a circle, and on each rifle, sword and knife, dropped a hibiscus. The smoke from incense sticks swirled around Pratima. She stood as still as the dark stone idol on the altar, knee-deep in hibiscus, in that perfumed smoke-circle, with her eyes closed. The courtyard rang with voices demanding her blessing, her courage, her spirit. Babul-sirdar stood up and drew a vertical line on her forehead with his bloodstained thumb. '*Jai Ma*,' he said softly, placing a hibiscus in her hand, and another one on his head. 'Come alive, now, for ever, for us. Now have your being, beloved mother of ours, queen of the night.'

On my forehead, draw the mark on mine. The boys mark each other's faces with red powder.

Close your eyes and see the altar, I say to them. The priest places a handful of earth on the clay pitcher on the altar. Then, a leaf, a hibiscus blossom, a fruit. The spirit of the Mother will enter the clay pitcher and make the cold clay come alive. He places a hibiscus on the mat he will sit on. He places a flower on his head.

It took nearly an hour of hard scrubbing to get the blood off Pratima's skin. Jamini threw the clothes out of the cave. 'I'll burn them tomorrow.' Pratima stood in the middle, still trembling. 'Are you cold?' Jamini wrapped a sheet around Pratima and made her sit on the stone berth. She let down Pratima's hair, combed it, wiped it with a wet cloth. 'Wash it tomorrow, first thing.' Pratima's body started to shake violently, her teeth chattering. Jamini put her arms round Pratima, held her tightly. How hard her body had become, all the softness gone after all these weeks of riding and running. Jamini stroked her shoulders and arms, ran her fingers down her back, pressing gently. So hard the flesh, like a man's. She could feel Pratima's ribs clearly, and her hipbones. She tried to ease the tautness around Pratima's neck and along her shoulders. Pratima's body was hot and breaking out in a sweat. 'Tell me what to do,' Jamini said against her neck. 'I don't know what to do. You're not mine any more.'

'It's cold.'

'What did you do, what on earth did you do?'

'I will n-not be afraid, n-not b-be afraid,' Pratima said gritting her teeth to control the chattering. 'I raised my arm – brought it down at the right time. The – the right time. There were lights on the lawn. The air was attar-scented. They were laughing, and looked up startled. It was over like that midsummer storm. Remember? When we were on the swing that day? A flicker of an eye. Kanai and Madhu knew where the money was, tax money – blood money.' Pratima struck her knee with her fist. 'Our horses had wings, Madhu said. We laughed and laughed.' She tossed her head as if to throw off something. 'Never afraid. I wasn't, I won't be, I'll do well, I did well . . .' She went on repeating, 'Never, wasn't, did well . . .' in a low chanting tone.

'Stop,' Jamini said. 'I'll get us out, I swear. Try to sleep now. I'll hold you, sing you to sleep, *shokhi*.' Jamini held her as tightly as she could and began to hum. 'Come sit on her eyes, bring some sleep, will give you rice from the rice tray, come sleep-carrying ones, come to our home, there's no sleep in her eyes, come sit on her eyes . . .'

Pratima stared at the darkness, her eyes shining brighter than the breathtaking dazzle outside.

'You must not – never again – with them – never.' Jamini gave Pratima a shake. 'Never – do you hear me?' Pratima lowered herself into the bubbling pool. Jamini rinsed the soap off Pratima's hair. 'Try to see them as they are. Do you realise what you did last night? We must get away from these men, from Sirdar. He's a man possessed. Don't let Kanai near you again. He – he – do you know he killed the woman who was carrying his child?' Pratima sank under the water, then came up gasping. She spat out water and laughed.

'That woman was making a nuisance of herself,' she said.

'You can't go around killing, just getting rid of people, just because they are getting in the way!'

'Funny you should say that, *shokhi*.'

'And what's that supposed to mean?'

Pratima looked at her and rolled her eyes. 'Kanai isn't so bad,' she said. 'He's a very good teacher. I never imagined I could even ride a horse, let alone jump on and off galloping ones. Babul-sirdar adores him.'

'He's a monster, like him. So why shouldn't he?'

'Monsters . . . yes, perhaps. They say Kanai may not be fully human. Only lightning can be as swift, only the air as invisible. Only a wolf can pick up scents like Kanai does, only a hawk can see as far. Perhaps some god snatched tiny pieces from these beings and churned them together in a magic vessel, and out sprang Kanai, shining like the night. That's what they say.'

'And Babul-sirdar must have sprung up from a butcher's back yard.'

'Don't speak of him that way!' Pratima slapped Jamini's hand. Jamini moved back with a gasp. 'He's the gentlest, most wonderful person I've ever met. He calls me Mother. He would lay down his life for me.'

'You are –' Jamini stopped. It was that same look on her face; whenever she would swing violently on that swing in the garden, or play those games – dressing up, running around the house with a stick, drawing that third eye on her forehead. The old ayah ready to swoon with shock, Pratima raising her arm, her eyes like the black midsummer storm. And that evening at the old temple, after the sacrifice, the goat's blood filling her cupped hands. Jamini never figured out the sensation coursing through Pratima during those moments. Elation, joy? Or was it sheer terror? 'Why?' asked Jamini, 'why?'

Pratima played with the water. 'See how it bubbles constantly? My interference doesn't change a thing. I divide it, splash it, make different patterns in it. It runs through my fingers and falls into its eternal rhythm.' Pratima splashed Jamini. 'When you slice through the air on a swing, fight the wind rushing at you, let the wind push you forward, you feel an inexplicable splendour dance through your veins because you know that if you didn't move your legs, kick the ground away from under you, quite a few times, feel the nothingness under your feet, you would never get into that swing-rhythm, never travel that arc – forward and up, down, back, and up again.' She splashed Jamini with water again.

'I don't know what I mean. I feel a third eye on my forehead. Can't see it, but I feel it seeing me.' Pratima threw her head back and laughed. Laughter echoed back and forth between the rock walls. Jamini put her hands over her ears. This was not Pratima's mischievous laughter. There was a frightening reckless edge to this laugh of hers. Jamini watched Pratima play with the bubbling water, slap it, splash it up, curl her fingers and try to grasp the water, squeeze it, hold it. 'I feel that third eye on my forehead burning me. Right here.' Jamini closed her eyes. There had been games of excitement before, running around the house with sticks, slashing at drapes – mere games, shadow-play. But now it had all transformed to a state of being; much like the old ayah had cursed, it was a pulsating reality.

'I'm part of that rhythm, that swing, that rush of air,' Pratima laughed. 'I'm burning.'

'Burning in a trap. You're caught, don't you see that? Don't you feel trapped in these caves, by these men? You think it's adoration, worship? That you're on the altar? Trapped on the altar, you fool! They encircle you like the goats they sacrifice, they surround you –'

'But it's they who are kneeling.'

'And what about you?'

'I burn.'

'Really? Not desperate any more, like when you sat brooding on your bed?'

'Desperate . . .' Pratima let the word out slowly, stretching it like a cobra's hiss.

Kamal is dancing as if the whole world were disappearing before his eyes, children, the soles of his feet burning on the fallen debris of incense and coal. His body sways, bends, twists, turns. He is the rising crest of a wave. He is a wave crashing on the shore. He is the whirling storm that levels villages, the crescent sweep of the flood that pulls the earth into the sea.

But he might fall. Chitra's fists clench. He might trip, lose his balance.

He'll fall on the altar, cut his forehead on its wooden threshold. The boys look at Chitra and bare their teeth.

Blood will spring up like a fountain of light.

I wish we could go there to see him dance, Chitra whispers. He dances as if tonight is all.

To see the goat's head chopped off, the boys laugh and shriek.

Perhaps tonight is all, tonight is always, and mine only.

Pratima drew Jamini into the cave. 'Come, I must read you the story on the walls. Remember how I used to read to you before?'

Jamini looked at Pratima in amazement. Was she coming to her senses? Was this remembrance a backward step forward, towards the past? So sudden – should she believe? But her eyes – so clear, oh, so disarming, just like before, yes, remember? Sit and tell stories, come, *shokhi*. That old look, that old voice. Perhaps this madness comes and goes. Perhaps now they could plan together to escape. Pratima sat down cross-legged in front of the left wall. Jamini sat down close to her, holding the lantern. 'Remember Arunav?' Pratima asked. ' "Arunav still doesn't know who I am." See, the narrator says, "Perhaps I have become someone else." '

'Who is the narrator?'

'Shh. "Arunav comes into the cave, all wet, asks me to dry him, give him his ochre robes. He sits on the bed as I comb his hair, just like before, except this is not my bed with its fine muslin sheets, all strewn with rose petals. Arunav doesn't blush at my touch, for he sees before him a boy on the verge of manhood. I wear these male clothes with such ease that I amaze myself. I look so handsome I could be a prince, like Arunav. I have to help him dress very cautiously, never allowing my fingers to stray. I close my eyes from time to time. I know this body of his so very well. Does Arunav really not know?" ' Pratima stopped and looked at Jamini.

'I can't believe this!' Jamini put the lantern down and touched the wall. 'What was she doing?'

' "Arunav asks me to bring his lunch to him under the tree outside. He leaves the cave slowly. I lean against the wall, my legs weak, my head swimming. His walk hasn't changed, neither has his lean, tall body. His hair is still flaming copper, and his copper eyes burn still, but with a different fire. He has glimpsed a crystal clearness, you see, because the hand of the great Narendra touched his head. Arunav searches for Nirvana.

' "That afternoon, three full moons ago, in the flash of an eye, Arunav lit up under Narendra's hand. Everyone had heard of Narendra. He had been all over the north, the south and the east casting the spell of Gautama, converting thousands. Kings had banished him, condemned him. But Narendra was still roaming free, stealing men away from their families, jobs, breaking through the promises of lovers, tearing them apart. Narendra, defying our king's decree, spoke to the people before the palace gates. Arunav was still asleep in my bed. Narendra's deep, musical voice carried over the temple courtyard, the wide stone steps, through the inner recesses, into my chambers. Arunav woke up with a start. He didn't even hear me call. He followed that voice to the palace gates. I ran after him, pleading, cautioning him. The King had outlawed the doctrines of the Enlightened One. He had banished all the followers, condemned them to death. —The prince has come! people whispered, seeing Arunav. Narendra went on and on, his voice making the people kneel, sway, raise their hands up in the air, cry, beg for Gautama's secret. I couldn't believe what I was seeing. Arunav was kneeling before Narendra, looking up at the old man's smiling face. And the wrinkled hand stretched forward, rested on Arunav's flaming head.

' "Then the soldiers were all over, their swords flashing. But no one tried to run. The soldiers looked around helplessly. These were their friends, brothers, fathers, mothers, sisters, wives, children. The soldiers fidgeted with their swords and spears and scratched the ground with their feet like frightened deer. Narendra led Arunav away from us. I walked back to the temple slowly.

' "Arunav came to the temple two years ago. He stood against a marble column and watched me dance. He sent me blue lotuses for three months, but never approached me, never sent a note or a messenger. You would expect a prince to be more assertive. He had won two battles against the border tribes already, and he was only twenty-three. The King had arranged his marriage with the Licchavis – a coveted alliance. But Arunav had refused to marry. So the King married the Licchavi princess himself, in order to secure the alliance.

' "It was so amusing to see Arunav with his burning copper eyes stand against that stone column evening after evening. But I started to miss steps, make wrong turns, lose track of the beats. The musicians began to swear under their breath, and give me angry looks. They couldn't believe that the best dancer was dancing like a novice. But what could I do? I had never seen such helpless eyes. I'd seen him ride through the city on his golden chariot, in his golden armour, his victorious head flung back, his triumphant army cheering, the crowds showering him with flowers. I never imagined he would look at me with such helplessness, as if he was lying on a battlefield, bleeding to death.

' "One evening I tripped and almost fell. I left the floor, embarrassed to tears. The other women took over the floor. I threw the flowers from my hair and wrists into the pool in the courtyard, and ran to my rooms. Arunav lay on my bed, his hands under his head. He had covered my bed with rose petals. He had lit lamps all around the room.

' "His hair used to slip through my fingers like long, warm flames. I would close his restless eyes. I wanted to erase that restlessness in him which made him run outside on stormy nights, and stand under the pounding rain. —What are you looking for? I asked him. —I don't know, he'd say. —It's just a feeling. He swore eternal love, and so did I. He practically lived in my rooms for a year and a half, abandoning the palace, enraging his father. Arunav always called me 'Priya', beloved.

' "Beloved. The word changed my life. Sometimes one has dreams; recognises them as mere dreams. But when a dream calls on you, makes you touch it, know it like you know the texture of your own skin and hair – then – what changes absolutely is your reason to be. So unreal. A dream living with me. Abandoning life as one knew it. What future? I dared not think. The present, so fragile, so breathtaking. Dreams always shatter, the other dancers said to me. Especially dreams like this one.

' "Arunav left the palace at night. He followed Narendra. The King sent his guards to the temple. They took my father, the priest, away. In court, the next day, the King accused my father of collaborating with the Buddhists. —You haven't got rid of the stone idol of Buddha, the King said. —It still stands in the centre of the courtyard. My father fell to his knees. —It's only a statue, he said. —We worship Vishnu in the temple. Look at the mark on my forehead – it's the mark of Vishnu. Buddha is an incarnation of Vishnu. How can I throw the statue out? My father was beheaded the next day. I gathered a few things and ran off with the other dancers to the forest. We knew the guards would come after us. The four girls decided to go west, beyond Magadha. But where was I to go? Narendra had taken all from me in one afternoon.

' "I went to the village west of the forest. I kept my veil drawn over my face so that I wouldn't be recognised. There were guards everywhere looking for us. I slipped into the goldsmith's house. He had always liked and respected my father. He and his wife let me stay for two days, knowing that we would all be executed if anyone found out about me. —You must go away, they told me. —You must leave the kingdom. They said they could help me escape to Varanasi. I asked them for men's clothes. I decided to find Arunav and Narendra and make my own peace in my own way.

' "I remember Arunav's face the night he left. He stopped by the temple to return a ring I had given him. I don't know what Narendra said to him, but Arunav was a man possessed. —I must find it, he said, —I must feel it, must know it. And there is only one way, Narendra's way. I threw myself in his path. But he just jumped over me and ran down the temple steps.

' "I stood before an old man's funeral pyre, dressed in a man's clothes, my once-knee-length hair now barely touching my shoulders. Men looked at me curiously as I stroked the pyre with a branch. They took me for an *acchut* who lives near the burning *ghat*. I threw my dancer's clothes into the flames, the gold pins with which I used to put up my hair and the silk bag which contained my cut-off hair. As my hair burned together with the old man's dead flesh, the acrid fumes scorching my nose, eyes, lungs, I exhaled hard. Priya was smoke now, vanishing into the darkness. I walked back through the forest to the palace gates where Narendra had captured the city with his words. I breathed deeply the night air fragrant with *sal* blossoms. I will find Arunav, and bring him back – to his senses, to me. And if I fail – if my reborn, stronger self too is destroyed – no, I will not let Narendra keep Arunav from me. I will find Narendra and learn from him his words of seduction.

' "It took me two weeks to find these caves, to see Arunav

again. I found the secret passage into the heart of the plateau by following a rabbit. When I reached that courtyard surrounded by caves, I saw Narendra sitting with his men. He was talking to them, telling them a story perhaps. I heard him ask them, — What do you remember? I don't know why I knelt, why I clasped my hands at the sound of his voice. Narendra turned to look at me. He smiled, his eyes half closing. —Come forward, he said, his voice sweeping around me like a drawing tide. He touched my head, asked me my name; but I couldn't speak; my voice failed. —You too cannot remember? He laughed, pulling me to my feet. —You will be called 'Smriti', boy, you will be memory.

' "Narendra asked Arunav to show me to my cave – this outside cave, away from the inner sanctuary. Perhaps they didn't trust this sudden memory! And alas, I was a pretty dead memory, it seemed, because Arunav's eyes were blank when he looked at me. Perhaps I had disguised myself too well, darkening my skin with walnut juice. There was no kohl lining my eyes, no jewellery adorning my wrists, throat, ears, hair, forehead. I must have looked quite plain.

' "Day after day I listened to Narendra's stories and sermons. —Don't let the fire of desire destroy your spirit, he would say, touching Arunav's hand sometimes, while I sat next to Arunav, my hand touching his feet. I didn't believe a word Narendra said; I didn't agree with a single idea. But I couldn't stop my mind from lapsing into this strange contemplation of the enchantment Narendra offered – a world without boundaries. No kingdoms or conquests, no untouchables or élites. All would think with this new light; minds would not be devoured by the flames of desire, but burn instead with a clear flame to distil the spirit for Nirvana. —Yes, it is a place, this Nirvana, Narendra said, touching Arunav's hand. —It is that something and somewhere we search for, that which is most intimate and ultimate – but we fail to discover it

100

because we grope for it with our hands, mouths, eyes. Close your eyes and release your mind from the trappings of fear, doubt and desire, and the light will wash you with its clarity.

' "But I don't want not to want, I wanted to scream. Through my desires, my fears, my doubts, I feel my self live, I feel my spirit come alive. What is most intimate and ultimate is what I shared with Arunav, and I want that back. Not your empty promises, Narendra, not your clear intangible light of Nirvana. I want to touch my world, taste it, see it, hear it, smell it, burn in it. I want to adore it, break my head against it in frustration. I don't want your clear light. I want turmoil and pain and anguish, yes, fears, doubts, all of that, the bad stuff, the madness, the longings, the uncertain happiness, passion, passion, passion, and I want –

' "—I still sense a flicker of hesitation in your spirit, Arunav. Narendra leans forward and looks into Arunav's eyes. —Does memory come in the way, Arunav? Narendra flashes me an amused glance. I start, freeze. The old man can't know. Just his weird sense of humour. —Something, someone? Narendra asks.

' "—No. Arunav closed his eyes.

' "I must reopen his mind, I said to myself.

' "I place a plate of food before Arunav. He nods his thanks. I sit down and watch him eat slowly. —You don't have to wait on me, he says to me. I smile, shrug. Narendra likes to see me attend to Arunav. I heard him whisper to Sachin, who is a monk like Narendra, and has been with him for fifteen years, —A little adoration and attendance will do Arunav good. After all, he was a prince. This Smriti will ease the path to Arunav's transformation. Sachin had shrugged.

' "—Arunav will prove to be valuable, Sachin said. —A converted prince is far more convincing than a converted peasant. More people believe in converted, good-looking princes. They turn out to be very appealing ideas.

' "Narendra had smiled wryly. —I would like to think that it is our ideas that are most appealing. I want them to believe in Gautama's vision like I do. But young resolute faces like Arunav's are far more attractive, I have to, alas, agree. You're a scoundrel, Sachin.

' "—I bow before the master. Sachin smiled, bent low and touched Narendra's feet." '

'Arunav will change his mind,' Jamini said. 'He'll go back with Priya. I know it. These men won't succeed in converting him. Love is stronger than all these doctrines and clear lights and all that. Arunav is young, Priya is beautiful, and there's passion.'

'I don't understand why you think that way,' Pratima said.

'Didn't you want that young poet as a lover?'

'He always said the same things over and over again.'

'Never mind the wretched poet. I know how this story's going to end. Happily.'

'Happiness is relative. What you consider happiness, Arunav may not.'

'But what of love?'

'Love?'

'Yes! Remember the young poet?'

'God, you're so trite.'

Jamini recoiled as if struck. The scorn stunned her.

'What do you know of love or passion, Jamini? The DM? Your numerous lovers?'

'And you, you – whom no man has ever touched – what do you know of it?'

Pratima narrowed her eyes and looked away. 'Dancers who dance over flaming incense, feeling nothing but the music, burning inside and outside, distilled to a pain of intense purity, then nothing matters but the pain, you move from one pain to another, birth to rebirth, pain loses relevance, and blood and fire become one.'

'You're mad. You make no sense.'

'Aren't you interested in the rest of the story?' Pratima raised a mocking eyebrow.

'I believe in Priya's power,' Jamini said, striking the ground with her fist.

'She is Smriti now – a memory like an old wound.'

'Why must you be so cruel?'

'Why don't I just read? "Arunav rested his head on his arm and lay down. I massaged his feet. He walks around a lot over these rocks, inside the plateau. His feet are callused, and the skin around his heels is chapped, cracked. Although he tells me not to attend to him this way – preparing his food, helping him dress, easing his tired feet and body with massages – he likes it all the same. He hasn't got used to the stark life of the monks and novices in these caves. It's not that he's led a soft life before – he's been through two wars. But this stark solitude makes him restless – more restless, I think, than he used to be on stormy nights in my rooms.

' "He asks me often why I serve him this way. —I find an anchor in you, I tell him. —You are a tangible reality to me, more endearing than the vision of that intangible Nirvana. Arunav laughs, ruffles my hair as if I were the boy who took care of his horses and his chariot. He asks me about myself. —There's nothing to tell, I say, because my life is just beginning. —What about your life before? he asks. —That lies in ashes, I smile and say.

' "—I'm glad you're here with me, Arunav says. —Sometimes when I'm afraid, I look at you, and your presence gives me new courage. Perhaps fate threw you in my path to help me along in my search for Narendra's vision.

' "—Yes, I say, —you and me, a trick of fate, surely. I can't imagine life without you any more.

' "—Boy, you talk too much! Arunav cuffs me on the shoulder lightly, laughing. I notice deeper lines around his eyes and mouth as he laughs. He looks older. That carefree boyishness has vanished. I want to kill Narendra. Rip him from throat to waist. I want to hold Arunav, kiss those lines away, whisper, Forget, forget, forget, come back to me. At twenty-three how can anyone give up life, love? How can a withered old man make you do so? What is evil – desire or negation of life? I cannot believe Gautama, who was a prince himself, preached that we should give up living.

' "—What exactly does Narendra offer? I ask.

' "—Peace. Peace that is beyond knowledge, Arunav said. —We have to free ourselves from material attachments. That's the way.

' "—The way is the way of life, of living. Freeing the self through the experience of living. Negating life is wrong – that's what I feel.'

' "—Because you're afraid of the wonder, Arunav says, touching my face.

' "—Have you ever known the wonder of love? I ask. I shook inside. But I had to give Arunav's mind a jolt.

' "Arunav didn't answer. He closed his eyes. —Well? I asked, giving his ankle a shake.

' "—I must forget.'

' "—Then you still love her.

' "—That's not an issue any more, he said. —Go away and take your annoying questions with you.

' "—I still love, I said.—And I won't give up.

' "—Then why did you come to Narendra? Arunav asked, sitting up. —If you can't let go then you must return to this woman you cannot shake off.

' "—There is a problem, I said. —Narendra's voice is as seductive as my love. I don't know which one will win yet. I must put both to the test.

' "—How dare you! Arunav caught my arm. —Narendra is like Gautama. He is not here to compete with mortal emotions.

' "—No, of course not. He merely wants everyone to leave their mortal attachments aside and follow him, adore him, believe in him, accept his word as the only truth. He is so above it all.

' "—Stop this. Arunav's fingers tightened on my arm. —You should leave, go away from here. Your mind is neither prepared nor ready to receive Narendra's vision.

' "—Why don't you, Arunav, teach me then? Your mind was transformed by a single touch, wasn't it?" '

'My God!' Jamini touched her throat. 'She is so brave. She has to win.'

' "—Narendra's voice opened my mind. His words entered my consciousness. Your mind is closed.

' "—If you convince me, I will believe.

' "—Only you can convince yourself, make yourself believe, Arunav says. —Narendra merely lights up the darkness inside with the wisdom of another.

' "—Narendra does far more, I'm sure, I said. —And yes, one must choose light over darkness. Searching for this light one's consciousness is re-created – yes, true. But do you know, prince, this search for the light can destroy, too. Wreck lives, dreams. What is this promise of a higher ecstasy that destroys living? The lover abandons his beloved. Seek the light that will re-create consciousness, Narendra says. Ah, but it destroys someone's reason to be, too, someone's very life. And what of her, what of her? How will she live knowing she's lost her life? What of that wrenching pain – I stopped, closing my eyes. I had said too much. I meant to be subtle. Pain can take over sometimes.

' "—Who are you? Arunav asked. —Something strange about your eyes, Arunav says. —Who are you?

' "Could I swear his voice shook just a little. Just my

desperate imagination. —Why, I'm just Smriti, I said with a laugh, – a poor, helpless soul wandering aimlessly, determined to love.

' "—You must learn to love differently. Love an idea, not a woman.

' "—I do, in a way.

' "—Who is this woman? Arunav's voice is strangely urgent.

' "—Why do you want to know? I asked, startled. He looked away.

' "—I'm sorry I asked. Sometimes I forget." '

'Do you remember, *shokhi*,' Jamini asked Pratima, 'how we'd lie in bed in the afternoon, making up wild stories?'

'Kanai's waiting. I have to go.' Pratima ran out of the cave.

The air grew stormy as Jaishta moved into Ashar, the month when the clouds gather. The thick curtain of heat began to quiver as sharp winds struck it. Pockets of coolness formed, as if stormy fingers had ripped in and made windy spaces. Brown clouds of dust blew over the cracked earth all around. Jamini sat in the shadow of the rocks and watched Pratima groom the horses with Kanai, Madhu, Tilak and the other men. They had drawn up a list of the future raids, and went over the details of each as new information came in every day. Were they getting their horses ready for tonight? Jamini wondered.

Kanai rubbed a horse down with a sack. He brushed the mane and the tail. He ran his hands along the horse's neck, back, rump, legs, stomach. Then he rubbed his face against the horse's neck. Jamini bit her lips and watched Kanai catch the horse's ears and pull its head down. Monster, she said to herself, and gave herself a reassuring hug.

Pratima ran up the rocks, past Jamini, into the cave. 'We're going now,' she said to Jamini, who had got up, startled, and followed her in.

'In the afternoon?'

Pratima got into a soldier's khakis and rushed out. When she walked back up the rocks again, as the dark copper light was vanishing into glowing indigo, looking as if she was carved in ruby, Jamini howled and fell to her knees.

'I was not afraid,' Pratima said softly.

'You could have had a husband, sons, a palace for a home, a happy life.'

'Why, I have twenty-two sons. How many more would you wish for me? They raised their fists in the air, Jamini, and called me Queen of the Night, beloved Mother. If you were only there.'

'Yes, I was there,' Jamini said, 'will always be there, next time, and every time. To see the madness, to rub your face in it till you come to your senses.'

'You'll see men on horses scatter in confusion. For a moment your vision will be obscured by dust and blood. Then, as if looking through a waterfall, you'll see the flash of crescent blades, bursts of flame, see bodies melt into red bubbling pools. You'll hear that stormy waterfall crash around you, and then you'll know it, just then, feel blood burn, and you'll find yourself falling, falling against laughter, laughter all around. *Jai Ma*.'

Was that what Pratima said? Jamini closed her eyes as the horses disappeared, trailing dustclouds. She knew exactly. Saw it clearly, as if a magic mirror was before her eyes. She could taste the tidal waves of dust from the hoofs. She coughed, almost choking. Her eyes watered. Smoke, stinging smoke. Wild neighing and pounding of hoofs all around. A warm red spray that eased your body. Ah, and the dancers were swirling, wreathed in sandalwood-scented smoke, swaying, spinning, their eyes half closed, their bodies arching back, back, until their hair almost touched the ground, trembling like bows drawn to breaking point, and ah, see how they spring forward through this lamplit darkness now acrid with burning flesh, the soles of their feet melting against flaming myrrh, and is this the blood burning, and are they heady, heady, is that what they are as they drop spiralling before the altar, a handful of tossed flowers, stretching out into this languorous stillness, resting their faces against the warm, wet stone to lapse now and for ever into this crimson dream?

What magic lies at the heart of this?

Would that I could feel this too, only to know and feel, to harness this magic, and then could I not transform you back with the same power, back to me, to what was?

Is it Kanai who entrances? Crouched on his horse, almost one with the animal. Could her – my – heart be still when Kanai turned his head to glance at her?

Kanai moving with that dream-swiftness from one point to another. Kanai in his own impenetrable magic circle, a dance whose steps you could not follow, because the music eluded your ears. Would that I were the music. Would stop you at will, snatch her away from you and this headiness which I can neither feel nor understand. What is this sway of dancers, a flood rushing across the land? Which god can I pray to? Which god will enlighten me?

Eyes closed, Jamini sat before the cave through afternoons and nights. Ashar was drowned by Sravan, and the rain thrashed ceaselessly. The dry fields around the plateau churned muddy under a foot of water. The plateau itself turned into an emerald forest. Bushes and trees sprang up from every spot that wasn't stone. Hibiscus blossoms spread out like red stains. The dark rocks steamed for a while, then turned shiny, cool. 'Senseless!' Jamini heard Kanai snap at Sirdar when the men returned from each raid. 'Senseless. If we lose our heads this way, we'll forget to be swift, careful, be discovered. We do this to survive. We're not butchers.' 'Stop!' she pictured him yell during a raid, 'Enough!'

'No!' she knew Pratima was yelling, 'no,' till Kanai rode over, caught the reins and turned her horse around. He must have reached out and caught Pratima's raised arm.

'Even She stopped,' he said to her, 'so you must, too.'

Jamini saw it all, through a red cascade, as the warm rain pounded all over her, in the closed darkness of her eyes.

Cannot stop, she heard Pratima say. This blood is necessary, Babul whispered, for this land, for the love of our mother. The horror, Jamini muttered, the horror. 'Yes,' she heard Pratima say, 'true, a lurking horror – living, breathing, then all cut short, something just not there any more. And I feel I've conquered that horror. Snuffed it out.'

'To be truly oneself, Ma,' Babul's hoarse whisper, 'to be truly oneself one must strive against all limits. To be truly oneself, one might have to be, in the definition of the ordinary world, bad.'

'You die and you die and you die,' came Pratima's faltering voice, 'till death gives up, leaves it all in your own hands. No other divinity but the self. This surrender that's a conquest, I think. Feels so strange. Do you understand? Strange and breathtaking. Not beauty, not ugliness. Just a breathtaking feeling that sweeps away everything else and you feel the ecstasy of death.'

Senseless, Kanai said again. But they couldn't hear him. They had spun off far far away with those dancers who danced on behind Jamini's closed eyes.

There's a price on Babul-sirdar's head, and he's a hero in three provinces, Jamini heard from Tilak. 'They all know about us, about our mother. They believe Kali has come to earth with her flaming sword.' Babul-sirdar showered Pratima with flowers, coins, powdered sandalwood after each raid. 'If you could hear what everyone says,' he said to Pratima, 'Mother, they believe you are with us. They believe we are right. They believe we – no, you – are the saviour. All the blood that flows, they say, will restore life to this devastated soil. Hail, Mother, bless us, be with us always.' Jamini hated these words that made Pratima's eyes burn like torches – these words that had swept her over to that other side, these words that had torn her from Jamini.

Children were told that if they stole pickles or didn't go to bed at the right time Babul-sirdar would eat them up. The district commissioners threatened the zamindars to speed up their search for Babul-sirdar's hide-out if they didn't want their lands to be annexed and turned into cantonments. In the villages many were tortured, shot, hanged. But no one could locate Babul-sirdar, who was always carrying off the tax money. He rides with Kali, they said. Kali's darkness hides him, protects him. When a zamindar dared to quote this to a district commissioner, 'You don't say!' the sahib said, slapping his boot with his riding crop, 'you don't say! A damn girl, with a damn sword? My dear fellow, taxes are taxes, have to be paid, and that annoying bunch be caught and hanged by the neck, I say.'

'Enough,' she knew Kanai was ordering, 'senseless, senseless.' But did he not feel this headiness?

'Jamini.' Pratima was before her again, drawing her close, holding her. Jamini withdrew sharply, recoiling from Pratima's sticky wet touch. Now these stains were on her sari, against her skin.

'Get away from me!' she screamed at Pratima. Her sari was covered with long red flames. She would burn to her death. She screamed and tore at her sari, removing it and ripping it to shreds. Pratima pulled her to the hot springs and down into the pool.

'What were my sins?' Jamini covered her face. Was she paying for her sins? Had she sinned, then, all her twenty-five years? She had only tried to survive the best she could. And for that, this? The water seemed to bubble up red before her, all around her. The strong sulphur smell, salty, hot, burnt her lungs.

'You swore to be with me, for ever and ever,' Pratima said. 'To stay with me. You swore.'

And so the madness went on, children, like those drums beating now with an ancient passion.

Ah, Jamini could not understand. What is this headiness? Something that takes you beyond yourself, beyond humanity almost? Like living in a dream and a nightmare at the same time. Losing yourself to a dream of passion. All boundaries disappear. Thought and action become one, fantasy reality. And you understand for the first time, for ever, that the meaning of life is this burning. So you let yourself burn. You let yourself be put on a pedestal and allow others to enclose you in a ring of fire; or you place another on a pedestal and encircle that creature with flames. There is no escape from that. In both situations, all burn together. No one gets out.

But Jamini hadn't learnt that.

Pratima had always known that, I think. When the choice is between one fire and another, what's the point in running away? Why not start the fire instead, and dream that you're burning the pain away?

I don't understand your words, Chitra whispers.

Don't worry, I say. It's not a matter of understanding, really. It's a feeling. A few among us have the dance in them. We call it madness.

Madness? Chitra's eyes widen.

Yes, girl. Madness, a forgotten way.

For ever and ever, Jamini muttered to herself night after night. What are my sins? How to get out? How to stop the dancers who spun ceaselessly inside her head? She sat against the cave wall and traced the etched script with her fingers when she was alone. Priya, she said the name out loud, Priya. You're so strong. You're so determined. You'll get your prince out of that old man's clutches. Priya. Jamini struck the wall lightly with her head. Priya, help me. Help me get her out. Help me get us out. How did you get your prince out of these caves? Give me your mantra, give me something. I see you leading him out into bright sunshine, back to the temple, then to the palace.

The King forgives you because you restore his son and heir. He won't behead you. He's grateful to you. No more bloodshed. Priya, I can't stand this smell. Nights, afternoons, all exude that sick red smell. When the wind brings the fragrance of *sal* blossoms, and I breathe deeply to fill my entire being with their sweetness, that red smell leaks in and chokes me, burns my lungs.

Perhaps I should have stayed back in the zamindar's house, stayed with the DM. Perhaps you, Priya, should have fled beyond Magadha, beyond Varanasi. Now in these caves, we live with strangers. Strangers! Who are these that we loved so dearly? Who loved us, too. What changed them? Words, cheers, the imagination of others? We used to run around the house, play all kinds of silly games. Silly games.

Ah, what games have I played to survive, to live well. A restless girl threw her arms around me, called me *shokhi*. I had never heard a word so magical. I used to sing to her, tell her stories. I shared all my secrets with her. She would look at me with wonder-filled eyes. She would say she couldn't live without me. How does she live now? How do I live now? You should have wondered about those strange games you played with her, I tell myself now. When she sat silent all day, her face darkening like a monsoon sky, you should have shaken answers from her. What is this darkness that takes over you? Tell me, *shokhi*. When she got on her swing and laughed that reckless laugh, you should have stopped the swing and demanded, What does this laugh mean? There was a madness you did not understand, you didn't quite notice. Ah, a headiness! What can I say to myself? You wanted to rise to the place she occupied and receive the same privileges. But the place she inhabited was not the place you saw her roam. It was not made of corridors and carpets and silver plates and silk sheets. When she held you close you thought she was drawing you into her realm. You wretched fool, look around you now.

Help me, Priya. I'll worship you as a goddess, if you like. Deity you might as well be, carved into this wall, your stone altar. Even if you aren't divine – if you are just a helpless spirit now – let me make you divine, all-powerful, all-knowing, with my desperation I create you goddess. You have to bless me now. Perhaps these words are your secret mantra to help us. If I only knew how to read them, knew how to – I'll pray to you, goddess of the secret mantra. Help me get her back. Help me draw her back into our lost world, the world where we played our silly games, sang our meaningless songs, where we peeped through shutters at a young poet with a sullen face. I choose you as my deity, as all others choose theirs for their particular purposes, because you alone can help me now. You alone listen to me now. Goddess of ploys, plans, listen to me, please, and get us out.

In the mornings, Pratima would run off to Sirdar's cave to meet with the men, then go to the temple. Madhu came with the food these days. When Jamini asked the boy why he came instead of Tilak, she learnt that Pratima had asked for the switch. So the boy came with the food, swept the cave, shook out the mattresses, polished the boots that had been 'acquired' for Pratima. He was shorter than Kanai, Jamini measured with her eyes. Wiry, with sharp dark eyes. A stubborn chin. Seventeen, she said to herself. Maybe. 'How did you meet Kanai?' she asked him while he swept the cave.

'Why d'you want to know?' He looked at her through narrowed eyes.

'Does he hit you?' Jamini asked.

'He might kill you,' he said, straightening up, 'if you ask too many questions.'

'Where's your mother?'

'In a tiger's soul.'

For a few days, when Madhu turned up, Jamini sat at the mouth of the cave, making sure he had to squeeze past her while she combed her hair. 'Come, let me comb your hair,' she said to him with a smile one day. He gave her a funny look and went away. She would smile at him, tilt her head to one side, laugh, when he worked in the cave. He began to smile awkwardly at her. Jamini ran her comb through his hair one rainy morning, and Madhu slapped her hand with a laugh. She caught his shoulders and pushed him against the wall. 'Silly boy,' she said, laughing, 'I like silly boys.' Madhu shifted uncomfortably under the pressure of Jamini's fingers. She ran her fingers along his shoulders, throat, down his chest. Madhu let out an uneasy laugh. Jamini played with the hair curling behind his ears, pressing herself against him. She saw Madhu's hands form fists against the wall. She traced the line of his jaw and moved her fingers to his mouth. Her fingers pushed against his tightly clenched lips. 'Come on,' she said. 'Don't be afraid of me.'

He opened his mouth, allowed her fingers to travel over his teeth. 'Aha,' Jamini said, and closed her eyes. Within a few hours I'm getting us out of here, Jamini thought. My new-found goddess must be helping me. Just give me a few hours and I'll have a slave at my feet. Madhu's teeth clamped down on her fingers. With a swift jerk, he disengaged himself from her, but kept his teeth sunk into her fingers. Jamini screamed in agony and fear. Blood streamed down her wrist, down his chin. He let go of her fingers and struck her across her face.

'Snake,' he said through his teeth. 'Kanai was right. Now we know for sure. We're going to slit your throat.'

Jamini clutched her bleeding hand and crawled moaning to a corner.

'Look what they've done to me,' Jamini wept when Pratima returned, holding out her hand. 'Are you going to stand and watch while they cut my throat?'

Pratima washed and bandaged her hand, calmed her down. She went out, got Madhu back. 'Why did you do that?'

'She tried to – to seduce me, to help her escape, get us hanged.'

Pratima slapped him hard. 'No matter what she does – no one is to touch her, ever.'

'Even if she touches us?' Madhu asked, rubbing his smarting cheek.

'Next time I'll kill you. Nobody touches Jamini – you tell them that. Now, out.'

Pratima sat down next to Jamini, held her close and rocked her gently.

'Pratima, Pratima.' Jamini cried on her shoulder. 'There's a price on Sirdar's head, on your head, too. If you're caught – what will that do to your father, your husband? The shame, the humiliation – we'll be hanged or shot, dragged through the streets, paraded like common criminals. They might call you Mother today in all the villages, but the day you – we're – caught and hanged, they'll cheer for the sahibs, the zamindars.'

'They'll never get us, never alive.'

'This place sickens me. Rocks on rocks, always inside rocks. If I could only walk through a bazaar, haggle with the silk merchant or the bangle sellers –' Jamini began to cry uncontrollably. 'Just once, Pratima, take me to a village, let me see normal people, just once. I'll drown myself, throw myself from these rocks, I can't live this way –'

Kanai shook his head slowly. 'She'll betray us,' Babul-sirdar said.

'She won't,' Pratima said. 'Because if she betrays you she'll be betraying me, too. And that she won't do. She won't risk my life.'

'Why don't we just get rid of her?' one of the men asked.

'I told you what she tried,' Madhu said, jumping up. 'She should be taken care of right now.'

'I think she's harmless,' Tilak said, scratching his head. 'But to let her go to the village, with that regiment twenty miles away –' He, too, shook his head.

'Please.' Pratima turned and faced the rest of the men, who were eating quietly. 'Please believe me. Jamini will not do anything to harm any of you, us, I swear. On my life. I will cut my own throat if something goes wrong.'

'All right,' said Babul-sirdar. 'One day.'

Much to Jamini's chagrin, she was blindfolded and carried like a sack over Tilak's shoulder to the village. By the time she managed to get the cloth off her eyes, Tilak had vanished. She had been dumped in the middle of a cluster of banana trees. Before her was a dirt road leading to a village. Behind her a dark forest with a solid wall of trees. She couldn't see any paths or clearing. She stood up and dusted herself.

The village was small, with only about fifty huts, and a bazaar that offered only vegetables and fruit. One stall carried crude soap and coconut oil. Ridiculous, thought Jamini. What am I supposed to do here? No real stores, no sahibs on horses. People stared at her the way people in such villages stare at strangers. Jamini blamed it on the rough cotton sari she was forced to wear, since all their proper clothes had disappeared. She walked around the village, sat near a pond for some time, and watched the goats and cows graze. Then, seeing the sun vanish behind dark clouds, she hurried to the clump of banana trees. Tilak sat there smoking a *biri*. 'You *chutiya*,' she yelled at him, '*sala chutiya, behunchud, gandu, harami*.' Tilak not only blindfolded her, but gagged her and bound her wrists and ankles as well, before throwing her over his shoulder.

116

'I won't be treated this way,' Jamini screamed at Pratima.

'We'll see what we can do.' Pratima laughed and offered her some lychees. 'Now get out of those soaked clothes and settle down.'

Somehow she would have to get them to trust her, Jamini told herself. Twice a day she whispered a prayer to Priya. Help me, goddess of a-plan-to-get-us-out. Help me, goddess of getting-my-own-way. They must let her out on her own, show her the hidden paths. She couldn't trust Pratima to plead on her behalf any more. She had become one of them. But Jamini would save her, she would. She combed her hair vigorously, braided it, coiled it on top of her head. She had won many a man's confidence in the past, and many a woman's. We will do it your way, she told herself. I won't give up. 'You think I'm afraid?' she asked Pratima. 'You think I can't deal with blood? You think you can't trust me because of that?'

From then on Jamini rode behind Pratima, holding on to her waist so as not to fall off the horse, gritting her teeth through the hard bumpy ride and keeping her eyes tightly shut. Jamini let the dancers spin out and fill her senses. She breathed in sandalwood-scented smoke, not dust. She heard drumbeats, not the thudding of hoofs or the sharp report of guns. Instead of startled voices, she heard the chant of adoration. Cupped hands lifting flowers, crimson hibiscus, and the blade that sliced down lightning-swift merely separated a goat from its head. And then they were supposed to take that blood, mark their foreheads with it. Must. It was the blessing. The smell made Jamini so very light-headed. She gasped with surprise as she felt, yes, almost felt her body sway, swirl without her consent, become almost one with those shadow figures circling inside.

When she heard the men cheer and laugh, Jamini let the words squeeze out through gritted teeth. '*Jai Ma.*' 'For ever and ever,' she whispered into Pratima's ear, 'for ever and ever, *shokhi.*'

'Stop,' Kanai was hissing. 'Now. Turn around. Senseless.'

But no one paid any attention. They disregarded Kanai's warnings and stopped only when Pratima leapt down from her horse and threw up her hands. Only Kanai moved his horse away. He stood and watched, his face inscrutable as always.

It's amazing, Jamini felt, that none of the men ever get hurt. Not even a scratch. They were fired on, but not one bullet grazed even a little finger. And nothing ever touched Pratima either, except someone else's blood. But perhaps that was because Kanai always rode next to Pratima, his sword or rifle creating a magic circle around her, and luckily around Jamini, by default. Babul-sirdar swore it was Kali's shadow that protected them, her blessing, our mother, Pratima. The men knelt before Pratima. She went to each one and touched his forehead with her hand. Kanai moved away when this ritual started at the temple after each raid. From time to time he would glance at Jamini. Jamini shook inside every time she caught Kanai's glance.

Yes, children, Jamini, beautiful as she was, confident with men as she was, shook every time she caught Kanai's glance – which was always, because she could never take her eyes off Kanai.

Jamini was surprised and frightened by Kanai's attention. She didn't know what to make of it. She didn't know what to make of the next surprise, either. 'You can go to the village by yourself,' Pratima informed her. 'No one will follow you. Madhu will show you the way.' Jamini threw her arms round Pratima. 'Kanai agreed at last,' Pratima said. 'I'll get you some spending money.'

Thank you, goddess of liberty, Jamini said to the cave wall, touching the carved letters.

Soon Jamini began to disappear for the entire day and return to the cave with silk saris, glass bangles, silver earrings, anklets. 'Don't betray us for these,' Pratima said to her.

'I'd rather die,' Jamini said. 'How can you even think that?'

Jamini found the second and third villages closer to her tastes. More people, more stores, and even an occasional sahib or two riding through the bazaar. They were from a cantonment twenty miles away. One day a tall, big-boned woman came up to her when she was flirting with the bangle seller. 'Jamini?' The woman reached and touched her shoulder. 'We know about you,' she said. 'Come with me.' So Jamini met Meena, Babul-sirdar's woman, and their two daughters and two sons. She also met Tilak's wife, Kajli, and the wives and children of the other men. They were all very curious about Pratima, and Jamini did her best to satisfy them. Moving her hands wildly while she talked, Jamini presented Pratima as no Kali had ever been presented. 'Does she breathe fire, then? Really eat their guts? Drink their blood from their own skulls? All they say is true, then. We thought there was more to it.' Jamini, taken aback by the response, left in exasperation.

But now her visits to the villages became more entertaining. She liked chatting with them. She braided their hair, they braided hers. They often gave her sweets and date juice for Pratima. Kajli was especially nice to Jamini whenever she was there. She liked to hear about Jamini's life at the zamindar's house, and Jamini would present her with a fairy-tale account. 'Such hardship now,' Kajli would murmur. 'Come, let me massage your poor feet. So rough and callused now. This life is all right for us. We grew up this way. But what adjustments you've had to make for the Mother's sake.'

'Well, yes,' Jamini would nod slowly. 'But when you love

someone, believe in them, well . . .' She would let her voice trail, breathe deeply, and let out heavy sighs. Kajli would rub hot mustard oil on Jamini's feet, massage her toes and heels. Then she would wash Jamini's feet with hot water, scrubbing them with a pumice stone. She reddened the sides of Jamini's feet with henna. 'Now this is how your feet should always look,' Kajli smiled and said. She even got hold of a pair of new leather sandals embroidered with gold thread and presented them to Jamini.

'I don't know why I like them,' Jamini said to Pratima. 'They are just village women – the kind I hardly ever spoke to before, you know. They're good company though, strangely. Wish you could meet them, Pratima. Well, maybe that's not such a good idea,' she added quickly, recalling the image of Pratima she had presented and the one they had in their heads from before.

'You seem to be taking care of your feet magnificently,' Pratima said, regarding the henna on Jamini's feet.

'Well, we sit and do these silly things now and then. I put henna on their feet. Sometimes, I even put it on mine. Remember how we used to paint our feet together? I'd wash your feet, then line them with henna. We painted our hands too, remember? We had to put our feet up and wait till it dried, or there'd be orange footprints all over. Wouldn't you like some henna on your feet sometime? How about now?'

'You've lost your mind.' Pratima stared at the henna lining Jamini's feet.

'Yes, I must have.' Jamini looked at her feet and smiled.

After two weeks, Tilak stopped Jamini from going to the villages. 'A new regiment has moved into the second village and set up camp,' he said. 'They are here to find us.'

No regiment had ever been sent to look for them before. But the raids had never been so frequent or so bloody either. Kanai and Madhu stalked the area night and day, checked out the secret paths in the forest, laid traps around the plateau. They would have to live as if they were one with the rocks, Kanai told them.

A week passed by. Jamini grew restless. 'Your pacing around is giving me a headache,' Pratima complained. A dull tension developed among the men, since no information was available about what was going on in the village with the regiment camped there. Kanai wouldn't allow any scouting beyond the forest. Sit and wait, was the order. At the end of another frustrating week, Jamini told Pratima that she was going into the forest to pick flowers. 'I'll make garlands, since I've nothing to do, and decorate our cave.' She promised not to go further than the *sal* tree that marked the middle of the forest. But she went beyond that, almost to its very edge.

Just a few miles beyond lay help, a way out of this, back to life. She bit her nails and looked around at the trees, flowers, the narrow, almost indistinguishable path that led out of there to the cluster of banana trees and the long dirt road. Tell me what to do, Priya. What would you have done? Think of my situation. Run out and find the officer in command, I know you're telling me that, goddess. That's what I should do. Pratima would forgive her later. There would be time enough to win back Pratima. Jamini took a deep breath and took a step forward, then another, and another. Then she stopped, her heart pounding against her ribs. Someone was stumbling up that path.

'Kajli!' Jamini took her hands and sat her down under a tree. 'What happened to you?' Kajli's sari was ripped in places, her face, arms and legs scratched as if she had run into thorn bushes. 'Take me to them,' Kajli said, gasping, out of breath. She wouldn't tell Jamini anything. 'Must see Sirdar.'

Kajli knelt before Sirdar and covered her face with her hands. 'Nobody talked,' she said. 'They couldn't get a word out of anyone.'

The men sat in a circle around Sirdar and Kanai. Kajli sat with Jamini in a corner. 'I can't believe it,' Jamini said over and over. Pratima sat on a basket next to them, her face cupped in her hands. An officer riding through the bazaar had overheard some of the children talking about Sirdar and his men. Sirdar's two boys had thrown stones at the officer. So the families were rounded up, questioned. Where are your husbands, fathers? All dead, really? Their huts were set on fire to get them to talk. The women and children reacted by throwing stones at first, then rushing at the soldiers with axes and sticks. After that the order was to keep shooting until nothing moved. Kajli had gone to visit her mother five villages north. She returned to witness the bodies being tossed into a freshly dug trench. 'They'll leave,' she said to Sirdar, 'in a few days, I'm sure. They never linger after these incidents.'

'No one's going anywhere,' Sirdar said.

'Don't be ridiculous,' Kanai said sharply. 'Do you want to join the corpses in that trench?'

'I'm with Sirdar,' Tilak said. 'I'll make them pay for this. I don't care if I die in the process.'

'I do,' Kanai said. 'The important thing is to stay alive, not throw your life away trying to get even.'

'What do you want to do?' Tilak asked the men. Kanai shook his head slowly as the men voiced their assent.

'I won't be part of this,' Kanai said.

'I will,' Pratima said, standing up.

'This is too dangerous,' Jamini said to Pratima when they were back in their cave. 'I won't let you go.'

'This has to be settled,' Pratima said grimly. 'We can't let them get away with this.'

But you've got away with killing sahibs for so long, Jamini muttered to herself. Those women and children – what had they done? They had made her alien life here bearable. Now the world was going to turn on its head again, it seemed, and the ground become unsteady for ever.

Can you see anything, children?

No.

It's the darkness of Kali. But suddenly the darkness explodes. Flaming tents, bodies on fire. Can you see?

Yes! The boys leap up, their eyes shining. They dance around the balcony, their small bodies writhing, twisting. Their faces are glowing as if the blood of enemies has drenched them for the very first time.

With one swift wrench it's out, in my hands, one says.

My hands, says the other, sweet, salty? Can't figure out.

I see Pratima leaning over with a flaming torch, says Chitra. Tent after tent burning like pyres. She wipes her sword against her legs. Smears blood on her forehead. She loves the smell, the taste.

Yes. She doesn't know when to stop.

Jamini rushed to the temple at the sound of running feet. No cheering, no laughter. Angry mutters, stifled groans. Pratima standing against a column, her eyes closed. The men were huddled together in the middle of the courtyard, bandaging each other's wounds. Tilak's bleeding shoulder was being tended by two men. Five bodies lay in the courtyard. Sirdar walked to each of them, knelt and looked at the faces. 'For the first time,' Kanai said. 'Take a look. Was it worth it?'

'The Mother wills it,' Babul-Sirdar said, lowering his head.

Kanai let out an exasperated sigh. 'We will not kill when it is not required,' he said, 'ever again.'

Babul-sirdar nodded. 'And now let's deal with a minor problem.' Kanai turned to a figure crouching near the altar. Madhu stood before him, his rifle pointed at the bowed blond head. Jamini drew her breath in sharply. She went towards the altar cautiously. Very young, couldn't be more than eighteen or nineteen. He kept wiping his eyes and nose with the back of his hand. His khaki shirt was unbuttoned, and his thin body shivered in those funny long underclothes sahibs wore when they went to bed. 'The best thing would be to slit his throat, put him in a sack and bury him.'

'Please, please –' He tried to stand up, but Madhu tapped him with his gun.

'Bring him to my cave.' Babul-sirdar motioned with his head and left the temple.

Inside the cave, they stood in a ring and looked at the pale young man wipe his eyes and nose furiously, and try to hide his head between his knees. 'Better get it over with quick,' Kanai said. Babul-sirdar didn't respond. 'Well?' Kanai turned and looked at him. 'Shall we take him outside?'

'Let our Mother decide.' Babul-sirdar turned to Pratima.

Jamini gripped Pratima's arm and pulled her back. 'You can't possibly consent to this!' Pratima pulled her arm away. Jamini caught hold of it again. 'Look at him – a boy. What's he done to you? He couldn't have killed anyone. He's frightened to death. Look at the way he's shaking, crying –' Jamini's voice broke. She covered her face and began to cry softly.

'I don't understand what the problem is.' Kanai went to the boy and pulled him up. 'I'll take care of this.'

'Say something, do something, for God's sake. How can you, you, let this happen? Have you forgotten everything?'

'Kanai –' Pratima stopped, biting her lips. Jamini gave her a push. 'I'll – I'll take – decide – I want to talk to him,' Pratima said. 'I'm going to take him to my cave.'

Kanai took his hands off the boy's shoulders. 'As you wish,' he said drily. 'I thought you liked the sight of blood.'

*

124

Jamini offered the shaking white boy a blanket. He shook his head. He drank the glass of water she handed him, and he also accepted the bowl of rice and lentils. He continued to shiver and wipe his eyes and nose with the back of his hand. He almost dropped the bowl of food when Pratima asked him his name in unaccented English. 'Tom Lowell,' he said. 'Please don't let them kill me, miss. I've only been in this country for a month, and me mother's expectin' me back home in two. Please, miss, don't let them. There's just me and me mum, that's all, miss.' He began to cry in a low whisper. 'I was jus' tryin' to get away – thought I'd get killed or somethin' – all that fire and the yellin' – but that damn horse – that damn horse –'

'Why did you get on to that damn horse? Why did you come here, with us?'

'I was going to get away – not get killed. But the horse just went whichever way it wanted to. I couldn't make it turn round.' He sniffed and wiped his nose on his sleeve. 'An' I was too scared to jump off. An' the chap in front of me wasn't quite dead – he was groanin' like he was dyin' or somethin' – and the horse was going faster an' faster – oh, miss, I never been so frightened in me life.'

'Did you help kill them – the women and children in the village?'

'I just help the cooks, miss, serve the food, do the dishes. I only wanted to see this country, miss. My grandfather was here with the Company and he used to bring back teak and silk and rubies. I just wanted to see this country, that's all, miss.'

'Why can't you let him go?' Jamini urged. 'The poor little thing. I've never seen a sahib this way before – whimpering like a tyke. God, what an awful sight!'

'He'll get us all hanged, you fool.' Pratima paced the cave.

'I never seen you, miss. Won't say a thing. I'll tell them I was unconscious, got knocked on the head, anything.'

The DM had appeared agitated when Jamini told him she was leaving with Pratima. Had offered her more money, even a carriage. Sahibs walked with their heads in the air, snapped orders, got people hanged by simply snapping their fingers. But this creature here was a snivelling crumpled heap. Perhaps he should be got rid of to save the reputation of the sahibs. Jamini chewed her nails. The boy was picking at the food, lifting it gingerly with his fingers to his mouth. Pratima continued to pace, to glance at him occasionally. 'What are you thinking?' Jamini asked. 'What are you going to do?' Pratima didn't answer. She sat down facing the boy.

'Why are you lookin' at me like that?' he asked. 'What you going to do with me?'

'Don't know,' Pratima said slowly.

'I won't tell a soul, miss. I've heard many stories 'bout you. You don't look like anything they say. You can't be much older than me, I'll bet.' He crawled closer to Pratima. 'You're not frightening in the least bit, miss. Why, you're awfully pretty, I'd say. How d'you come to be with these bandits?'

They sat looking at each other. 'Never seen a girl in breeches before.' Tom smiled. 'Never seen a girl ride like you, either. Me mother'd be somethin' awful shocked if she saw you.' Pratima smiled back at him. 'You've pretty eyes, miss. Real bright, so bright that they look like torches, miss.' He laughed. 'My cousin, miss, he wrote a pome 'bout this girl's eyes, an' we all laughed at him. He was so smitten-like, you know.'

Pratima looked away. 'Remember?' Jamini asked, 'remember that young poet in your father's house? Weren't his poems exciting? Remember how we laughed?'

'What's she sayin'?'

'Nothing.' Pratima shook her head. She reached out and touched the yellow lock of hair falling over Lowell's forehead.

'Soft,' she said with an odd half-smile. 'Very soft.' He smiled and reached forward as if to touch her face, but moved back at the sound of footsteps.

Kanai and the sirdar appeared with four men. 'Well?' Kanai entered with his fists at his waist.

'Blindfold him and dump him somewhere. I don't want him harmed.'

'You're mad.'

'We'll do as she says,' Sirdar said.

'Then you are mad too,' Kanai said softly and left.

Jamini's fists clenched slowly as Sirdar chose two men to tie up the boy and dump him near the village. Goddess, Jamini said to herself, oh, goddess, have I been blind! Here you are flinging an answer, no, your mantra, in my face, and I am refusing to look or hear. If I don't seize this opportunity, goddess, you have every right to abandon me. Your mantra is ringing in my ears now. I hope the words have magic enough to catapult us to our lost world.

Tom Lowell was blindfolded, gagged and trussed up. Then one of the men lifted him and threw him like a sack over his shoulder. Jamini wrapped a blanket around the boy. Nobody noticed how close her mouth was to his ear for a second.

'He'll never be able to help them track us,' Pratima said. 'He has no sense of the place, where he is. Don't worry. He didn't kill anyone either,' she said to Sirdar. 'He's just the kitchen help.'

'I hope the Mother will protect us,' Sirdar said, touching his forehead. 'I hope we are doing the right thing.'

Pratima caught Sirdar's arm. 'Why do you doubt?'

He looked at her face for a few seconds. 'Five good men have died. First our families, now our comrades. Death on death. I feel this terrible twisting in my heart, as if we have taken a wrong step somewhere.'

'We'll recover. Trust me. We'll be fine.' Pratima held Sirdar's hands firmly. 'We'll be fine.' Sirdar nodded slowly.

'I will continue to believe that,' he said, and touched her feet.

Kanai kept to himself after that night. He and Madhu would wander off together during the day, and return to their cave after dark. Sometimes, they would go off at night, too. And then if you listened, closed your eyes, concentrated, really listened, you could hear their flutes. Jamini lay awake night after night trying to catch that sound that Pratima claimed she heard, but it always eluded her. She did not leave the plateau for two weeks now, in case they thought she had hatched some plan with the sahib. Everyone seemed to be waiting for some kind of retaliation. But nothing happened. The regiment – what was left of it – packed up and left. 'Let's try to have a normal life,' she said to Pratima, 'even in hell.'

Pratima gave in to oil-massages at noon again, followed by long, luxurious baths. Jamini went off to the villages and got hold of some books that Pratima liked to read. 'Sing with me,' Jamini said. After dinner, with Sirdar and some of the men for an audience, they sang together songs they used to sing while sitting on window ledges, on the swing. Jamini enhanced the lull that had entered their lives. Gradually, however, the men began to grumble about the restricted cash-flow. They wanted the sirdar to investigate the possibilities of a raid soon. But both he and Kanai decided to lie low for some time. In any case, they assured the men, no information about travelling groups or tax collectors' visits to the local zamindars had come through yet. Jamini helped distract the men. She began to cook delicious meals for them, and entertained them with stories. Kanai was never around for any of this. But Jamini could usually see him sitting on a distant rock painting his pots, or lying with his head on Madhu's knee while the boy played his flute.

'I know you miss all of this,' Jamini whispered into Pratima's ear while washing her hair, or combing it, or just when Pratima was lapsing into sleep. 'Wasn't it nice when that boy said you were pretty?'

'Don't be silly,' Pratima said.

'Why don't you read that story to me again,' Jamini said. 'I don't know what happened to those two. I want to see Priya get Arunav out of there.'

Pratima gave her a crooked smile and sat down next to the cave wall.

' "I have come to realise that Arunav hasn't quite crossed over to Narendra's point of view. He has asked Narendra to help him clear his mind. —The past touches me once in a while, he said to Narendra. —How do I overcome it? —But there is no need to overcome your past, Narendra said to Arunav. – Accept it, because it is over. Every time you feel its pull, think how weak you were, how vulnerable to devouring flames.

' "—Flames, I say to Arunav, —flames. Haven't you ever burnt for another? Have you forgotten ecstasy?

' "—Go away, he says to me. —You must leave, or I will ask Narendra to ask you to leave.

' "—But Arunav, I only want to learn from you. Convince me. Make me understand.

' "—I can't, he says agitatedly. —It's not a matter of understanding. It's a feeling inside. It's this longing for peace. Love doesn't bring peace.

' "—Not if you run away from it. It chases you and torments you. But love is something real. You know it's there to hold on to. Nirvana is a mirage in the desert.

' "Arunav throws me out of his cave, his face dark with anger. I return to this cave and sit against these walls. Only the stone accepts my words without resistance. But I will not give up.

129

' "Narendra asks Arunav to meditate, to concentrate on a circle of light above his head. I drop flowers in Arunav's lap when he sits against a tree with his eyes closed. —Open your eyes, I tell him, —breathe in the fragrance of this flower. He frowns. Asks me to go away.—Enlightenment, I murmur, —astounding brilliance when that light hits you. Your self disintegrates into a shower of light. Ah, like angels of light. But trying to be such angels, perhaps we become worse than beasts. Trying to be god-like, become destructive. Possible, do you think, even remotely? Have you ever thought of the pain of others, the pain of the abandoned ones? Arunav's back tautens and he lowers his head.

' "—Am I too self-absorbed? he asks. —Am I too –

' "Sachin appears suddenly, cutting him off. —You must not distract Arunav when he meditates, he says to me. His voice is tinged with anger. Sachin seems to follow us around these days. From a distance, he watches me bring Arunav his meals, ease his body with massages, make Arunav laugh with stories. Sachin came up to us today, when I was in the middle of a story. He caught my shoulder, pulled me up and sent me off to sweep Narendra's cave.

' "I have to be careful about Sachin. He has asked Narendra to separate Arunav from me. Thank heavens Narendra laughed and disagreed. Sachin looks at me with a twisted smile during the morning prayers. He steps in like a sword between Arunav and me much too often." '

'Oh, God,' Jamini said, holding Pratima's hand tightly. 'I think Priya should kill Sachin. Creep into his cave when the monster's asleep and kill with one swift stab.'

'You approve of killing, Jamini?' Pratima widened her eyes, dropped her jaw.

'Go on,' Jamini said, making a face. 'I wish I could be in there and help Priya.'

'The next section is two weeks later, I'd say, looking at the moon sign. "I am shaking with fear still, although Arunav stepped in to protect me. But I fear he may not be there all the time, if it happens again. I had roused Arunav from his meditation again. —Not again, he said, almost smiling. —I want to tell you about her, I said to him. Arunav looked at me as if he was seeing someone else. He reached out and touched my face. I closed my eyes. All of a sudden, I felt nails dig into my neck, hands drag me to my feet. Sachin! He had leapt out again. He shook me hard. —Didn't I tell you not to disturb him? He flung me against a rock. My head reeled from the hard contact. Sachin's fingers tightened around my throat. —We should have known better, he was saying. The sunlight was vanishing into a thick dark cloud that was pressing against me. —Sachin! I heard Arunav's voice. And then I was coughing, breathing in gasps, trying to clasp the hard, flat ground against my body.

' "Arunav laid me down on the stone berth in my cave. He gave me water. Stroked my forehead and sat beside me till I closed my eyes. Soon, I heard angry voices outside. —Are you mad? Arunav asked Sachin. —Why were you trying to kill him?

' "—That thing in there is a poison root, Sachin said. —We must get rid of it.

' "I heard Narendra's voice next. —I know the King's men are hunting for us, he said. —And a life in hiding makes all of us tense, angry. We must attempt to make our minds serene. We must not break the law of *ahimsa*. We must not hurt each other.

' "—That boy is not with us, Sachin said. —He could be an infiltrator.

' "—No. Arunav's voice was firm. —You are wrong.

' "Arunav returned to my cave. —Sorry, he said, stroking my throat. —Are you in pain?

' "I shook my head. —Look at the dazzling night outside, I said, —and think back on the wonder you once felt. Arunav closed his eyes and moved back.

131

' "—It can't be, he said.

' "It is, I said. —Look at me. Do you really feel nothing?

' "—Why? he asked, pushing his fingers through my cropped hair.

' "—No questions, I said, —there are no answers.

' "I stayed awake and watched Arunav sleep. He used to sleep just this way, his face against my shoulder, one arm thrown across my waist. Before I could lapse into sleep, Arunav woke up with a start, and scrambled to his feet. —It's not even dawn, I said, pulling him down, —come back to sleep. He pulled himself out of my grasp.

' "—Why? he whispered, covering his face with his hands, and left the cave slowly.

' "The darkness faded. The sun has risen and set. The cave is glowing with an iridescent copper light. Arunav has not returned. I have sat here writing on these walls with my knife all day. I wanted to go and look for him. But I was so afraid: that I would not find Arunav. Now, on the glowing copper rock surface outside the cave, a shadow has fallen. Someone is standing to the left of the cave's mouth, and his shadow falls long across the ground. Is it you, Arunav, come back to take my hand? Or is it –" '

'What? Who? Why did you stop there, you wretch?'

'There isn't any more.' Pratima turned up her hands and smiled that same crooked smile.

'I don't believe this!'

'I've read all that is there on all three walls, honestly.'

'Is there a dragging mark? No.' Jamini traced the letters on the wall. 'I mean, if she was dragged away . . . What about the other caves? Perhaps the rest is written on some other cave wall.'

'No it isn't. I've checked all the caves here. I, too, wanted to know what happened. So I ran to the other caves. But in those there were only the teachings of Gautama carved on the walls by monks who hid in these caves centuries back. Nothing else.'

'You must have thought about this over and over again. No wonder you used to lie awake at night staring at the darkness. What did you imagine happened?' Jamini squeezed Pratima's hand. 'Tell me?'

'I couldn't imagine. I couldn't see any more.'

'Well, I'll tell you why there isn't any more to this story. Priya was too happy to write, that's it.'

That evening, after dinner, Jamini made everyone sit in a circle. 'We have to share something with all of you,' she said to the men. 'We have discovered the most incredible story on our cave wall.' She raised her voice to make sure Kanai, who was sitting with his pots further away on a boulder, heard. She handed out *paan* to all of them. 'A special one for you,' she said to Sirdar, handing him his *paan*. Then she climbed over rocks and handed one to Kanai, who tossed it to Madhu. 'You start the story,' she said to Pratima, 'after all, you're the one who did the translating.'

'Yes, you tell us the story,' Babul-sirdar said. 'On your cave walls? How amazing. Go on, we want to hear it from you.'

Jamini watched Kanai turn his head as the story progressed. Slowly, he put his pots aside and came and sat with the men. 'We don't know what happens after that,' Pratima said, smiling, hitting the ground with her fist.

'I think it's Arunav's shadow,' Jamini said. 'Arunav comes to his senses, comes back, runs off with Priya. They kill Sachin before they leave, of course.'

'Do you think they kill Narendra, too?' one of the men asked.

'Perhaps Arunav comes back and tells Priya to leave,' said Babul. 'And she leaves. So there's no one to write on the walls any more.'

'No!' Jamini shook her head vigorously. 'Arunav comes back to go away with Priya.'

'Well, the shadow could also be Sachin's,' Tilak said.

'I think,' Kanai cleared his throat, 'I think you're right, Tilak. The shadow is Sachin's shadow.' The men turned to look at Kanai in surprise. 'Sachin comes into the cave. The wretched woman freezes in fear, naturally. He simply pushes her head back and slits her throat, just like she deserves.'

'But what about Arunav?' Sirdar asked.

'What about him?' Kanai raised his eyebrows. 'Why do you think any of them ever existed? That story on the wall could be just someone's invention, just to liven up an otherwise dull existence. Perhaps the narrator was a man, a lonely old monk fantasising in a barren cave.'

'Then why would he not finish his story?' Jamini asked, her voice rising in anger.

Kanai looked her up and down coldly. 'Perhaps he wanted to frustrate the reader – plain vindictiveness: why should anyone else get satisfaction if he wasn't getting any? He had grown old searching for this Nirvana promised him by some charlatan seducer. And the poor fool had followed the trail. But, say he found nothing, absolutely nothing. Just emptiness, loneliness. So he wrote, to give himself something to do, to create a world around him that he could control. And, of course, he hoped that someone someday would beat their head against those cave walls, dying with curiosity to know what happened in the end.' Kanai spat on the ground. 'You've played his game, and you're stuck in his trap.'

'Why do you have to ruin our fun with your sour thoughts?' Jamini made a face and turned to Pratima. 'You tell them – I mean us – what you think?' Jamini gave Pratima a shake. 'What does Arunav do?'

'I can't say,' Pratima said. She stared at Kanai walking back to his pots.

'What do you imagine?'

'I can't. I cannot foresee the end. In that story it was all now, with no before or after. I mean in the telling of it.' Pratima's fists clenched slowly. 'It wasn't like this had happened, but as if it was happening while she was writing. So she couldn't foretell either. And I could never see Arunav's face.'

'Oh, come on.' Jamini stood up. 'Here is this young prince with coppery hair and eyes. He is restless, passionate, overwhelmed by his emotions – he can't give up love. He's realised he's still in love. He couldn't see his own face for a while. Narendra's withered hand blocked his vision. But in her eyes he saw his face again, recognised himself, his love. So what do you think he would do?'

'I don't know. I can't see his face.'

'Imagine him looking into a mirror, a pool, into a pair of shining eyes.'

'Stop your silly imaginings,' Pratima snapped. 'I'm tired.'

Kanai watched Pratima disappear into the dark cave.

'So it's just a matter of seeing someone's face,' Jamini muttered to herself. 'Like looking into a mirror, and getting a shock and saying to oneself, My god, that is me, that lost, forgotten me.' She looked intently at Pratima curled up on the stone berth. Yes, she was fast asleep. Jamini wrapped a dark cotton shawl around herself, covering her head. She stepped out of the cave quietly. 'Help me, Priya,' she whispered. 'Don't abandon me now, goddess. You sent me a clue and I'm acting on it. Help me get my lost world back, just as you did.' The half- moon, slipping out of the clouds occasionally, gave the dark rocks a slippery shine. Jamini's shadow fell in front of her, moving swiftly before her footsteps as if leading her, showing her the way. 'Be there,' Jamini whispered.

'I know what to do now. This time I'll win. It's just a question of a mirror.'

Information about a possible raid came from the village within a few days. Sirdar was surprised when Tilak brought the news. Tilak couldn't pinpoint the source of the information. 'Everyone in the villages is talking about a loaded party that will be passing through the forest down south.' The following week, Madhu and Tilak were sent out to bring back specific information. Sirdar held a meeting in his cave after they returned. Kanai appeared to be uncomfortable about the raid. 'Too little information,' he said. 'What kind of a party?'

'Some kind of an escort for a group. Not more than seven or eight altogether,' Tilak assured them.

Jamini helped Pratima get dressed. She combed Pratima's hair slowly, carefully. 'So beautiful,' she murmured, 'like dark rain-clouds.' She coiled it, then put it up with pins, allowing wisps to escape around Pratima's face. Then she crowned her head with chains of gardenia and hibiscus, even pushed in a large gardenia behind Pratima's left ear. 'May I?' she asked gently, and lined Pratima's eyes with kohl. Pratima sat mutely, staring through Jamini.

'There,' she said, moving back and looking at Pratima, 'flowers, after so long. You look magnificent.'

'Do I?' Pratima smiled faintly. Jamini caught her breath. It was that old smile.

'Would you –' Jamini stopped and bit her lips.

'Would I what?'

'Would you go back home if it were possible to go back now, free, with no charges on our heads, if all of this could be forgotten?'

Pratima reached and touched Jamini's lips with two fingers, giving her that half-smile again. 'After a certain point, *shokhi*, there is no turning back.'

136

'There is no such point,' Jamini said, holding Pratima's hand tightly. 'There is always turning back. There are only turning points.'

'Do you intend to come with me today?' Pratima asked, disengaging her hand gently.

'Naturally. I will always be with you, you know that.'

The temple glowed with sunshine. Babul-sirdar lit the incense, placed the flowers on the altar. Pratima rubbed each man's forehead with sandalwood paste. Kanai put up his hand and moved back when she went towards him. 'Don't refuse the blessing,' Sirdar said to him.

'I'll survive.'

As they knelt, eyes closed, hands clasped, before the altar, a tall, lean figure entered the courtyard. 'Babul,' he called from the back. The *tantrik* had appeared again.

'I didn't think we'd see you again,' Sirdar said.

'It's time to stop.' The *tantrik* raised his hand. 'Don't go for this raid today.'

'Why not?'

'I don't know. When I woke up this morning I saw your face in the sunlight. So I came.'

'As long as she's with us nothing will happen,' Sirdar said.

'May the Mother do what's best.' The *tantrik* touched his forehead and his chest with his right hand, and left slowly, his wooden sandals clattering over the stone courtyard.

As they neared the forest, the afternoon turned stormy. 'Thank your lucky stars,' Kanai said to Sirdar. 'The darker it gets, the better. Let's not do anything we don't have to,' he said firmly, turning to the men. 'We are just going to grab and run.' They took their positions behind trees and waited for the sound of hoofs and boots.

An odd chanting became audible soon. An up-and-down cadence, Hein-ho, hein-ho, hein-ho, hein-ho. Rhythmic foot-steps. Pratima lifted her rifle. 'Don't.' Jamini forced the gun down.

'Not more than four horses,' Madhu said, picking up the sound of hoofs.

'Wait,' Kanai said. 'I'm certain there are more than that. I sense more.'

Four turbanned men on horses came into view. A palanquin followed them, carried by four men. None of the riders carried guns. 'No shooting,' Kanai whispered. 'Let's go.'

Within seconds the group was surrounded. The bearers dropped the palanquin, and huddled together. The four riders circled around confusedly on their horses. 'The money.' Sirdar extended his arm. One of the men removed his saddlebag and handed it over. Another appeared to be doing the same. But, instead, his hand went to his mouth and a whistle went off with a loud shriek.

Uniformed men on horses shot out from clusters of trees on the other side. No one was sure who or what they were shooting any more. Horses slammed against each other. Jamini scrambled off the horse. 'Get off, don't shoot.' She tried to drag Pratima off the saddle. Pratima kicked Jamini off and, lifting her gun, aimed at the palanquin.

'Miss,' she heard, 'miss, come along, everything's going to be all right.' Two hands from either side were pulling at her legs. 'Get off the horse, miss.' She pulled the trigger. A woman stumbled out of the palanquin.

'Don't shoot, miss.'

The woman was running towards them waving her arms. Her red sari was practically falling off her. Her hair came undone. Pratima held her rifle tightly and watched the woman trip over a man in khaki lying on the ground. She fell on the body, then scrambled to her feet. She tried to rearrange her sari clumsily, the yards of red-gold silk tumbling over her shaking hands.

Pratima let Jamini pull the rifle out of her hands. 'Look,' Jamini was saying. 'Take a good look.'

'Oh God, get off the damn horse, miss!'

Jamini screamed, seeing Madhu run towards them with an axe. Tom Lowell shot the boy with his pistol at two yards. Jamini looked wildly for Kanai. She saw Babul-sirdar making for the woods. Pratima struck the blond head at her knee with her heel. She moved away from the falling body, and turned her horse around. Jamini scrambled back on the horse. 'You've ruined everything,' she screamed. 'You've destroyed the very last chance we had. Oh, what I went through to arrange –' Her voice cracked.

Pratima pushed Jamini off the horse and dismounted before the plateau. 'Wait. Stop.' Jamini caught Pratima's arm. 'We must go back. They're waiting. How could you hit that boy after all he did?'

'What did he do? What did you do?' Pratima removed Jamini's hand roughly.

'I got us out – that's what I did, with his help. *Shokhi*, listen to me.' Jamini touched Pratima's face. 'I met that sahib four times. We made plans. He talked to his officers, arranged the ambush. But I was afraid you wouldn't come to your senses – you had lost yourself so completely. So I begged them for the palanquin, the bearers and a girl in it, any girl, so you could see where it all started, where it all ended. Come with me now. Let me take you back.'

'Take me back where?' Pratima smiled that wondrous half-smile of hers again.

'*Shokhi*.' Jamini reached out to take Pratima's hand. Pratima moved backwards, that flashing crescent smile vanishing, her eyes growing opaque.

'I trusted you.'

'And I have lived up to that trust. I promised, vowed to myself I would save you, us. Don't you see?' Jamini caught her shoulders and shook her. Pratima freed herself gently.

'Promises, vows, honour – all fall on their knees at the onslaught of life, don't you know by now?'

'Listen to me –'

'The burning – you'll feel it burn, too,' she said.

'What are you talking about? You listen to me now – after all this – do you know what I've been through – look at me –' Jamini grabbed Pratima's arms, digging her nails in. 'Look at me. What is to become of us? Think, you little –' she shook her violently, breaking into hysterical sobs. 'You are coming with me now – I will beat it out of you if I have to – you'll not ruin everything now –' Pratima struggled out of Jamini's grasp, stopping her short. Jamini gasped as she felt Pratima's skin tear under her nails. 'No – stop. I didn't mean to hurt you.' Pratima backed away slowly, smiling. 'You're bleeding – wait – I didn't meant to hurt you.' But Pratima was smiling, and moving away, almost swirling away as she turned, her feet picking up sudden speed. 'Stop!' But the dancers swirled in again and spun Jamini's head into a sudden dizziness, making her lose her balance, fall to her knees.

'Too late to be late again,' Pratima said, running to the rocks and then down towards the temple. Jamini scrambled to her feet, ran a few yards, stumbled, slipped, fell, finally crawled the rest of the way, unable to walk, having twisted both ankles badly. She reached the temple courtyard to see Pratima in the alcove beyond the altar. She was removing the blade from the stone figure's hand. 'Still burning,' Pratima whispered to the black stone statue.

Screaming hoarsely, Jamini crawled towards the altar. Pratima

140

fell before her, sideways on the altar, a thin stream of blood running from under her head, her unmoving hand clasping the curved steel blade.

Jamini started at the sound of footsteps. She scrambled behind a column. Babul-sirdar ran to the altar. He knelt, touched Pratima's feet, then her head. He was whispering, 'Ma, Ma, why, Ma?' He removed the crescent blade from Pratima's hand, touched his forehead with it. He wiped the blade on his clothes and raised it, stretching his arms out, offering it to the statue in the alcove. 'Take, Mother,' he whispered, 'this complete surrender.' He touched his throat with the blade. Jamini saw a silver flash edged with red moving from the left to the right. Sirdar fell forward on the altar.

Jamini crawled back to the altar and pressed her face against Pratima's forehead. She sat with Pratima's head on her knees, ran her fingers through her hair, over her shoulders, along the red line across her throat. 'Come sit on her eyes,' she crooned, stroking Pratima's eyelids, 'sleep-carrying ones . . . Priya, goddess, come, speak to me like you used to . . . why don't I hear your voice any more? Where are you? You must come to me now, take my hand, show me the way, come, come, come sit on her eyes, sleep-carrying ones . . . dance us away, dance us away . . .'

She felt herself dragged up by the hair. It was dark all around. Hard fingers held her jaw as if they wanted to crush her face. 'Perhaps it was you all the time,' Kanai said. His face was so close to hers. 'We thought it was her. Because she used to burn with it. All passion, that girl. Drunk. But you did it the way I did it. The *tantrik* was right. Perhaps it was not Her blessing that came among us. I knew it would all end if you were allowed free rein. I wanted it to end, you've no idea how much, especially when Babul placed her on his special altar which none of us could quite see. And she, well – she had that smile.' Kanai's eyes held a strange soft light.

141

So beautiful. Jamini touched his face. His skin so soft, the bones so finely etched. Kanai removed a knife from his waist. Jamini tried to twist her face out of Kanai's tightening grip. 'I'll give you something to live with,' he said, 'I'll give you your third eye,' and, digging the knife-point in near her left eyebrow, cut a deep crescent line down to her chin. 'How limp you are now. The soul gone from the vessel.' He let her go.

Kanai smiled. Only a god could smile that way while passing through a dark desolate battlefield marked by knots of flame, its silence deepened by the Om-om-om of whispered chants. Kanai walked out of the temple swiftly. The dazzling indigo all around swallowed him up. No one ever saw him again.

Hours later, boots marched into that courtyard. 'What a terrible thing to happen, miss.' Jamini felt a finger touch her face.

Where is that forest? Chitra asks.

Is the goat's head off yet? The boys are leaping around. The drums are a rolling, thrashing river now. The chanting grows louder and louder. *Come, Mother, come.* Blood and flowers on a silver plate. Calcutta explodes all around us. Machine-gun rattle echoes like distant thunder. Fountains of light in the sky.

Where is that forest where life can change between one bird-call and another? Chitra asks, holding my shrivelled hand.

The night has lost its darkness and silence, on this night of nights, flaming with your beauty, beloved mother, roaring with the voices of your children.

The boys are wrestling, hitting each other viciously, knuckles slamming against nose, mouth, eyes, ripping each other's clothes, hair. I do not understand. No, don't hurt each other. Stop! What are they doing, hurting each other like that? Beasts, animals, worse: monsters, monsters. They feel no pain. Their faces are bleeding. Stop, stop, no, don't hit him with that. Chitra claws at my hand. 'Where – that forest?'

The boys tear out of each other's grasp and rush to the balcony as the priest's agonised chant cuts through all sounds. '*Ma –*' The crescent blade is descending. The speakers pick up the muffled sound. '*Ma! Jai Ma!*' A thousand voices.

Kamal falls in a slow swirling cascade, his body trembling, his hair sweeping the dust, and Shanta running to touch his face, his hair.

Ahh – this burning in my lungs.

'That forest – that shadow before the cave – what is that shadow?' Chitra clutches my arm, her nails digging into my withered flesh.

'You tell me, girl,' I say, wincing with pain, trying to tear my hand from Chitra's nails. 'What do you see?'

'I see –' Chitra arches backwards, closing her eyes, her fingers curling, clenching. 'I see the shadow entering the cave. It is Narendra. He stumbles in, half carrying, half dragging Arunav. He drops the body before Priya. —Why? he asks. Arunav's body is ripped from throat to belly. —Why did you push him to this? Narendra asks, his voice shaking with grief. —This is your doing, Priya says. —You destroyed him the moment you placed your dead hand on his head. She drives her knife into Narendra's throat and tears him open to his navel.' Chitra crouches forward on her hands and knees, her hair sweeping the floor. 'Priya lays Arunav down in the centre of the cave. She covers him with flowers. Kneeling beside Narendra's body, she dips her hands into his chest, lifts up the gushing redness as if lifting water to her mouth.' Chitra drinks from her cupped hands this night air ringing with voices, gunshots and exploding rockets. ' "Now I will go back to the city," says Priya. "I will go to the temple and light lamps all around the marble figure of Gautama. Cover those stone feet with flowers. Then I will dance before you, oh lord." '

Chitra sways as if dancing to some unheard music. 'The guards will run to the temple. Priya is dancing like a stormy river. She knows she will be killed. She knows she has entered the forbidden courtyard. When the soldiers rush forward, when their swords come down on her head, ah –' Chitra gasps, laughs, rolls on the floor. 'Priya will fall – the very last flower – at the feet of the Enlightened One.'

Enlightened, annihilated, don't know any more, but my lungs burn. No, not this way, the end. Don't put this curse on me. My Priya escapes free with her love, free, yes, and my body, oh so light, light, no pain, racked with this coughing, but no hacking agony, ahh, coughs like jolts of laughter, blood speckling my palm, dancers falling on burning myrrh, not my Priya, not her, spare her. You take her away from me for ever on this night of nights as blood streams across the altar, and all my stories bleed into one another, leaving me, quite leaving me –

And now, a slow exhalation of breath, from the speakers, the priest's voice cracking, harsh. '*We can never know how to invoke you, quite how to adore you. And when you come, through our bodies, uniting, we do not know how to release you again, how to end this meeting, break this bond, with what words to say farewell. We have loved and acted imperfectly, our adoration flawed, beloved Mother, but believe us, it was passion, it was pure, if for this moment only, from our hearts, in all sincerity. So forgive us our flaws and all our ignorance. In Hari's name, the supreme being, forgive us.*'

'But the priest doesn't tell us if She's on our side,' Chitra says.

'Now the priest will shake the clay pitcher,' I say, 'releasing the spirit. Then, and then only, you can touch her feet, when there's nothing left.'

'But now there's no life on the altar –'

'Run off, hag,' says Shanta from the door. 'The riots have spread to this side of the city. And what's going on here? Stop

144

that, you two. What have you done to your faces, you little monsters?' Shanta leans against the door, swaying a little. 'You can get lost now, hag. Hurry to your shack. Riots have broken out near the Muslim quarter and might reach the slums this side.'

'Kill the bastards,' the nine-year-old says.

'Shut up,' says Shanta, her voice rising. 'What have you done to each other? How could you have hit your brother so hard? You little –' Shanta swings a fist at the younger boy, who ducks deftly and laughs.

'Where is that cave?' Chitra asks, her face lighting up for a moment with a curved flash of a half-smile. 'Where is that forest? You think I don't know?' Do her bright eyes taunt? I don't know. I don't see very well. Eyes so bright with that inner darkness.

'Tear-gas,' Shanta says. 'Look over there.' Clouds of white smoke rise in the distance. The machine-gun rattle grows louder.

I must be on my way, back to my unlit shack. We've chosen our gods and thus our special deaths, this I know. I'm as light as a dry crumpled leaf. The gutter waits with its careless smile. And your crescent blade, beloved Mother, with its crimson edge shines at the corner of my eye, always. Much like a smile that drained my blood. Much like a voice that startles my dreams with just one word – *shokhi*.

The Basket Weaver's Letter

'Something's up,' the old man, sitting cross-legged inside the *paan* stall, said to himself as he saw the basket weaver nod her head up and down and side to side and walk out of the rich doctor's house on the other side of the park. He could see the doctor's wife with her latest hairstyle, curls piled upwards like a temple *gopuram*, still calling out to the basket weaver from the door, her mouth opening and closing. '*Sala*,' he muttered, 'if only I could hear what she's saying to the crazy basket weaver.' He watched the basket weaver walk slowly towards the park, walking her particular slow walk, dragging her footsteps, her hips swinging ever so slightly, her back erect, head straight, as if she was carrying a pitcher. The servants, hawkers, slum kids, who had all spread themselves on the warm dry grass this late-February afternoon, all shifted positions to glance at the basket weaver making her way towards the pipal tree in the centre of the park. 'Ah,' the old man said to the *paan* leaves in his hand, filling them with crushed betel nuts and spices, 'to her royal seat as usual. Look, look, better be satisfied with looking, you lazy no-goods. There she's going to sit and stare into space with her crazy, vacant eyes.' But the basket weaver did not sit down under the pipal tree. She stood and looked around at the people smoking, playing cards, chatting, and called out, 'Oy, dhobi.'

The old man dropped the leaves on the wooden board before him. A deep whispery voice with a light crackle to it – a voice he had never heard before, that no one had heard before, because the basket weaver never really spoke to anyone, just nodded, or let out Hmm, *na, accha*, now and then when spoken to.

The basket weaver adjusted her green-and-white-striped cotton sari and knelt under the tree to stack her baskets and separate the unfinished ones. The dhobi, who had been shaken and woken up rudely by the barber, who had nearly sliced the throat in his hands at the sound of the basket weaver's voice, sat up in shock. '*Kya?*' the dhobi asked, 'has the sky fallen or what?' 'Dhobi,' he heard, and turned his head to look at the basket weaver.

The old sweeper stubbed her *biri* and watched the suppressed excitement all around. She made her way to the *paan* stall, asked the old man for a '*zardawala*' and sat down on the bench near the stall. 'Did you hear?' the old man asked her.

'I hear many things,' she said in a lazy grating drawl, 'inside houses, outside houses, and, now that my hands have swept and mopped the marble and mosaic floors of eight houses, I intend to sit and chew my *paan* and doze. You go ahead, Dauri Lal, and do the hearing and the lusting, like those *chutiyas* out there.'

'I can't help hearing,' said Dauri Lal, a sullenness coming into his voice, 'it's a matter of proximity, Lachman's mother.'

'Of course. And one's ear does perk up, doesn't it, at alien sounds?'

'Thought she was a deaf-mute. Silent all these years. And now she's speaking as if a spell has been broken.'

'Or a spell cast.' The old sweeper's face twisted to a smile. 'Silence ruptured. Like an omen, maybe. Could be bad for your health, old man.'

'Could be lethal for yours, too, bitch. How much blood did you cough up today?'

'Blood? What blood? I cough up dust, the dust that is my body, the dust I sweep away. You watch out for that pain in your head, Dauri Lal, the pain you don't quite understand.'

'I take my pills,' the old *paanwala* said gruffly, and drew back into his stall.

'Dhobi,' the basket weaver called again, hesitant between words, 'can you – can you find – find me someone to write a letter?' The dhobi scrambled to his feet. The barber, Bheem Singh, flung down his razor, his soap-scum-and-stubble-covered towel, and ran to the basket weaver.

'I'll write, I'll write, *meri jaan*,' he said. 'Let me get pen and paper, then I'll write all the words of love in the whole wide world.'

'*Sala, behunchud kahinka.*' The barber reeled in shock at being called 'sister-fucker' in a snarling whisper. The basket weaver is definitely mad, he told himself, like we always thought. For two years under this tree, hardly a word to anyone, fingers weaving in and out with cane strips, the woman is certainly mad, and now plain filth is coming out of her mouth. She might even tear his throat out if he said one more word to her, the way she was looking at him now, with eyes burning.

The dhobi came up to her and touched his forehead. 'I'll get a pen and paper, Rajni, in two minutes.' He had always liked her, from the day she turned up under the pipal tree, liked her silent still form and her constantly moving fingers.

'No.' She shook her head. 'Not you. A letter in Angrezi.'

The dhobi opened and closed his mouth. The barber sat down with a thump. The parkful of people moved a little closer to the pipal tree. Dauri Lal in his stall froze with his hand in mid-air, reaching for spices. The sweeper stretched out on the bench and closed her eyes.

151

'In English.' The dhobi scratched his head.

'Yes.' The basket weaver sat down with an unfinished basket, and lowered her eyes.

Kiran, the prostitute from the slums behind these palatial houses, crawled towards the basket weaver on her hands and knees. 'Rajni,' she said, 'I know who can write your letter in English. But then, if I get him, say you'll let me sit near you and listen, please.'

'Listen,' the basket weaver said, concentrating on her fingers twining around strips of cane.

'Here he comes,' Kiran said, as a young man in jeans and a cream shirt came riding round the park on a bicycle. 'He's on his way home from college.' She ran after him, calling, 'Lalit, Lalit, stop, one minute, the poor and oppressed need you today,' covering her mouth with her hand to hide her laughter.

What a woman, the sweeper thought, half opening her eyes. She's a sharp one, that Kiran. She's noticed, aha, the boy looking at the basket weaver, every afternoon, as he cycles by, on his way home from college, once a week when he stops and hands her a bottle of aspirin so that her arthritic fingers can weave on insensible to pain. Young men develop these fancies sometimes, when they talk a bit too much about equality and sharing the wealth and cast eyes on silent women under trees who look but never speak. I wonder, though, if Kiran ever noticed the look in the basket weaver's eyes every time that boy rides by on his bicycle? It's an odd look – not of lust, but of longing. To touch the past, maybe. To tell of the past, maybe.

Tch, she makes me dream sometimes, this basket weaver. She's past her prime, her hair silvered at the temples, but her face is still smooth, her body still as a frozen wave. I was like that too, decades back, and men looked at me, and when they took me home or came to my room, they filled my hands with crisp notes and silver jewellery, even gold sometimes. But somehow, I think the basket weaver's had a different kind of luck. Her walk is too aloof and never signals welcome. That coldness of hers makes my heart twist now and then; twist like pliant cane in her hands. I could have been like her, cold, alone, had life permitted, had my first husband not been the scum he was.

Dauri Lal folded the *paan* leaves carefully, wrapped them in silver paper and set them in rows on an aluminium tray. Letter – who to? Who does she have, that crazy woman? No one that I know of. But how much do I know, except that – sometimes – when this knotted pain throbs in my head I, too, feel like writing a letter? But where is she now? She was a bit like that basket weaver, with those same eyes, when they are not blank, her eyes now carrying in their darkness the restlessness of bamboo groves before the rains come. What can I say to her now, to her who vanished years back when I was the foreman in a sahib's tea estate? She never listened to me, just like her mother before her. And now, this crazy woman with her baskets, her interweaving fingers mesmerising my eyes, trapping me like the cane in patterns I want to forget, wants to write a letter, in a sahib's language – If I could stop this bile from rising to my throat.

The young man got off his bike and followed Kiran to the pipal tree. 'Something wrong?' he asked the basket weaver, taking off his sunglasses. 'You need to write a letter in English? Applying for something, reporting something, something stolen?'

'No,' the basket weaver said. 'It's time now. Must write.' Her hands left the cane strips for a few seconds and clenched slowly.

A little puzzled, 'Why of course,' he said and sat down, taking out a notebook and pen from his satchel bursting with books. 'Who are you writing to, Rajni?'

'To my son.'

'In English?'

'Yes.' She paused, coiled a strip of cane round her fingers. 'He's there.'

'There?'

'Lon-don,' she said slowly.

Lalit stared at her, his lips parting. Kiran let out a gasp. Clothes and feet rustled the grass as people moved closer still to the pipal tree. Dauri Lal sat with clenched fists. The old sweeper raised herself on one elbow, slowly twisting her body until she could see the basket weaver's face.

'Fifteen years now,' the basket weaver said, a little breathless, her forehead wrinkling with concentration, her eyes intent on the strips of cane between her fingers. 'He was only three. Don't know if he'll remember. The doctor's wife called me and asked me if I would like to go there, to work there as an ayah for her sister's baby. If I say yes, I can go there and work there, and see him. Wonder if he remembers the river.'

Lalit looked down at the notebook. 'Doesn't make any bloody sense,' he muttered under his breath.

'I'm going to strangle you,' Kiran said, 'if you don't tell me how all this came about. Your son over there? How? That husband of yours spent most of his nights in my bed till that truck hit him five years back, that night when he was stumbling home drunk. He said you never let him touch you – so where did this eighteen-nineteen-year-old boy come from, eh? Talk.' Kiran pinched her arm gently.

'Does he know who you are?' Lalit asked. 'I mean – did you sell, I mean give, him up – you stayed in touch – I mean, does he remember?'

154

'*I* remember,' the basket weaver said. 'Remember swimming in the river, the sickening smell of rubber trees.'

Lalit's eyes narrowed enquiringly. 'Rubber trees, hmm. A plantation?' The basket weaver looked back at him blankly. 'Tell me,' Lalit said, reaching out and taking her rough, chapped hands. 'I've wondered about you for months now, you sitting here every afternoon with your baskets, and I've always felt that someone had done something to you, because your eyes are always so blank, as if pain had annulled every emotion. I think I know your story, Rajni. But tell me in your own words.'

The basket weaver smiled hesitantly at the intense face before her. 'I don't think you will understand.'

'Your son won't either,' Kiran snapped.

'If I understand, then he will too,' Lalit said. 'But only if I understand.'

'Sometimes I think of him when I see you,' the basket weaver said to Lalit, disengaging her hand from his. She reached and touched his face lightly. 'Your eyes are always angry.'

'Ridiculous,' Lalit said, rubbing his eyes. 'Just explain, and I'll decide how to put it in English, so it makes sense.'

'Sense . . . yes.' The basket weaver resumed weaving. 'To go back a thousand –' she stopped, her fingers pausing for a second, '– miles. Rubber trees, and the river.' She frowned in concentration. '*Irra – wadi*,' she said haltingly.

'Burma!'

'I asked my father,' she said, 'What do gods look like? Because he would call on them night and day and blame them for his aches and pains, my mother, us. He would carry buckets and buckets of the sticky fluid, pour it into vats. And every time a bucket appeared not filled to the brim, he got beaten.'

'I get it.' Lalit shut his notebook. 'It's all crystal clear. You grew up on a rubber plantation where your father was one of the abused workers, and you were abused as well. I should have guessed.' He rubbed his chin against his knuckles. 'All so simple,' he said to Kiran.

'A monster,' the basket weaver whispered, 'sweat pouring down in dark streaks from matted red hair into bloodshot eyes.'

'So what did this man do, Rajni?' Kiran asked, exasperated. 'Get to the point.'

'He had a black shadow,' the basket weaver continued, as if in a trance. 'Together, they beat many to death. The black shadow stole women from the village. Nobody ever saw them again. Black shadows, always, all around the monster when he rode in.'

'Were you abducted by the sahib and his foreman or whoever that was?' Lalit asked, his voice urgent. 'I mean, we understand that you were in a rubber plantation in Burma, abused by your father and the sahib who owned the plantation. But what about this son of yours, and how did that come about exactly?'

'How did that come about exactly?' Kiran mimicked Lalit's urgent tone and rolled her eyes. 'What kind of an ass are you, kid? And you're supposed to be educated.'

'Gods,' whispered the basket weaver. 'Very different from those two monsters, my father said, the gods. They look like they are made from light, pure sunlight, and in their eyes they contain the blue of the sky. They are golden, shining creatures, and they always protect you. And very different from you, my father, I said to myself. They do not beat the mothers of their children or their children. We'd wait every night till he passed out, then drag him, throw him on his bed, the only bed in our hut, then huddle next to our mother on the floor and fall asleep.'

'I knew it was something like this,' Lalit said, frowning.

Yes, yes, Dauri Lal said to himself, bringing the *paan* leaves down with a sharp slap on the aluminium tray before him. The man is always the beast, beating his wife and children, coming home drunk and throwing things. What if the wife has been making eyes at truck drivers, and even disappearing for hours in the afternoons? What are you supposed to do when the tea pickers whisper to each other: Did you see the foreman's wife, did you see that new sari, that new gold chain, the earrings, the bangles, she was getting into the saab's jeep, did you see? What is a man supposed to do, tell me – take a deep breath, walk home, get into bed and close his eyes? I was the foreman, the man in charge. At one time those tea pickers would shake at the sight of me. Now they giggled and laughed.

These *paan* leaves are the only things that behave. Stay folded when I fold them, hold still when I lay them down. And how does that cane feel in your hands – good? Bending, twisting, weaving in and out as you want it, yes, just as you want it, that pale green strip you are placing in between the yellow and the purple-tinted one – that green one, that same pale green of tea leaves.

'The bangle seller came two or three times a week,' the basket weaver said. 'Sold my mother bangles. He held her wrists and hands, stroked her fingers, slipped those glass and silver bangles over her hands so gently, so gently, and my mother would laugh, smile, and the bangle seller sang of the rain-wind, the full moon on the sands, lotuses shining on the lake. My mother, smiling, singing his songs, till my father came home at night – We wished for shining gods – to come and save us.

No one's going to save you this time, I said to my wife, the day I saw her, with my own eyes, getting off the sahib's jeep. His assistant had approached me once, about my wife. My wife is not for any sahib's pleasure, I told him to his face. But money had seduced her, and power, I guess, and I was not going to pretend any more to be deaf or blind.

That strip of green cane, so twisted now in your hands, so meshed in with that yellow and purple, would break if you tried to drag it out. It's something else now, not just one strip of cane, criss-crossed by purple and yellow. Almost a blur, a sharp blur – of leaves, through which I saw her as she stepped out of the jeep, laughing, clinging to the sahib's hand. His arm round her waist, pulling her back into the jeep. She, still laughing, pulling away, then falling against him, laughing, laughing, laughing – can hear it clear as gunshots, as crisp and slashing as cane, a bamboo pole cracking against your head. Couldn't move, couldn't look away. Broken glass under my feet, for miles and miles.

I didn't mean to let my anger get the better of me – just teach her whose woman she was.

Just like my husband, the sweeper hissed in her head. The bastard, like this old Dauri Lal, who I can bet killed his wife – he has that look in his eyes: 'I didn't mean to, it happened.' What woman wants to keep house for a filthy drunk? I ran away. Who wouldn't? My poor daughter, don't know what became of her, perhaps my *chutiya* husband raped her, sold her off. He tried to sell me off, only I found out in good time, and ran away with that construction worker. Ah, I thought he was a god, beautiful, strong. When I leant against him, he stood rock-steady, like a god on an altar. Too bad I couldn't adore him longer than a few months.

Started beating me too, drunk, foul-mouthed. The local constable, however, turned out to be a decent fellow. He shot my construction worker accidentally during a strike. Yes, the constable was OK. He didn't mind my seeing the rich folks occasionally. After all, I was bringing in good money. But that idiot had to go get killed in a riot – someone jammed a broken bottle into his throat, *hai*, so I had to move in with the sweeper and pick up his trade. Thank God, he had that stroke that took him up there or down there or wherever. Now my body's only good for lying in the sun and cleaning floors and bathrooms.

Rajni, I'm so glad to see you under that tree, you've no idea. I hope my daughter's sitting calmly under some tree, her life quite uninfested with men. Ah, I could have run away and sat under a tree and woven baskets, I could have, and told wondrous stories of monsters and gods, but I don't remember any gods, any more.

'Gods,' Lalit said with a dry laugh, 'yes, they better save us.'

The basket weaver smiled vacantly. 'Our mother sent us off to play near the river and when we came home, she was gone. The bangle seller never came again. Father broke things, slapped us so hard we spun away . . . Five years , for five years I prayed for this shining god to appear and kill my father.'

Kill your father. Dauri Lal spat on the ground. So you could go and wrap yourself around every man in the neighbourhood. Didn't I know my daughter, with those restless eyes? She had learnt all the tricks from her mother and, with her mother gone, had decided to take her place in the new sahib's bed. So I made a decision – only a man of my choice would be allowed to own my daughter. I found a man I felt would be the right husband. He used to train the sahib's horses. I was going to teach the slut's daughter a lesson.

'I know the rest of the story,' Kiran said, rolling her eyes. 'So your father sold you to the sahib, and then he, in turn, sold you to –'

'I used to take the water cart –' the basket weaver cut her off – 'a cart hitched to a cow. Poured water into cupped hands once every two hours. Men would be gasping, collapsing all around me. So terrifying, the rubber trees, that black shadow looming behind me.'

'So the other man bought you, eh?'

The basket weaver raised three fingers. 'Sold yesterday, three, to the doctor's wife. She'll buy more she said, this evening.'

'It's quite clear to me,' Lalit said to Kiran. 'It's the same old story. Poor thing, it must have been suffocating, that sort of life.'

'Yes, suffocating.' The basket weaver looked at him, surprised. 'That smell. Tree after tree oozing that thick yellow glue. A smell of milk gone bad. I ran to the river for its fresh breeze. So bright the water. No longer drowning in hot glue.' She closed her eyes and drew in her breath slowly. 'Forgot the heat, the steaming mud. Could breathe again, move, see. My father breathed that smell and became the oozing yellow glue. Could smell it in his sweat. So I ran.'

'Away,' Lalit added.

'You ran for days,' Kiran said.

'Yes, there you are running –' Lalit grabbed the basket from Rajni's hands. 'It's all here! Look, Kiran, isn't that a river, and these, trees? And look here –' He picked up another basket woven in muted green, yellow, and purple. 'A man, another, a child –'

'I don't see a thing in it,' Kiran cut in, 'it's not in these baskets. It's in her head. I can see her running in there, for days, months, years.'

'I ran to the river,' the basket weaver said. 'And I stuck my fingers into my throat, retched and retched to get that smell out. But it clung to my nose, tongue, throat. Lying limp on the soft silt of the riverbank, so cool against my burning face. The river breeze washed that frightening smell away.'

'It's all here. Look at this basket, here, this one. You lying on the riverbank, and who is this, someone in the river, wading towards the bank?'

'Here, let me have another look, Lalit-saab, maybe I can start seeing things too, if I try hard enough.' Kiran pulled the basket out of Lalit's hands. 'Ah, this thing coming out of the river has got to be –'

'The shining being my father had told me of – he appeared. Golden, shining with water and sunlight, he turned and looked at me. His eyes, yes, you could say they had captured the evening sky. I felt a stunning coolness, the very first slap of the rain-wind.'

'OK. Now we're getting somewhere.' Kiran rolled her eyes.

'The monster's arm went up when I tripped –'

'No, no, you were looking at the shining god, woman!' Kiran slapped her hand.

'I closed my eyes when I saw the cane coming down,' the basket weaver whispered, 'but it didn't touch me. There was a very loud sound. The shining creature was standing near my head.'

'And what did you do?' Kiran asked with a sneer. 'Did you touch his feet and beg to be saved?'

'I made sure the floors were always clean, the food hot and on the table at the right time, the books dust-free, clothes washed and pressed. He told me his house was near a river. He told me not to be frightened any more because the monster was dead.'

'*Arré*, your future was made then! So what's the tragedy? Why so silent all these years? How much money did the sahib give you? *Arré*, your life began that day, Rajni.'

' "Don't go back home," he said. "My father will kill me," I said. He smiled. "I'll simply shoot him, he said." '

'You don't mean – I knew it. Same old thing.' Lalit took hold of her shoulder and gave her a little shake. 'You let him use you, that's what you did. You didn't think, didn't stop to think about what was really happening.' He turned his face away and let out a light laugh. 'You're conditioned not to think, and you rewrite the narrative over and over.'

Yes, your life began, like my daughter's, who was now going back and forth between the foreman's shack and the sahib's bungalow, and I had to witness it all, grit my teeth, lower my head, walk on. Barbed wire twisting around me, tighter and tighter. What is a man supposed to do – sit back and twiddle his toes while his daughter drags his *izzat* up and down the street like her mother did before her? Easy cane twisting in your hands. Even a hammer isn't sufficient sometimes, or an axe. Can you smash or chop off the searing in your head?

Ay, Rajni, your body has felt gentle hands. Mine did, only once, for a few months with that construction worker. No wonder you've sat cold and aloof ever since. You don't need anyone any more. Your sahib turned you into a block of ice, didn't he, with gentleness and kindness, freezing you up for ever after, so you could never be with another man. And you say your life began that night. Woman, come talk to this withered old piece some day, and she'll point out a thing or two.

'Men in black robes came to us,' the basket weaver muttered. 'Angry voices.'

'Of course.' Kiran gave a sly, knowing smile. 'Missionaries never liked it when the sahibs mixed with our kind. But I'll swear your sahib picked up his gun –'

'What gun?' Lalit asked, his voice tinged with puzzled anger.

'All sahibs have guns,' Kiran affirmed. 'So he shot at them, I'll swear.'

'He raised his fist to his face,' the basket weaver muttered.

162

'Ah – I can hear him. "My bungalow, my woman, my plantation." And then he fired. The missionaries ran off like frightened mice.'

'Two monks came up to me at the bazaar.'

'And your sahib picked up his gun and fired again. God, I can see them, their saffron robes flapping, running off cursing. Oh, they curse all right. Sahibs and guns – anyone would curse, even God. "There," your sahib said, then, right? "There. Let's see who comes next to mess with my stuff." Kiran raised a fist, pushed her blouse up her arm and flexed her biceps. 'There.'

'You're mad,' Lalit said to Kiran, scorn flushing his face.

'Mad? Why? Look at this basket. Wouldn't you say, Lalit-saab, that this straight line in golden yellow is her sahib with his gun shooting at these purple criss-crosses, the monks and missionaries? It's quite clear to me. You see vague shadows of rivers and people. I just see these things more specifically, that's all. These baskets of hers do carry tales, I'll swear now. You found them first. And, well, I see them now; a little differently, that's all.' Kiran played her tongue over her lips. 'Perhaps I read minds better than you do, kid. Maybe I'll prove it to you sometime, when I feel like it.'

Stunned anger filling his eyes, Lalit clenched his jaw.

'Let me see now,' Kiran continued with a broad wink, 'then you went to see the village midwife, and then all the trouble started. That's how your father found out, right? And your brother told you to drown yourself. "Was the sahib worth his salt? Can he save you?" he flung at your face. And you were frightened, you poor thing. You were terrified.'

'My brother was terrified,' the basket weaver said haltingly. 'Confused.'

Lalit tore a few tufts of grass and scratched the ground with his thumbnail. He twisted strands of grass between his fingers. Of course, confused. There's no rational, analytical approach to things. They've broken off the engagement. His father's voice had been mildly bitter. His sister was beside herself. She couldn't understand, couldn't, couldn't, nothing made sense, they had been seeing each other for a whole year now, and he'd sworn he loved her, more than life, and this was not an arranged marriage, so now this withdrawal didn't make sense, any sense – All a question of money, can't you see? Lalit had snapped at her. All this bullshit about love. We just won't dish out that much money. We don't have it. It's wrong, anyway. And if he ever meant what he said, why doesn't he have the balls now to tell his parents to go to hell and run off with you?

Twenty-four and a broken engagement. A catastrophe. That was his mother's and his aunt's response. Twenty-four and a bloody fool, said Lalit. Twenty-four and hysterical. Twenty-four and irrational, immature, just can't see things as they are. Five years older than me and you don't know what the real world's made of. Why do you want to sit at home with an MA in political science? Get a job, teaching or something, and forget about that asshole. Pull yourself together.

Like to beat the shit out of that spineless bastard.

'Shall I tell you what happened then?' Kiran stretched out slowly on the grass and pulled a basket to her chest like a pillow. 'So your father went to the sahib's bungalow. Well after midnight, you heard the door crack and splinter. But he didn't get past the drawing room with his axe, did he? Your sahib shot him.'

'His face cracked open,' the basket weaver whispered. 'I got that sickening rubber smell. Sticky yellow oozing all over.'

'Then your sahib dragged him outside, down the gravel drive, out of the gates, and rolled him into the gutter. "That's that," he

164

said, with an odd one-sided smile. And after a few months, the baby was born, right? Right there in the sahib's bungalow.' Kiran smiled triumphantly.

'A large brick building,' the basket weaver said, running her fingers over the basket on her lap, feeling the criss-cross interweave of its surface, 'and inside, the walls, doors, beds, the clothes the people wore – all white. A strange sharp smell that hurt my throat. Bright, shining metal, the prick of needles, and a white mask coming down on my face. A heavy sweet smell that took away all pain. Then laughter, and a tiny, wrinkled face that was so pink ... so pink ... I stared in wonder at a pale, alien creature.'

No one knew for sure, the old man muttered to himself, washing *paan* leaves in a bucket under his stall, whether it was the sahib's child or the new foreman's. Every time I went to the bazaar, I heard people smirk, titter. How long was I supposed to grit my teeth? Doing away with one's wife didn't do away with shame. Shame, younger, more brazen, flaunted this baby like a flag before my face. Your grandchild. What could one do in a place full of laughing faces but turn slowly away and leave? In my heart, I knew what I had to do, and I would do it. I had to get rid of this awful wrenching shame.

The only way to save face now is to get her married off quickly, within the next three months, and I have always had this young doctor in mind, Detroit-based, and his family's not expecting big money. A far better prospect, let me assure you.

Just how some aunts rush to the rescue!

Ever thought of presenting a paper on commodification and product mobility? Lalit had asked, arching an eyebrow. You ought to be running one of those special domestic-service agencies that cater to Kuwaiti sheiks, dear aunt, and head their damage-control divisions as well. You're quite wasted at afternoon teas.

I thank God for you, his mother said to his aunt. You know how to turn curses into blessings.

Do gods bless or curse? I wondered, staring at that tiny shining alien. It didn't look happy at all, but there was laughter all around. 'Was that the laughter of the gods? Were they happy then, or –'

'What shit you talk.' Kiran threw the basket aside. 'Gods! Gods!'

Gods, woman, what do you know about gods? I've adored gods in my life. And I've learnt to forget them to ease my soul. And why shouldn't we forget them, eh? They forget us in seconds, changing our lives in one night and then just vanishing, going about their daily business – like nothing had ever happened – changing heart, mind, body, Oh, so what, these things happen, shaking the earth, just part of the whole routine, my sweet, splitting the ground occasionally, crumbling mountains to dust, and you lie on the floor unable to connect nothing with nothing, blinded by a strange dust, and your gods laugh their merry laughter.

Every floor I sweep, I sweep with vengeance, clearing the dust that must have dropped from the feet of some such gods. The dust rises with each stroke, however careful I am, and still stings my eyes. Such is the dust of gods.

'Hang the gods for a second. Your son was beautiful and gold – his skin, his hair. And his eyes were a laughing blue –'

'His eyes were as dark as the river silt. They carried in them a strange sullenness, almost anger.' The basket weaver's hands

166

clenched. 'It lingered in his eyes like that sticky yellow smell that clung to you.'

'But all the people in the village looked at you, at your son, with a simple, clear envy. A Buddhist monk stopped you at the bazaar one day. What's to become of this boy? he asked. Send him to our school. But you shook your head. Never.' Kiran swept her hair back with both hands, twisted it and put it up. 'No one was going to shave his shining hair, and take him away from you. Those monks, they're always stealing boys from the village, shaving their heads, putting them in ochre robes. You better decide about him, the monk threatened you. The Japanese are moving in. These sahibs will have to run soon. Remember us, when they come.

'I remember much talk of the Japanese, those days,' Kiran added confidingly to the people around her, 'much talk of planes, bombs, digging trenches. I was only about two or three then. But where you were,' she turned to the basket weaver, 'you saw missionaries leave in truckloads. The plantation workers started to run away and cross the border into India. You ignored all that, I know, swam in the river with your son on your back and laughed at them. Now what was his name? What did your sahib call him . . . let's see now . . . what does D'Mello-saab call his dog? "Jack". I've heard that name a lot. But I don't like the sound, so let's call him "Roop", or beauty. Because your life was perfect then, and beautiful.'

'A sound like distant thunder.' The basket weaver looked up at the clear blue-gold light of February.

'Yes, one afternoon, when you were feeding Roop, you heard a rumbling far away. Minutes later, your sahib rushed into the bungalow and asked you to pack. Got to get out, he said. Didn't realise those damned yellow fiends were so close. He threw some clothes into a bag, while you hurriedly packed a few things for your son and yourself. He drove the jeep as if there were demons after you. You asked him where you were going, and why, but he asked you to be quiet. Later he said he had to reach the river. But he didn't tell you which river. You drove through plantations, towns, swamps, nights, days. You'd never seen the sahib so tense and anxious. You saw his face relax when at last a muddy silver streak appeared near the horizon. India, he said, as you drove over the bridge.'

The people, drawing closer and closer, listened crouching, open-mouthed. Kiran's face glowed; her eyes were startling bright. 'Through forests, dawns, villages, twilights, cities, driving like a demon –' She arched her head back, sucked in air and let it out with a long hiss.

'Rice fields,' sighed the basket weaver, 'rivers, days and nights of flat green land. No rubber trees or swamps. Fresh, dry air.'

'Where were you?' Lalit caught the basket weaver's arm. 'Which city or town?'

'Police station.' The basket weaver's eyes became glazed. 'A piece of paper in my hand. I crumpled it, threw it on the road. Everything disappeared into a golden haze.'

Yes, gods disappear, don't they? They abandon you when you're most confused. Why did he save me? you wonder. Why did he bring that golden gentleness into my life, only to vanish into that golden haze? Sweep, sweep hard the ground, sweep away the dust of gods. I spit on this dust every day, curse every day this dust that stings my eyes. Sit and weave, basket weaver, endlessly let your fingers weave. Watching those restless fingers intertwine with sharp cane, I feel myself twist and turn in those patterns. How will you now weave us out, woman?

'Forget,' said Kiran, stroking Rajni's arms, shoulders. 'Your son's better off with him, there. I've given up a son, too. Sold, really, to a rich cloth merchant. He and his wife were childless. And I know my son's better off with them. Forget. Like we forget dreams. Like we forget the only man we ever loved. Don't sit here brooding any more. Two years under this tree, God knows all these years from where to Delhi. Enough. Come with me. Taste some money. Taste something salty.'

'Don't be absurd,' Lalit said. 'From one brutal exploitation to another.'

'Sahibs like that ought to be done away with,' the old *paan* seller said to the sweeper lying on the bench.

'And how many have you executed in your time, eh, Dauri Lal?'

'With one short swing of my axe, the head from the shoulder.'

The old woman got up, picked up her broom, straightened her clothes. 'Peace to your heart, old man,' she said to him, and touched her forehead with her hand. 'You don't look too well. Why are you breathing so hard?'

'Too many miles, and too many years. They can't catch me now.'

'Of course not, and I won't tell either, *pyaré*.' She winked at him broadly. 'Now don't choke on one of your *paans*.' She cleared her throat and spat. 'That one's for you up there, or down there or wherever you are, we don't have a clue,' she said.

'Clouds of golden dust – do you understand?' The basket weaver clutched Lalit's arm.

'Perfectly.' Lalit disengaged his arm, laughing drily. 'Don't know how to restore gods, or anything else.'

'A house by a river that's always full of boats, he said . . .' the basket weaver's voice trailed.

'Hell of an address that. Knew she was crazy,' Kiran muttered to Lalit. 'Tell the doctor's wife you can't go, OK?' she said, shaking the basket weaver's shoulder. 'I'll tell the doctor's wife, OK?'

The basket weaver nodded slowly and stood up. She looked over their heads, over the houses, at the distant uneven horizon of the city. 'Yellow,' she whispered, 'always the sunset is sticky yellow.'

It is a system of appropriations – that's how you have to look at it, Lalit had explained to his sister. With all these hysterics and tear-shedding you're simply reinstating yourself into the cultural narrative – the narrative you need to write yourself out of. Stop this lunatic sobbing. Stop it, stop it, forget the jerk – he dumped you like a – like a – Shattering, splintering glass. Blood streaming down his wrist. He had driven his fist through the window pane. Unbelievable. Stop this insane sobbing, stop! Smashing the windows with the cricket bat, sweeping the books off the shelves, then just hitting the walls, the doors, throwing chairs, stools, his mother's scream of panic like brakes screeching, and then the hard slap, no, three, sending him reeling down the stairs – Get a hold of yourself. His father's eyes, hard and blank.

To look at these situations rationally, analytically. Not to get sucked into –

To kill that bastard.

What did I do? What happened to me, I can't quite explain. Where my daughter went, I don't know. I had to run to save my skin. They would have hanged me had they caught me. A sahib's blood on my hands. A darker sin than killing a god. Perhaps my daughter's sitting under some tree today and staring vacantly at the sky. Is there ever any forgiveness? Weaving again? What else is there? I wrap my leaves, you make your baskets. Sometimes a cool green smell wraps around me. Slender fingers tearing the newest leaves from the top of the bushes for the freshest, heavenly fragrant cup of Darjeeling. Voices singing in rhythm with those swiftly plucking hands. Entire hillsides to be sun-dried, strained into a cup. Why is that basket weaver getting up? Walking towards –? No! What – *paan*? Never asked for one before. Here – here, this one, extra sweet, have this one on me. *Namaste*.

It was just a *paan* leaf that she took from my hands. Our fingers touched for a moment. Funny, that cool green smell again, wrapping so tightly round my head. Rolling down an emerald hillside, once, I remember. A dazzling spinning cool all around. Look at that sunset, Dauri Lal – the sky's cast in gold and copper, a god descending in full armour. I can barely breathe. My eyes – am I blind or mad – ?

'Dauri Lal's falling off his stall,' Kiran said, pointing. She ran towards the *paan* stall. The crowd that had pressed close in a circle exploded into exclamations and scattered like shrapnel.

'Heart attack or a stroke –' Lalit stood up. 'I'll call an ambulance. Rajni –' he turned to the basket weaver. 'Did Dauri Lal say anything to you?' She looked up at him and smiled, her eyes empty as the wind.

'You know what to write? *Understand?*' she asked, her eyes widening expectantly. 'It's time now – you understand? Must understand.'

'Right,' Lalit said. 'Tomorrow. We have to save the *paanwala* today. No god will come to his rescue.'

'No, not from a yellow sky,' whispered the basket weaver. 'Tell him to wait for the blueness.' She unwrapped the *paan* leaf, shook it, and watched the filling of crushed nuts and spices scatter on the ground.

Destiny

A tidal rush of high-pitched voices made Nisha Paul drop the notebook in her hand and run outside and towards Lachmi's house. 'Why? Why? Why this, oh lord?' she heard Lachmi scream as she ran up the red dirt road leading to Lachmi's polished teak door. The entire village was at her door, watching Lachmi beat the red dust, tear her sari, scream and sob.

'Where is that husband anyway?' an old woman asked. 'She'll scream herself to death. Did she dream something?'

'I saw her open that window,' the dhobi said, turning to Nisha, 'as I was passing by. The look on her face made me stop dead in my tracks. Contorted –' he pulled and twisted his cheeks with his gnarled hands to explain, ' – in pain.'

'We heard the window slam all the way from the bazaar,' the flower boy said excitedly. 'Bang!'

'That door burst open with such violence that I,' the dhobi touched his chest, cleared his throat, 'thought I was going to have another one. One should treat teak doors with more respect.'

An old woman shuffled forward with a basket of eggs. 'If you had seen how Lachmi flung herself on the ground –' She drew her breath in sharply, and touched her forehead. 'And then the scream, the scream of a wounded animal.'

'Could something have happened to Kanu?' Nisha asked in a low voice.

'He'll turn up all right,' said the barber, and spat on the ground. 'Must have passed out on the way. Send those brothers of yours to find him,' he said to Lachmi, raising his voice.

'But he always comes home at night, however late, always.' Lachmi struck the ground with her fist. 'Always. He always sleeps in his own bed at night.'

Someone tittered in the crowd.

'Perhaps my brother has seen the light at last.' The sneering, high-pitched voice made Nisha turn her head sharply. Nirmala – who could never miss such an opportunity. Too bad Nisha had left her tape recorder and notebook behind. What a fabulous crossfire of voices – and at the point of their intersection lay Lachmi, crying, beating the red dust.

'Get up, Lachmi,' said some of the older women, 'get up, bathe, go to the Shiv temple with flowers, light a lamp, ring the bell.' But Lachmi continued to tear her sari, cry, strike the ground with her fists. 'Did you dream something?' the old woman with the basket of eggs asked again, 'some terrible dream?'

Nisha looked at the crowd gathered around Lachmi. What could this dream be that the old woman seemed concerned about – yet another superstition? The people here didn't appear terribly concerned; they gave casual advice, but did not try to console this woman who was crying hysterically. She had learnt in the past two weeks that Lachmi, although regarded with awe because of her money and her house, the only two-storey house in the village, her thuggish brothers and a flourishing dairy – forty cows and a contract with the government dairy – was not liked. They considered Lachmi arrogant and unfeeling. She had refused to help out during the ploughing; three families had pleaded with her to lend them four oxen for three weeks, but she had shaken her head the wrong way, and closed the door. Her late father had been the same. And her brothers, somewhat slow-witted but built like their well-fed bulls, did whatever their younger sister said. Lachmi's husband, Kanu, was popular, but pitied now, since he had turned to the locally produced *tadi* to drown his frustrations – his curtailed freedom. He had to work in the cowstalls during the day. His days of wandering along the riverbank with his flute were over since the moment he put the garland round Lachmi's neck. So people watched, shrugged, made concerned noises, but did not go towards Lachmi to help her to her feet and wipe her tears.

Jealousy, Nisha had entered in her notebook a week back. *Rich, owning house, property, independent in spite of being a woman. Orders the husband around. Silent, aloof.*

The first thing since my arrival to disturb the lazy calm of Binjhar, Nisha noted mentally. Must enter, enquiry about a dream, missing husband, fate-oriented possibly. Use in project. She squared her shoulders and pushed her way through the crowd to Lachmi, who was now striking her head against the hard red mud.

Nisha had developed more than a fondness for this tall, statuesque woman who always walked with her head tossed back. Lachmi, she had noticed, never looked up with her eyes. She would raise her head, but keep her eyelids lowered half-way, giving her eyes a partly languid, partly scornful look. Lachmi brought her dinner twice a week; she would enter slowly, holding out a plate made of bell-metal on which the food had been neatly arranged. A hibiscus or a spray of basil was Lachmi's special touch on the side of the rice. 'This is how it will be,' Lachmi had told her, placing that very first plate of food before her. 'Twice a week from my house, since Ramu will take two nights off and will not be able to make you dinner.' A slight lowering of the head, a flicker of a smile, and then that slow withdrawal, as if she was leading a retinue out of a palace.

Nisha Paul looked at herself in the mirror after Lachmi's first visit. She saw bamboo groves sway as the wind moved through them; she saw banyan trees with their dark leaves and long hanging roots shade and cool the cracked earth below them on the scorching afternoons of June. The fading gold of the twilight played tricks in the mirror. Peacocks fanned out their dazzling tails against a lightning-splashed sky. A forgotten world swept in and out in Lachmi's wake. Nisha had closed her eyes and swallowed. Colonial eyes would have dreamt up such visions. She must not. But in the hazy shine of the mirror, she saw Lachmi walk on through her own slender boyish form, a swaying, mythic, dark gold wave. She felt a rushing in her head, as if the River Dakhin had swept in unawares and Lachmi, too, was pulling her along into something. Unbelievable – she shook her head. For Nisha had moved on to another world.

Unbelievable – for Lachmi to make such a public display of herself; unless she had sensed something terrible, beyond her control. Nisha felt strangely unnerved by the sound of Lachmi's uncontrollable sobbing. Not choking, hiccupping bursts, but a sustained rushing moaning like the river out there, a movement of sound dragging everything along towards some unknown destination. Lachmi's fists echoed each tumbling word, 'My – husband – always – comes – home – at – night,' with a dull fatality.

'Stop,' Nisha said, kneeling beside Lachmi. The village population stood and watched the student in her blue jeans and white cotton shirt smooth Lachmi's hair and put a few Kleenex tissues in her hand. Then they nodded, shrugged, made a few tch-tchs, laughed, concluded that such was Lachmi's fate – the dhobi shaking his grey head slowly, murmuring, 'Fate, fate, how can you force, really, what was not meant to be, shouldn't have forced, well, tricked the man to marry you, tch, tch' – and slowly dispersed to take care of their cattle and crops and stores and children. All went away, except for one young man who sat down under the mango tree a few yards from the two women and lit a *biri* with a shaking hand.

'He'll never come home again,' wept Lachmi on Nisha Paul's shoulder, 'never.'

'Why do you say so?' asked Nisha, mixing a few Oriya words with Hindi and Bengali. 'What do you suppose has happened? Did you say something to him, did you fight, is there, perhaps –' she cleared her throat, '– you know what I mean, another . . .'

'No, no,' Lachmi groaned, 'but there was, and maybe I should suffer.'

'Don't be silly,' Nisha said with a laugh. 'Go inside, bathe and, well, why not go to the temple with flowers? You'll feel better, and I'm sure Kanu will be back before the cows come home.' She stood up, pulling Lachmi with her. She helped Lachmi adjust her ripped green silk sari. 'This sari's ruined,' she said.

'Who cares?' Lachmi dropped the tissues on the ground and wiped her face with one end of her sari. 'I'll get another one next week. But –' she blew her nose into its crumpled wet corner, 'but –'

'He'll be home, I'm sure, and soon. You go in now.' As she walked away she saw the young man under the mango tree for the first time. He stubbed his *biri* and ran towards Lachmi.

'Lachmi!' he called, his voice half excited, half frightened, and stopped her by grabbing her arm. 'Lachmi – don't cry.'

'Ramu!' Nisha called after him, surprised. 'What are you doing here? You were supposed to fix my bicycle!'

'I will, *Nisha-didi*,' he said, scratching his head and looking down at his feet. 'I will, in half an hour.' She showed him a fist, shook her head and left for the bazaar. Missing husbands and village life, she thought with a wry smile. Husbands were still hideously important. The letter from her mother yesterday certainly affirmed that. 'We've found the right boy for you. He has a decent job, is dedicated to his work, just like you are. We like his face, and the person who made his existence known to us is thrilled after seeing your photograph. His parents are both dead – a good thing in some ways, considering all the dowry deaths in the past few years. No in-law hassles for you. He's stuck in some village right now, but not for long. Will make good money soon. You can decide whether you want to live here in New Delhi or not after the wedding. Your father could help relocate him here. After all, you do want to live in a city you're familiar with. We would like you to get married this summer, so you'd better come home. It really is time for you to get married. We don't want you to go back to America – and if you do, you will take a husband back with you. Otherwise we will consider ourselves so ill-fated as to lose all hope . . .' What could they do, really? Could they tie her up and throw her into the river? That was how arranged marriages had always struck her: a ritual offering, a petrified form swathed in yards of red and gold silk and tossed into unfamiliar currents. Mothers! Husbands! What would they say if they knew about Drew and the year she spent in his studio apartment? She quelled her laughter as she walked into the bazaar, in case they thought she was mad, and proceeded to buy soap and fruit.

The apples and pears looked good, the bananas were pure sugar the man swore, and the flower boy pressed tuberoses against her legs begging for 'Only five rupees for a bunch, please, *didi*, rice is expensive these days, just five rupees.'

'I have kept the leg for you –' said the man in the meat stall to her. 'Send Ramu when you get home.'

The flower boy wrapped all her purchases in a newspaper,

including the flowers. 'Special for you,' he said in English, smiling as she laughed.

They all treated her 'special' ever since she had arrived and moved into the half-constructed school at one end of the village. Ramu, the bangle seller, in a pair of over-sized khaki shorts and a dirty white T-shirt, had turned up at the station the moment she stepped off the train in the next village west. 'Who are you?' she had asked, a little apprehensive about surrendering herself to this skinny sprite's mercy.

'Ramu, *didi*,' he had smiled, touching his head with his right hand. 'Dishtri magitray say you train come Shailen-doctor jeep I am.' Nisha Paul had blinked twice, taking a few seconds to decipher his words.

'I can follow Oriya,' she said, stringing Bengali, Hindi and Oriya together.

'Slow down! Oh, my god!' she had gasped as Ramu swung round a corner of the uneven dirt road, almost overturning the jeep. 'No worry,' he had assured her, grinning widely, fingering the copper amulet round his thoat, 'charmed life mine.' What about mine? she wondered, closing her eyes.

Ramu brought her to the school and helped her settle in, turning a classroom into her living space. No school, he had informed her. The city contractors had stolen all the money, so the school was never completed. The local children went to the school in the next village, which was bigger, with many more people, a post office, a police station, a small hospital and the train station. Here in the village of Binjhar, there were none of those brick buildings one could run to for survival when the floods and cyclones hit every year, when the river swelled and roared and swept away huts, cattle, disobedient children, rice fields. But this unfinished brick school-house was here, and the dispensary a quarter-mile away, where the doctor worked and lived.

181

Ramu worked there for the doctor – 'Shailen-doctor', as he called him – taking care of the household chores and helping with the patients. 'Sui lagai,' he told Nisha, poking his forefinger into her arm, 'do injections.' The doctor had taught him how. He had also taught Ramu to drive the government-loaned jeep, and was now teaching him to read and write English.

Nisha hadn't met the doctor yet, but knew a great deal about him. He got out of bed at six, liked shrimp and fish, had delivered thirty-five babies in the two years he'd been there, and possessed a television. Every Saturday and Sunday evening the village trooped to the doctor's quarters to watch movies; to learn about the latest riots in the cities, a civil-war-torn Kashmir, predicted drought in the east; and to relish the cricket highlights.

Although invited by Ramu, Nisha had refrained from walking over to the dispensary to join the ritual TV-watching. Ramu urged her constantly to meet the doctor. 'You must, *didi*,' he said, 'you must,' while sweeping the floor of her room, cooking her dinner, bringing her tea in the mornings. He handed her malaria pills and told her the doctor's instructions – four tablets a week, just for prevention. Dettol had appeared, too, from the dispensary, a first-aid kit, and diarrhoea and dysentery pills. *Wants to move into my territory*, she had jotted in her notebook, adding, *with discomfiting ease, hate to admit, bottle by little bottle, just as he has taken over this village. They like him and respect him, trust him too much. He's usurped the place* – It would be difficult now to have free rein: to question their faith in lore, make them doubt their beliefs, try out the experiment she had carefully planned with Professor Lennox. If they didn't like what she said or asked, they could always run to their beloved doctor for reassurance. Perhaps they already had.

Nisha felt a little uncomfortable while eating dinner – was the doctor eating the same stuff? Did Ramu narrate her daily routine

182

to Shailen-doctor? Had Ramu turned her into a story for the doctor, just as he had turned the doctor into a myth for her? Did he tell that doctor all the little things she had asked Ramu – Why do you think you have a charmed life? Do you think there's really something that shapes your life? Ramu had laughed and giggled. Yes, yes, yes. Why? Just because they say so? Are you sure things happen this way, because things are meant to be? Test them, Sylvia Lennox had told her, question their beliefs, be detached about it. Don't coax, force or pressure, just be matter-of-fact, detached, give them explanations, see how they react.

There can be quite logical explanations, really, Nisha had said to Ramu, for everything, yes, let me give you an example . . . The doctor be damned. She knew how to do this. Otherwise Professor Lennox wouldn't have chosen her, or gasped when she outlined her project. Even Sylvia Lennox, the wily, sharp – For your book? she had asked Lennox. At least three chapters out of six – you think? A systematic introduction of chaos: first the questions, then the doubts and then the confusion. Can you leave right away? Lennox had asked. Go now? What about Drew? OK, get me the money, Nisha said, and I'll do it. Let's put the spirit back into anthropology. Like you say, let me make the most of a humanities dissertation. Just a little bit of psychological devilry, that's all. The third world exists for exploitation – what else? Startled by her tone, Sylvia Lennox had forgotten to ease back against her chair and languidly cross her Fredrick's-of-Hollywood-clad legs. She had cleared her throat and leant forward instead. Within the week Nisha held a grant package in her hand. I have dollars, I have cents, wonder where the third world went? she had sung to Lennox. For a moment, a river flashed against her eyes, a river she had heard stories of as a child. She had damned that river up for years. And all of a sudden, in less than a month, she stood face to face with that mad river.

Let me give you an example . . . Nisha would blink away the swirling waters, lean forward and tap Ramu's shoulder. But Ramu continued to laugh at her questions and suggestions. The barber's wife, who had turned up to take care of the laundry, much to the dhobi's chagrin, was more receptive. She'd cock her head to the side and listen intently as Nisha devalued destiny. You're different, the barber's wife said, partly shocked, partly fascinated. Nisha smiled, inclined her head. She was special, as alien is special, unreachable to some extent, but special as she was quite approachable. What is it like over there? What's your family like? How many brothers and sisters? When will you marry? Why do you cut your hair short? Nisha happily answered every question, some openly, some evasively. She wanted them to like her, because she liked being here.

During the half-hour ride to Binjhar from the station two weeks back, Nisha had surveyed the territory with clenched fists as if expecting something to happen, something inexplicable. After all, her coming here was inexplicable – just like that, a snap of the fingers, when she was not quite prepared to make this journey, right now, leaving Drew just when she felt the relationship was out of control, animal attraction, call it what you will, and Sylvia Lennox asking, What's happening to your dissertation? Are you here in my office or in that obsessed artist's bed? So Nisha flew twelve thousand miles, from neat Ephesus in upstate New York to this tiny straggly village that wasn't even marked on the latest map of Orissa.

As soon as they had left the station – one long platform with a tin shed at one end and a forest of banana trees and bamboo groves at the other – with its stale-urine-and-coaldust smell, the red dust came wind-borne to your nose and eyes, an eerie, sweet mixture of rain and blood and mud. This angry red belt – that was the perfect soil for rice, when the rains rushed in on time. Fine dark dust from drying dung cakes on hut walls touched you now and then when a strong gust of wind swept in, a pungent but grassy odour. And then you looked up, startled by this mingling of smells, and found an undulating landscape – a jade and turquoise horizon, blazing copper with the setting sun, the ground rushing by red, sometimes a coppery brown, dissolving in the distance into gold and green mustard fields. And the River Dakhin, with its warm, red, silt-laden waves, filled with treacherous cross-currents, infested with crocodiles and harbouring the secret island of the goddess Manasha, swept round south of the village. 'Island of No Return,' Lachmi's sister-in-law, Nirmala, had said, nodding her head slowly. '*Nisha-didi*, Ramu's mother is there.' And Nisha had scrambled for her notebook and tape recorder.

'When Ramu was three, *didi*,' Nirmala had said, wiping her son's runny nose with the corner of her sari, 'his mother – and the less said about her character the better – brought him to my mother one morning. Burning with fever, throwing up, Ramu was almost dead. His mother put him in my mother's arms and said, I'm going. I've made a raft, and I'm going to Manasha to bring back my son. My mother clapped her hand over her mouth in shock. Don't say these things, Ramu's mother, you don't know what curse you'll bring down on all of us! Ramu's mother vowed that from that day on nothing would harm Ramu, that he would have a charmed life. My copper amulet, here, for Manasha's protection. You can't take death away from him, my mother told her, you have to give a condition – you can't say nothing can kill him. Only another man, Ramu's mother said, no illness or calamity will strike my son down. We watched in horror as the river pulled her away among its rocks and crocodiles. We never try to go there, you know, never pray to Manasha for anything. For if you ask for something, be prepared to lose something similar. Manasha takes when she gives, sometimes life for life. A few days later Ramu's fever left him, and the dhobi found his mother's blood-stained sari caught on the rocks near the bank. Wrapped in its folds – ohh –' Nirmala had drawn in one horrified breath, 'one bloody toe.

'Ever since that day,' Nirmala had carried on, 'Ramu grew up with us, and me and my brother Kanu treated him like our younger brother. Ramu has a charmed life – everyone knows, because of his mother's sacrifice. He swims in the river, comes back alive. Crocodiles never go near him. Once Kanu tried to drown him – well, boys, you know. Then another time, Ramu got bitten by a cobra, and the cobra died. And Ramu was always jealous of the bigger, stronger, popular Kanu, and I think he thought Lachmi was going to marry him, but –' Nirmala made a face and rolled her eyes. 'Well, Ramu was always at Lachmi's beck and call, running around bringing her flowers, calling her Radha, himself Krishna, saying that they were meant to be, not Lachmi and Kanu . . . Yes, well, who knows what fate, destiny is such a trick – you never can tell.'

'Destiny a trick? Really?' Nisha had raised an eyebrow. 'But what you really mean is that Lachmi married the man she wanted to. Ramu was merely deluding himself, fantasising all along. Right?'

Nirmala had looked at her, puzzled. 'Well – yes – well, I'm not saying anything about Lachmi, that's she's manipulative or anything like that –' Nirmala shook her head vigorously. 'Just that she always gets what she wants. Rich people, you know, fate favours them.'

'I think you should think hard, Nirmala,' Nisha said. 'Perhaps it has nothing to do with fate. Perhaps some people are good at getting what they want. Maybe through money or cleverness, or maybe they know how to create favourable circumstances for

186

themselves. Think about that. Start putting two and two together.'

'Yes.' Nirmala nodded slowly. 'Two and two, I see what you mean. Three villages south, you know, a man became very rich after his wife drowned while bathing at night. He said he found a chest full of jewellery under a banyan tree. He said a god came to him in a dream and led him to the tree just as his wife was drowning. The god was compensating him for the loss of his wife, he said. That man was hanged, *didi*, by the district magistrate there. When the district magistrate started asking all kinds of questions, it all came out. You see, he had lost all his money gambling, so he asked his wife for her jewellery. She wouldn't give him any of it. Late at night, she went and buried it under a banyan tree. He had followed her, and watched her bury the chest. Then he knocked her out and threw her in a pond, and went back to dig up the chest.' Nirmala rocked on her heels. 'The district magistrate wasn't too bothered about gods in dreams. I guess he put two and two together. But Ramu says so many things, *didi*, about fate, about who's meant to be with who, what's meant to be and what's not. Well, so much for believing and not believing, but as for people – who can tell why he's this way, and she that way? Those brothers of Lachmi – *aar ki boli* –' Nirmala touched her forehead and her sternum, her voice rising to a higher pitch, 'seen them?'

'No,' Nisha said.

'They are always in the cowshed, and in the evenings at the liquor store. Of course, you don't go there, why should you or I ever go that way? They and the father – the father died, you know, six months back – made plans, and well, there was my brother, bewildered, puzzled, putting the garland round Lachmi's neck. Those brothers are hot-headed, you know, very strong, and they do have, well, some say, a nasty vindictive streak, ah, well, the less said the better, I'm not one to bad-mouth anyone, I mind my own business, yes. But what Lachmi wants she always gets, yes. Except for a child. Been married for three years now, and seen many doctors, including Shailen-doctor here.' Nirmala had adjusted the sari over her shoulder and tucked its end in firmly at her waist.

This was the right spot, Nisha decided, the perfect subject for her dissertation – the ideology of destiny, what makes you believe, what makes you doubt, a survey of belief, how belief functions now in the third world. In spite of television and injections and malaria pills, the island of Manasha haunted Binjhar, and the general ruling this morning was that this was Lachmi's fate – what was not meant to be can't be.

She had taken photographs, taped their songs and stories, entered their rituals into her notebook. She went to the river in the evenings when the women floated clay oil lamps downstream, praying for the well-being of their husbands and children. When Nirmala suggested the ritual winter oil-massages, she frowned for a second and then surrendered. They wouldn't trust her if she didn't give in to some of their stuff, she knew. However, oil-massages were a special luxury. Nisha's grandmother used to insist on oil-massages for the children. Hot mustard oil and the afternoon sun. An ecstasy lost since the age of seven, when her grandmother died of a stroke. Nisha's ayah had been trained by nuns in Goa, and she did not believe in exposing the bare bodies of children to the world in winter. But here, under Nirmala's deft fingers, that old warmth resurfaced. Her grandmother's eyes misting as she spoke of a river called Dakhin with its secret island.

Tell me more, she urged the men, women and children. They had surprised her by telling her of their admiration for the doctor, who, in their opinion, was 'special'. Special, though in a different way. He is one of us, Ramu had said to her, and she had entered his discourse on 'special' in her journal. He listens, really listens, ear to the ground, Ramu said. He makes us find the solutions. Doesn't tell us what to do, like the district magistrate. The dhobi and his wife had said the same, and many others. He was special as native is special. You are special, too, Ramu had assured her, catching her frown. But as an alien, Nisha knew. And that made her uneasy. *A doctor who sometimes allows nature-cures*, she entered. *How very interesting.*

Thinking about this ideology of 'special', and listening to comments about Lachmi's virtues – or lack of them – over bananas, rice and spices, she counted her change, paid the flower boy. Instead of snatching the money with glee and touching his forehead, the boy jumped up and pulled her back.

A long moaning scream assaulted the bazaar from the left. 'My brother – ohh, my brother – aiee – ee – ee!' Nirmala, her hair dishevelled and streaming behind her, stumbled past Nisha and the flower boy.

'That witch – that witch – she's killed him – it's her fault – her curse – she's cursed – !' Nirmala staggered to the middle of the crowded bazaar, holding up a tattered portion of a wool *kurta* stained with blood. 'Look,' she screamd, 'Kanu's – this is Kanu's – the dhobi found it floating near the bank. It's all that bitch's fault.' Men, women, children touched the bloody fabric with wonder-filled eyes. 'I'll not be quiet,' she screamed at them. 'On my brother's blood, I swear I'll get even.' And with that, Nirmala whirled around and raced out in the direction of Lachmi's house. The bazaar seemed to lift off the ground and follow her. Mouth open, Nisha watched the whole village run to Lachmi's door again.

'Let's go, memsaab,' the flower boy tugged at her sleeve. And she followed.

189

Standing in a circle, the village of Binjhar watched Kanu's sister, Nirmala, drag Lachmi out by her hair. Lachmi swung out and struck Nirmala on the side of her head and freed herself. Nirmala moved back, gasping, clutching her right temple. 'You whore!' she shrieked. 'Are you satisfied now? You weren't happy taking my brother away from me, you had to kill him too? Just like you killed the woman he was supposed to marry. Rich father, powerful brothers – and Lachmi, to whom no one can say no. "No" – a word forbidden, yes? I'll tell it all today – what have I got to lose now? My brother's dead, and why? Because of that witch, that whore!'

All eyes glistened with excitement and, though Nisha tried to intervene, the dhobi asked her to just listen to the poor sister's story.

Beating the hard red mud with her fists, Nirmala screamed out her accusations. 'You tell me, if Kanu didn't want to sell his land, why should he? Yes, yes, when rich people want, they must have – so all the wiles began. Lachmi had set her sights on him, and on that piece of land that's now that cowshed. How to rope a man in – she knows how to, quite well, can teach you and me a thing or two, I can tell you.'

'Get off my land,' Lachmi hissed.

'Stop this.' Nisha raised her voice and tried to force her way in. 'Nirmala – you have no right – you can't just – stop this – this is terrible –'

'Why terrible?' Nirmala turned and faced Nisha. 'I'm merely putting two and two together. Lachmi might blame fate. Let her. I know who's to blame and why.'

Nisha blinked and stepped back hurriedly as Nirmala took a step towards her. Putting two and two together – the phrase had an ominous ring suddenly. The men and women around Nisha insisted it was important to listen to both sides of the matter. 'But

this is only one twisted account, and what really is the matter?'
Again, shh, listen. Two women fighting – why get in the middle?
Could turn out to be fatal – to get between two women such as
these.

'Did my brother want to marry her? His marriage to someone
else had been arranged the day after he was born. Kanu had never
wanted to marry Lachmi,' Nirmala yelled.

'Liar, jealous bitch, get off my land or I'll have you kicked out.'

How dare Nirmala carry on like this? Nisha fumed inside. She
would never accept a massage from Nirmala again, she decided,
never.

'This is how it happened –' Nirmala tore out a tuft of her own
hair. 'My brother sits drinking with two of her brothers –'
Nirmala struck her forehead, '– my brother lost, *hai*, ever since that
night! And the next thing I know, screams and yells from this
house here. Angry father, murderous brothers, my poor Kanu's
nose bleeding, and that whore shrieking about robbed *izzat*.'

Lachmi stood with her chin raised, silent, her mouth curled in
a sneer.

'I know for a fact,' Nirmala stood up, 'that Kanu was led into
her room that night and locked in. Drunk and helpless, drunk for
the first time, mind you, he didn't know what was going on. And
I'll bet she even got Ramu to help her, Ramu, our own adopted
brother. What did she promise Ramu? What? Can you think?
What else? He was in love with her, so what else?' Nirmala pulled
the old dhobi forward from the crowd and slapped his chest,
making him cough and buckle. 'What else? You tell me.'

'Careful,' the barber said, pulling the old dhobi back and
massaging his back, 'don't kill the old man, his heart's not so
strong these days.'

'Get off my land,' Lachmi said softly, 'before I call my brothers
from the cowshed and have you thrown out.'

'Throw me out – oh yes, go ahead, go yell for your brothers. Who knows – perhaps you called them last night and told them my brother had dared to raise his hand. Why are his clothes bloodstained and he not in them? Just vanished, has he?'

'Get off my land.'

'My brother, good man that he was, believed what he was told and married the maharani here. The woman he was sworn to drowned herself in shock. And then he started to drink, night after night. Because of you and your doings – with – with those city contractors!' Nirmala paused, then turned and looked at her audience, whose eyes had widened considerably.

Nisha remembered Ramu once mumbling on about Kanu smashing the windows of the schoolhouse after hearing some talk at the bazaar about Lachmi. One of the junior engineers had bought a pair of silver anklets for Lachmi, and had made no secret of it. Silly talk, Ramu had said. I heard Lachmi tell Shailen-doctor that. Lachmi tells Shailen-doctor everything. Nisha had scribbled that down. Why?

Nirmala didn't give her time to worry over that. Her penetrating voice hit a high note again. 'Why did my brother disappear a few nights after he beat you up? He beats you up in anger and grief, and then disappears, and all that's left of him is a piece of this wool *kurta* – which I made for him – all red with his blood. Blood on your hands you have.' Nirmala rolled on the ground, tearing her sari, pulling her hair, crying and cursing Lachmi, who stood surveying the horizon with half-closed eyes, her chin up. 'My brother, oh, my brother –'

'Yes, your brother,' Lachmi said with a laugh that sounded like a snarl, her face still turned away, 'don't we know what went on between brother and sister. Don't we know why you didn't want him to marry me, or any other woman for that matter. Brother, indeed!' Lachmi ran her fingers through her hair, twisted it and coiled it on top of her head.

Nirmala's wailing stopped. The second-worst insult in the country had been thrown on her head. Nisha heard the crowd suck in breath loudly. Nirmala slapped the ground. 'She's going to tear her sister-in-law's head off,' someone whispered.

'You killed him – had him killed,' said Nirmala, and started a fresh bout of sobbing.

'Who killed who and who is dead?'

Everyone turned at the sound of the voice. Nisha saw the crowd move aside swiftly for a slender man in a black T-shirt and khaki trousers who walked, with a very sure stride, up to the two women.

'Shailen-doctor,' cried Nirmala, reaching for the doctor's sandal-clad feet. 'My brother is dead.'

'Really? Where is the body?' he asked, cocking an eyebrow, avoiding her hands. The dhobi stepped forward and touched his forehead.

'No body,' he said, clearing his throat. 'Crocodiles must have eaten him. Only a piece of his *kurta*.'

Who saw him last night? Half the male population, at the liquor store where Kanu lay on a bench and emptied a football bladder of *tadi*. Sucking at the long rubber tube attached to the bladder, lying on the bench, singing of his *dil diwana* and the garland of thorns, Kanu had entertained them as usual. Then he had staggered to his feet, muttered something about a deal or a meeting or setting something straight, and wandered off, taking his usual route home by the river. 'Did you find anything, any object?'

'A broken branch on the bank, a large one, from the *neem* tree there. The wind was strong last night, and the branch was old and cracked,' the dhobi said. 'And it's possible,' he added, 'that he wandered too close to the river, slipped on the mud and fell in. After that – well, who can escape the crocodiles? Especially this time of the year, so close to the goat sacrifice, the crocodiles swim close to the bank now, waiting. Last year this time Raji's mother got eaten. We warned her not to wash clothes in the river. The water pump had been installed –'

The doctor raised a hand and cut him short. 'Was anyone near the bank last night?'

'Ramu,' said many of them. 'Ramu's always there in the evenings.'

'Search the riverbank,' he said firmly. 'I'll speak to Ramu.'

Nisha regarded the intruder closely. So this was Shailen-doctor. Amazing how he just walked in and took over. Perhaps it was the air of calm determination about him that made them pay attention. So unlike the delicate and fragile desperation that defined Drew's face.

The crowd broke up and went away. Nirmala got up, straightened her sari, tidied herself, muttered something about hell being here in this life, and walked off. Lachmi stood there, her face expressionless, one hand at her waist. The doctor, his hands in his pockets, his face lowered, studied the red dust around his feet intently. Very slowly Lachmi moved a few steps closer to him. The doctor raised his face and looked at her.

Nisha waited under the *neem* tree. She waited for the doctor to say something to Lachmi, for Lachmi to say something to him. The look in Lachmi's eyes puzzled Nisha. It was as if Lachmi desperately wanted to ask the doctor something. But she didn't utter a word. Nisha shifted from one foot to the other. *Lachmi tells Shailen-doctor everything.* Ramu's words rang in her head. She took a step forward, and went up to the two of them hesitantly. 'Excuse me,' she said to the doctor in English, feeling as if she was stepping into a cordoned-off space between two figures who held each other's gaze without blinking in spite of the blowing red dust and the dazzling light. 'Excuse me, you don't know me, but –'

194

'Nisha Paul,' the doctor turned, breaking a spell almost. He smiled and stretched out his hand. 'Indeed, I hear of you night and day!'

'Well, the thing is,' Nisha said, taken aback, 'shouldn't you inform the district magistrate and have him send a team over to search the river?'

'Will the Binjhar people – Nirmala, Lachmi – be satisfied if a torn-up body is found, even a skeleton? Will the district magistrate explain why fate worked this way, feel inclined to hypothesise? Like you do – as I understand from Ramu – hypothesise, analyse, quite regularly.'

Embarrassed, Nisha frowned. That *chutiya* Ramu had no doubt built on little things she had asked him now and then. Why do you think Manasha will always protect you? Do you think your mother redesigned your fate? Ramu, solemn-faced, had said, but my grandfather used to say, *didi*, and so it's said in the Mahabharat, destiny cannot fulfil itself without timely effort. You work with it, you pay attention to it, to its call, don't resist it, learn how to protect yourself with its guidance. I wonder if it is . . . she had probably said something then to Ramu, yes, like Shailen-doctor said, hypothesised.

And now this man was smiling at her, his dark eyes crinkled in the bright late-morning sun. 'Well, what do *you* think?' she asked him a little fiercely, fighting her embarrassment.

He touched her elbow gently. 'May I,' he said, 'invite you to come have some *chai* at my pathetic clinic? I have to take care of Chandra's brat's leg so he can go climb another tree. This time he'll break his head.'

Nisha listened to his voice carefully. Just a faint trace of a Bengali accent. A voice almost musical with its deep gentle tone. When the words rushed out – and yes, they rushed out, for he spoke fast – she heard the rush of the river. 'Well?' He tilted his head and looked at her. Why is he one of them? she wondered. Why does he know Lachmi's secrets? Did his voice have something to do with it? Or was it the way he spoke, very fast, words tumbling out, just like Ramu and Nirmala and the rest of the people out here?

'But what about Lachmi?' she asked, walking a few steps with him.

'Someone's always there to take care of her,' he said, with an odd coughing laugh that sounded almost bitter, as Ramu came running up to Lachmi.

Seeing them, Ramu touched his forehead, but he turned straight to Lachmi. 'Lachmi,' he said, 'listen,' and gently pushed her back to the steps of her house, 'sit.' They sat down together, Ramu stroking Lachmi's hands as if consoling a child. 'Listen,' he said, 'he won't beat you any more. It's all taken care of. You and him were not meant to be. I had always known he wasn't for you – so God has taken him from you. He heard your cries and took pity, don't you see?'

The doctor frowned, catching Ramu's words. He went back to them. 'What are you saying, Ramu? What have you been up to? Tell me right now, before you get into trouble with the district magistrate.'

'Shailen-doctor,' Ramu said softly, 'do I look the kind of person who would dare to even try to kill a *mastan* like Kanu? He used to beat me when we were kids. I would cry and hide, and Lachmi would hug me and make me feel better. I've never hurt anyone in my life, you know that, everyone in the village knows that.'

'But where were you last night? They said you're always near the river at night.'

'Yes, I was there.'

'Well?'

'I was there.'

196

'Don't play the fool with me, Ramu. How come I didn't see you then?'

'I was sleeping – you were there too?' Ramu looked up at the doctor in surprise, and so did Nisha. 'But you never go for a walk that late, and I didn't see you, or anyone.'

'Are you sure you didn't see –' the doctor caught Ramu's shoulder, '– didn't hear anything, a noise, maybe a cry, a shout, someone falling into the water, someone slipping –'

'No. The river was so loud. I didn't hear a thing. I slept. That's all I remember.'

The doctor shook his head and went back to Nisha, standing a few yards away.

'I don't think Ramu did anything,' Nisha said to the doctor. 'It really is possible for someone to fall into the river if he was very drunk.'

'Yes, that's true,' the doctor nodded, 'but sometimes I don't know what to believe – the muddle that surrounds them, us.'

Nisha stopped and looked at the young doctor's face. The sun glancing off his sharply defined cheekbones and jawline high-lighted the anxiety tautening across his face, flitting from eyes to mouth. She sensed a sudden impact like a crash. Something was happening here that she couldn't put her finger on.

'Something wrong?' she asked.

'No.' He shook his head.

'Odd that you and Ramu didn't see each other or Kanu last night.'

'Hardly,' the doctor said sharply. 'It was very dark, and, like Ramu said, the river drowns all other sounds at night.'

'I guess.'

'Oh –' he stopped and looked at her. 'Let's not talk about that any more.' His mouth twisted to a smile, his head tilting to the side. 'How are you coming along here?'

'Why did you send those medicines and first-aid stuff?' she asked, as they walked towards his dispensary.

'I wasn't sure if you had anything with you in case something happened,' he said. 'Ramu said you seemed most disinclined to meet the doctor.' His eyes shone when he said that, almost twinkled, Nisha could swear. 'The water's not the safest –' he continued.

'I make Ramu boil the water,' she snapped.

'Of course, a very wise thing. You can't boil the river though, you know.' The doctor's eyes narrowed and glittered. 'And the river is very, very dangerous. It steals your mind away, enslaves your spirit.'

'I'm sure you'll send me an antidote for that soon enough, won't you? What else can save me but your arsenal of pills?'

'I've figured out what you're doing here,' he said as they went up the cement steps and into the dispensary. 'But why did you choose to come here? Where are you from?' he asked, putting the kettle on the kerosene stove in his consulting room. The room contained a large table, a medium-sized refrigerator, three chairs, shelves of bottles and medical supplies, wall to wall. There was a black telephone on the table, Nisha noticed, surprised. The only phone in Binjhar.

'Well,' Nisha said, 'I don't know if it matters where I'm from. My family – parents and two brothers – live in Delhi, and I've been in the States for five years. I'm here now because my grandmother used to tell me about a village near hers, a village on the River Dakhin, about the island of Manasha, and that the people of the village were always trying to keep that goddess happy.'

He handed her a cup of tea. 'So –' he looked at her, his sharp dark eyes narrowing. 'Your grandmother told you of a mythic island on a river called Dakhin. It's a little hard for me to believe that someone would come all the way from the States to find a

198

river and an island on a whim. You've been asking a lot of questions, I hear.'

Nisha put her cup down on the table. 'Although it's none of your business,' she said, 'I'm here to do some research for my dissertation.'

'Ah. So I thought. Not a sociologist, I hope?'

'A graduate student trying to put together an interdisciplinary humanities dissertation.'

'Little bit of this, little bit of that. Must be interesting.' The doctor inclined his head slightly.

Nisha decided to ignore the condescension. Was he trying to provoke her? She wasn't sure. But she was not going to waste time or energy by getting into an argument that would put her on the defensive. 'Where is your patient with the broken leg?' she asked, raising her eyebrows.

'Oh my goodness.' The doctor opened a door on the right. 'Please,' he said, 'welcome to my surgery.'

The surgery was a small room with a long table raised with bricks in the centre, wall-to-wall shelves and some cupboards containing more supplies. A boy lay curled up on the table. The doctor turned on the light above the table. The boy groaned and rubbed his eyes. 'Let's see now, Tulu.' He straightened the boy's right leg.

'Why is he sleeping here?' Nisha asked, 'all by himself? Where are his –'

'Shh – his father works in the city, his mother has to mind her store at the bazaar, and he was very tired when she brought him in.' She watched him give the boy a lollipop from a jar on a shelf to distract him, then feel his ankle carefully and bandage it. 'Just a bad sprain,' he said. He removed a pillow and a blanket from a cupboard, put the pillow under the boy's head and covered him. 'Sleep.'

He ushered her back into his consulting room.

'No patients.'

'No, no patients right now,' he said. 'They must have forgotten their ailments, listening to Nirmala carrying on in the bazaar.'

'How do you do anything here?' she asked, a little shocked. 'There's nothing here. What if someone has a heart attack or needs surgery or –'

'Ah!' he said. 'See that?' pointing at a hammer on a shelf, 'one knock on the head and then the axe follows. That, I keep outside – do it outside, under that *neem* tree, no need to clean the blood, you know, the ground soaks it up. Why do you think it's so red?' He laughed and poured himself a cup of tea. 'Last month I had to run to the old dhobi's house. Gasping, choking, he was blue in the face when I got there. Pumped in some morphine, Lasix, hooked him to an IV, stuck nitro-glycerine under his tongue, threw him in the jeep with Ramu holding the oxygen mask and tank and the dhobi's son hanging onto the IV bottle, and drove to the village west of here, to the hospital. Checking the mercury rise and fall every few minutes, you know, change gears, turn a bend as gently as possible, turn and look, phew –' He pushed his fingers through his hair. 'Heart jumping up to my mouth with every jolt, let me tell you, while the old man went on muttering about living till a hundred and two, it was written in his palm. He's walking around now, and thrashing dirty laundry on the stone beneath the water pump.'

'Where do you live?' she asked him, accepting a refill of the strong black tea.

'Oh, I sleep in there.' He opened the door on the left and showed her a room with a bed and a table and shelves. The windows in all the three rooms were large and barred, and brought in stunning light. 'What else interests you?' he asked, closing the door.

'Right now,' she said, picking up her teacup, 'that island is very interesting to me. Especially the power it seems to have over everyone here. And Lachmi interests me – how all these people reinvent her every day –' she broke off laughing, then stopped, catching his frown. 'Well, the island has always fascinated me. So you could say I'm acting out an old, imaginary script; but now I call it research.'

He smiled faintly. 'No one really knows if there is such an island, you know. I mean, there is some kind of tiny landmass somewhere downstream just before the river plunges towards the sea, but whether there's a temple there, who knows?'

'But surrounded by television, your instruments, cars, trains, they continue to believe in the whims of Manasha.'

'Very much. The cyclone last year was due to a rather frightful incident, you know,' he said, maintaining a straight face. 'There was this wretched young man, rude, crude, unbelieving – he kicked a lit lamp from Tulu's mother's hand as she was about to float it on the river after sunset. He said that was all nonsense, superstition, all that sort of thing. Well,' the doctor refilled his cup and spooned in sugar, 'within a month the cyclone hit, and after the waters went down and people returned to their homes – what was left of them – from the next village you know, we have to rush to the school in the next village in case of floods and cyclones, it's the only building that's on raised ground, and after a week or so, that particular young man was found dead in the bamboo groves out there. I examined the body: his left leg had turned black from the bite as usual – a cobra. Manasha's pet animal had struck in revenge.'

'If you wander into bamboo groves you can very easily die of snake bites.' Nisha put her teacup down.

'That is correct.'

'I heard Ramu got bitten and the snake died.'

'Oh, yes, of course. Now that was a sure miracle. Would you like some of these?' He offered her ginger biscuits from an orange and black tin marked AMPICILLIN. She took two. Quite entertaining, she thought, now the anxiety that had clouded his face earlier had disappeared. But there was an air of restlessness about him, the way he moved his hands while he talked, the way he flicked back his hair. 'I get them from Cuttack, occasionally, when I have to go there for supplies,' he said, rattling the biscuits in the tin. 'Yes, about that snake bite. Ramu wandered into the bamboo groves, flute in hand, *tadi* in his stomach, hours after sunset. He crawled in through this door after midnight, his leg swollen under the tourniquet. He was having fainting fits, shivering, sweating, all the right symptoms. From what he said, he'd been bitten almost two hours before. I'd give King Kong fifteen minutes if a cobra sank its fangs into his thigh. But there was Ramu, groaning and cursing after two full hours or more. Since he hadn't left this world for the next by that time, I figured he'd make it. When I asked him why he didn't come to me right away, he said it took him some time to kill the snake. He applied the tourniquet himself, slashed open the bitten flesh and set about his snake-hunt. If I die, it dies too, he said to himself. Ramu, filled with anti-venom, was hopping around the very next day! But then, he has a charmed life – you know that.'

'Why don't you have them clean out the bamboo groves, cut the bamboo, you're the doctor, they listen to you –'

'What!' The doctor clapped his hands together and touched his forehead. 'I gave up asking them to boil their water after three weeks of being here. I've succeeded only in forcing them to feed their children eggs and milk at least three times a week, so now the kids' spleens are less enlarged. But to ask them to remove the precious lovers' grove with all its secret passions and fatal consequences? Star-crossed lovers would lose their status.'

'Star-crossed, hmm, I wonder what stars are crossing over my head,' Nisha said with a laugh. 'My mother has fixed my marriage, chosen the husband and informed me of my future status.'

'Can they drag you kicking and screaming – I don't think –'

'Shailen-doctor, *eije*, Shailen-doctor.' A voice from the door cut the doctor off and made him shrug and turn to his agitated patient.

On the way back to the schoolhouse, Nisha went past the riverbank, where some of the children were mud-wrestling while their mothers oiled their hair and occasionally screamed warnings at them. Nisha stood near the shiny, slippery black rocks and looked at the rushing waters. Was Lachmi's husband somewhere in there, full fathom five? Neither Ramu nor the doctor saw anything or anyone, heard nothing, yet both were here last night. Wasn't anyone going to look for him? Couldn't the doctor use that phone on his desk and – The river was so loud before her, raging, sweeping her head clean of every sound and thought but itself.

Dakhin was never calm. Tossing, whirling currents dragged everything down the river's journey to the Bay of Bengal. Fishing or ferry boats did not go further east than this point. You had to depend on more than man to navigate these waters eastwards. Two or three times a month steamers and motor launches carried city people to see the swamps and the forests. Sometimes speedboats were seen to skim the surface, glimpsed for a few seconds like birds swooping down to lift a fish off the waves and disappear. These days, with the warm spring-summer breeze on the waters, small, motor-powered fishing boats whirred by quite often, and the people of Binjhar said that they were trying to intercept the Hilsa on their way in from the sea. Some would be swollen with eggs already. The crocodiles, Nisha heard, were swimming close to the shore, waiting for the goats to be thrown in. Don't step into the river, don't try to row downstream. Only if you wanted to make that journey to Manasha's island would you make yourself a raft and turn yourself over to the river's whim.

Dakhin: when you spelt it that way, Dakhin, not Dakkhin, said it with that sound – Da-khine, like a whisper or a rush of wind, Dakhin, south, or was it the south wind that brought the first rainstorms and cyclones? She recalled a song her grandmother used to sing. My heart touched by the south wind – *dakhina hawa*. Some kind of madness. What was meant to be will be, what was not will not. And what of Ramu's words that without timely effort destiny cannot fulfil itself? Was her mother's determination a hideous timely effort that could fulfil a destiny beyond her control? Or was timely effort in Nisha's own court, right now? What about her PhD? What about the rest of her life? What about this moment in time on the banks of Dakhin? 'Time for you to get married' – who decides that? Marriage and death are determined by something else, her grandmother used to laugh and say. Your life in your own hands – look! she said, tracing the lines on Nisha's palm. Free, and not free, to do what you want. But then, how do you know when you should do what?

Timely effort – but how do you know what is the right time and what the appropriate effort? A sense of destiny, her grandmother would say, laughing, a sense of reconnecting with that something intimate, ultimate. Nisha ran her fingers through her hair and gripped a tuft of it above her left temple. She was allowing her mind to ramble, her own mind, which she alone controlled. She had come here to do research in order to write her dissertation and provide Lennox with some interesting stuff for his book. This rushing noise all around – the waters, the wind – was confusing her, that was all. Must stop this rushing feeling somehow. What she had decided to give up, she must give up. She had crossed over to that other world. Left this maddening confusion – political, social, mythical – behind five years ago. Chosen that other, clearer, neater world from where you could easily define this space that now surrounded her as an area of research, of experiment, nothing more.

The next day, the district magistrate arrived in his jeep with a truckload of policemen behind him. They questioned everybody, searched the riverbank, and when the launch arrived got aboard and searched as much of the river as they could. Nothing was found.

The district magistrate, a little porker of a man with thinning hair, paced the short grassy strip in front of the dispensary, fists at his back, head bowed. He nodded twice at Nisha sitting on the steps. The doctor stepped out after bandaging a bleeding knee and smiled tightly. The DM shook hands with the doctor, and thanked him for reporting the 'nasty business'. 'Why don't you, you know, make out the, I mean, death certificate,' he said, 'and we can get on, what do you say?'

'I can hardly make out a certificate of death without a body.' Shailen-doctor put his hands in his pockets and looked the DM straight in the eye.

'Now, now,' said the DM, trying to pull his khaki trousers over his pot belly, 'there's no sign – nothing left of the man. I need that certified. I mean – how can I write a report – no body, I mean the report must have some certainty, validity, I mean, closed. Otherwise, this'll go on and on – no, no, no. Missing person means search, launches, helicopters for days, weeks – who's going to send the necessary – ?' he rubbed his fingers and thumb together. 'You're the doctor. All I'm saying is I need a certification.'

'Then you certify it.' Shailen-doctor turned on his heel and went inside.

'Phew –' let out the district magistrate. 'What a doctor! Your replacement will arrive soon, I've received a telegram, he'll be here soon, I hope,' he said to the doctor's back.

'Eaten completely, possibly,' was the DM's report, which he signed with adequate flourish, and put a purple stamp on it to make it valid. Then he collected his men and got into his jeep and left.

'So you did report to the DM after all,' Nisha said to the doctor.

'Of course,' he said. 'After all, I work for the government you know. And you,' he said, touching her shoulder, 'are getting far too involved.'

'No I'm not. I like Ramu, I like Lachmi, and I thoroughly dislike Nirmala for behaving like a harpy and insulting Lachmi that way. I wanted to thrash Nirmala. The nerve!'

'You'll need a tranquilliser, one of these days,' said the doctor, his dark eyes growing darker.

'Well, you like Lachmi, too.'

'She has a way about her.' He lowered his eyes.

'Well?' she asked, tilting her head as if to look under his lowered glance.

'Well what?' he asked looking up.

'What way, er, does she have about her, or about you?'

'Are my thoughts necessary for your dissertation, too?'

'All right, none of my business.'

'Thanks,' he said with a half-smile.

As they walked along the bank, she asked him if he was going to leave soon, and he said that he'd been hearing that for a year and a half now. 'I was supposed to be here for only six months, but as you see –'

'Why don't you ask the DM to get some funding for a hospital here? How can you do anything here with only first-aid equipment and malaria and dysentery medication?' she asked.

'Ask that oaf? It's all right now. We manage, like I said before. I drive people over to the hospital in the next village in cases of emergency. The doctors there understand the situation. There were two heart attacks, and eleven necessary Caesarians over the last two years. That's what I call an emergency, and if anyone splits open their skull – that happened once. Kanu hit someone on the head with a hammer.'

'Was he violent? I thought he was really popular.'

'The two go hand-in-hand sometimes. But life is not violent in that sense here. No murders, no violent fights, no robberies. But Dakhin River strikes you down, or Manasha's curse. The bamboo groves lure you and you find yourself hypnotised by glittering jewelled eyes. And look,' the doctor pointed at the waters, 'my God, look!' Two slow-moving tree trunks seemed to float close to the bank and then away again towards the dense forests of the other shore. 'You never know what it is until you're practically torn in half.'

'Where is your family?' she asked him, wanting to move away from this talk of death.

'My family? There's no one left. My mother died two years back.'

'I don't even know your name,' she said; 'Shailen-doctor is what they call you.'

'That is my name.' He smiled and shrugged. 'Shailen Roy. I was born in Assam, where my father worked on a tea estate. He was killed by the Assamese during the unrest – well, it's still carrying on – and so we Bengalis had to leave Assam. I grew up quite poor, as poor as the middle-class in this country can get, but managed to go to medical school in Delhi – yes, I know Delhi. We used to hang out in South Extension markets and the M-Block market in GK.' He stopped and laughed. She laughed too. So unreal that world seemed, standing on this bank and listening to the

207

growling, snarling Dakhin as the sun went down and turned the waters copper and vermilion. A salty wind was coming in from the east that evening, drowning the mud and grass and cow-dung smell. 'Well, I came back to Calcutta and started working in Medical College. About a year later, my mother seemed to be losing weight, getting dizzy spells. Tests showed cancer.' He looked down at his sandals. 'You know,' he said, raising his face, 'she had come in for more tests, the specialist seemed hopeful, and I was in the middle of a difficult C-section – I trained to be an ob-gyn, but here I have to be a GP plus that – when she stepped out of the hospital to go get some *paan*. She was hit by a bus while crossing the street. You know how traffic is on a north Calcutta street, especially that street. I was told after my surgery was over, successfully over, thank God. The only other consolation was that the people around had pulled the bus driver out and beaten him to a pulp. He was in intensive care but no hope, they said, a couple of hours maybe. Now tell me what to believe, you who are analysing destiny.'

She told him about Lennox's half-written book, her dissertation. 'Oh, so you're fast turning into a western orientalist, too,' he laughed.

'I'm not western anything,' she said sharply. She had always sold the east back there, eastern, oriental, together with its mythical mystique. She had sold the east better than anybody she knew. Exploit what they exploit, and exploit them as part of the game, she had told an Indian friend. That's the way to get on here, if you want to make it. Post-colonial – that's the name of the game now. Academia has discovered the third world. The west doesn't interest me any more, Sylvia Lennox says in that languid drawl of hers. The interesting stuff is coming out of the east. The post-colonial voice, the subaltern subject-position. Nisha tossed her hair back. Post-colonial – I can be it then, pretend it.

Appalling, that right now she was 'it' truly, wasn't she? Redefined, reinvented, colonised utterly to post-colonial, that's what it was, thinking in English, thinking this river foreign?

The merciless river breeze slapped her face now, hissing out some irrevocable curse on her head. What were you selling? it seemed to ask. She had always known the answer so very well. Shailen had touched the rawest nerve. 'Just because I was there for a while doesn't make me western anything,' she said. 'Haven't you ever wanted to go there?'

'Where – to the modern Mecca? I should, shouldn't I?'

'Shut up,' she said, punching his arm lightly. 'Why did you become a doctor anyway?'

'I'm not sure any more,' he said. 'What should I say when someone standing on the banks of this wild river asks me that? Should I sit down on one of those rocks out there, rest my chin on my knuckles, look into the fading light and say – what? Well, maybe that when I was eight I walked into a room. I don't know how I managed to get into that room where a certain woman was lying, exhausted, weak, barely able to talk. She used to tell me the most fantastic stories, and she would give me money in secret to buy kites. I thought she was the most beautiful woman in the whole world. We used to say she had hair like dark rainclouds, and lotus eyes. What impelled me to sneak into that room and hold her hand as she lost consciousness? It was about three in the morning and I was fast asleep. But I woke up, for no reason at all.'

Nisha felt that rushing feeling in her head again. Shailen laughed, a light coughing laugh. 'Will that do?' he asked, 'mythical enough?'

'Possible enough.'

'Yes, possible only by the banks of Dakhin in the darkness of Binjhar. But how can you believe so easily, you who are supposed to question everything?'

'I believe –' She stopped. 'I believe there's more going on here than some people would like to admit.'

'Really? Like what?'

'A man disappears without a trace – well, except for a piece of bloodstained cloth. Nobody seems really concerned. They are almost relieved, it seems. And Lachmi, well, I don't know quite what to think about Lachmi.'

'What about her?' His voice was cold and flat. That gentle tone had vanished like a snap of the fingers.

'I – I – you seemed –' Nisha scratched her head. 'I mean, what *did* happen to her husband? Ramu was here that night, so were you, on this very riverbank. But even so, no one heard or saw anything, anybody.'

'Ah!' Shailen ran his fingers through his hair. 'Why don't we examine the bank? Aren't you curious about that broken branch the dhobi mentioned? Let's see now . . .' She followed him to the *neem* tree, walking fast to keep pace. Under the tree, just like the dhobi said, a large branch lay on the hard mud. 'Here it is.' He picked up the old cracked branch. 'It's quite heavy.' She took the offered branch, held if for a few seconds then dropped it on the ground.

'Someone could have hit Kanu on the head with this,' she said. 'Everyone seemed to have had some kind of a grudge against the man.'

'But of course – the motive.' Shailen stepped closer. 'I think I have a better story. A simpler story. Do you remember what they said – what was it that Kanu said just before he left the liquor store? Something about a deal or a meeting? Perhaps I arranged to meet him here. Then, oh, I could have taken his arm, just like this,' he caught her arm just above her elbow, 'very friendly, man to man, you know. And before he knew it, or ever quite felt the pin-prick, I was pumping in some lethal fluid.' He let go of her arm. 'He's limp in my arms within seconds. How many seconds

210

more did it take to drag him over and throw him in?' He moved back a few steps. 'You've already worked out my motives in your head, haven't you? It's so easy to fill in the blanks sometimes, isn't it, especially when you feel so adept at analysing, arriving at conclusions, when you feel so sure that there's always a logical answer –' He broke off, turned his head and looked into the river. 'Well, perhaps we all had our motives concerning Kanu, or Lachmi.' Stepping forward swiftly, he caught her shoulders and gently pushed her against the tree. 'Is that what you think?' A faint smile moved from his mouth to his eyes, then disappeared. Nisha flexed her shoulders. So chillingly calm his face was. 'All these questions,' he said. 'I could do the same to you, couldn't I? It's so dark now, and not a soul around.'

'I'm not getting very scared, by the way.' Nisha forced a smile.

'No, of course not.' He released her, stepped back. 'You drive away all the demons, don't you? But think hard, Nisha, must we question our beliefs with your questions? Why must you make these people – us – think the way you think? Those are the real questions.' He moved away a few steps. 'And let me tell you something. Kanu's good riddance for more than one reason, and I don't think there has been a murder or an accident.'

'Where is he then? He is now certified dead.'

'How can I change the DM's report?' he asked, interlocking his fingers, forcing them backwards and cracking his knuckles. 'If he's alive somewhere, anywhere, I can only wish that he'll come back to clear up suspicion and blame. And if he is – well, I don't know, life will still go on, Lachmi will still walk the way she does, look at you, me, them, the way she does, with her head up and eyes lowered. These things are beyond my control.' He shrugged and moved away. 'Come,' said Shailen, his voice softening, 'it's dark, and you should be in your room, where Ramu's feast is steaming on your table. And I must wait for my replacement to arrive so I can take off for Puri and walk in the sand.'

Ramu opened the door as they reached the stone steps of the school. Nisha stood and watched the doctor vanish into the darkness of banyan trees that hid the road leading to the dispensary. She could still hear his deep rhythmic voice, the words rushing out like the river current. And that rush, that restlessness was an inseparable part of him. No stillness about him. Had he always been this way? Or had the river breeze made him so? She could have asked him that. Maybe invited him in for dinner, made him stay and talk a little longer, maybe sit on these steps in this river-scented darkness. But he had stopped so abruptly before the steps, turned, left.

What if – What if he had told the truth on the riverbank? Syringe in hand, he had waited and – no, impossible, not him. But what if it was so? And what if – She stopped her thought and let out a gasp of laughter. What if Shailen turned out to be –? Some of the details matched: his parents are dead, her mother had written, and he is dedicated to his work, now stuck in some village. Trick of – no, just her mother's unique manipulation. A master-plan all right. And then her mother would turn around and say, Well, it was fate, destiny, dear. What if it was Shailen – good lord, when you let the craziness take over, anything is possible, and why should she even think this way? Just a hypothesis, really, and one must always be able to hypothesise. But why should she even allow herself to think this way? Madness, madness, it was the river, its sound, its smell. But somehow everything seemed inexplicably connected, coincidences piling up – No. She was doing the connecting. It was in her own mind, confused by this nightsmell, this riversound. She was giving in – reading things in where they weren't, just like

212

everyone else. No, never. Shailen, syringe in hand, waiting under the *neem* tree – Nisha shook her head.

'Looking at him, ah,' Ramu murmured. 'And why are you looking at him that way – do you know?'

'What on earth are you muttering, you idiot?'

'Yes, I mutter on,' he replied, ushering her towards the steaming food. 'I mutter on, Dakhin rushes on, life goes on, fate takes over.'

She mixed the rice and dal with her fingers and began to eat while Ramu sat down near the window. He sighed, took a deep breath and sighed again. 'What's wrong?' she asked, taking in his pensive face.

'Lachmi does not understand,' he sighed. 'She does not understand that we were meant to be. And now, even now if we resist what we were meant to be, we'll be destroyed, I know, happiness will be destroyed, if we fight the inevitable. The moment I saw her, when I was four, I knew. She knew, but she denies it. Kanu was a boor. Yes, he was tall and strong and had an enviable face. But he wasn't meant for her. He wasn't meant for this life for long either – why else? Do you know how many times he beat me up? They all thought he was so entertaining, and funny – yes, funny, when he tried to hang me from a tree, shouting with laughter all the time, saying, Little idiots should be hanged. Perhaps Manasha heard, after all these years, and struck out.'

'How do gods strike?' Nisha asked. In the village, they said he was crazy, he was silly, not quite there, a good heart but something not quite right since he had almost died, perhaps really died and then come back to life. There was something elusive about Ramu, sprite-like. He would appear and disappear according to unuttered wishes, as if he sensed what you wanted. She was amazed by the food he brought every day. It was as if he knew what she wanted to eat, which fish or meat or vegetable. He

213

had also conditioned her palate somewhat. For breakfast he would bring her tea, but along with it bread, and thick, sticky date syrup for dipping. Sometimes he would bring puffed rice mixed with coarse date sugar and bananas. She did not miss toast and eggs and cereal any more. He would cook cabbage with shrimps and coconut milk, and she would long for it if a week went by without it. He revived for her her grandmother's cooking, a taste she had almost forgotten, a flavour her mother had denounced as too extravagant with spices, salt and sugar and far too complicated for everyday fare. Nisha cursed herself occasionally when she imagined Ramu as her reincarnated grandmother.

'Gods strike through instruments,' Ramu said, his face changing from pensive to resolute. 'They choose instruments who then carry out the will of the gods.'

'Like snakes?'

'Sometimes.' Ramu reached into his pocket and removed a screwdriver. He studied it intently, turning it slowly, letting the light catch its point, which, Nisha noticed, had been filed and sharpened.

'Instruments like rivers, the weather, wild animals?' she asked, staring at the screwdriver.

'Sometimes.'

'You mean something could fall on someone's head? A man could slip and fall – he might just be somewhere, er, dangerous, just arrive there due to –'

'Something like that.' He held the screwdriver in his fist like he was holding a knife. 'You ask too many questions,' he said. 'Yes, gods destroy. But they protect too.'

'I hope so.' Nisha swallowed.

'Manasha has protected me three times already – saved me from Kanu twice, and once from the snake. Now I think I'm on my own. She won't step in again. They never do more than three times.' Ramu put the screwdriver back into his pocket.

'Well, what about Kanu – why didn't any god or goddess help him? What do you think happened to Kanu?'

Ramu looked at her blankly and shrugged. He removed her plate and cleaned up. Nisha washed her hands and took out her notebook and pen. Ramu came back to her room and sat down on the floor. 'We saw another part of the Mahabharat, *didi*, on TV. I know this part by heart. Kanu's grandfather used to recite it every evening. But when I saw it on TV – oh!' He clasped his hands. His voice rose in excitement. 'Right in the middle of the two armies, bow thrown down, the great warrior kneeling. I don't know, he said, what to do? What is my duty? How can I kill those people out there? They are brothers, cousins, uncles, teachers –' Nisha recalled the episodes she had seen and squirmed. The production was so crude, garish, the metaphor completely lost under a hideous melodramatic literalisation. She let out a soft 'Ugh.'

Ramu continued at the same pitch. 'And then he, the other, he dropped the reins and stepped down from the chariot. He touched the warrior's shoulder, his face. Listen, he said. They are already dead. You are not killing anyone. You cannot kill or be killed. No arrow can pierce the life that informs you –'

Nisha looked at the impish form sitting on the floor hugging his knees. A gleam had entered his half-closed eyes. His voice was like a soft chant. She began to write as fast as she could, yes, Lennox would like this – belief perpetuated, yes, seconded by television.

'No fire can burn it, no water drench it, no wind can make it dry,' he recited from memory. 'What you think you are about to do now, next, has already happened, been realised, the action has been originated and completed, what you think you do is the echo, simply the echo. What you see is what you want to see, it is just an illusion. You will think of heaven and of hell and of destiny. Finally you will arrive there; you will wonder, is this it? Then you will sit there and say, I'll go no further. Then a voice will say, This was the last illusion.'

'Ramu?'

'What you can't see is flying all around, the wind is the beating of its shining wings.'

'Ramu?' His eyes were glazed as if in a trance. Nisha wanted to give Ramu a shake, but the cadence of his voice, the rhythm and flow of the words, held her to her chair, unable to intervene or write any further.

'The lake was shining. The brothers were thirsty. They drank without answering the questions, and fell dead. But Yudhishtir said, I will answer the questions. And the voice from the lake asked, Tell me, what is the greatest wonder? Yudhishtir said, Every day death strikes and every day we walk as though we were immortal. That is the greatest wonder. The waters bounced in joy. What is madness? His eyes lighting up, Yudhishtir replied, A forgotten way. The waves swirled, rose, sparkled. The voice from the lake asked again, Tell me, for all of us, what is inevitable? Yudhishtir, without even a moment's hesitation, answered, Happiness, happiness is inevitable.'

'Ramu?'

'Like it? I learnt it by heart.' His eyes were sharp again; he was crouching forward in excitement.

'What I'd really like, Ramu, is if you would tell me what you think happened to Kanu.'

'You should ask Manasha,' he said.

'I'm asking you, Ramu. Do you think someone killed him? Say, Shailen-doctor?'

Ramu sat up. He removed the screwdriver and held it up near his ear as if he was about to throw it. Nisha sat very still, unable to look away from the screwdriver.

'Don't try this stuff on us,' he said softly. 'We are your own people. If you have so many questions, ask fate, destiny, that which one can't control.'

'I will try my damnedest,' Nisha said, holding her notebook in front of her like a shield.

She lay in the uncomfortable *charpai* and looked up at the mosquito net arranged so neatly all around her. She saw the screwdriver in Ramu's fist, a syringe in Shailen's hand, Lachmi walking through swaying bamboo groves. And Dakhin seemed to leap up and dance, a sinewy shining body with a copper and silver wave fanning out like a cobra's head, wiping away all the questions she had prepared and asked. The heaving river glowed beacon-like, urgently calling her to some almost-forgotten place where the mind lapsed to a left-behind otherness. Her research was transmuting to different questions: who, why, how? Ramu had changed her eating habits, but she hadn't been able to change his thoughts. Her dissertation seemed to be going down this river as well. Perhaps it had been swept away long before. Perhaps her attempt to salvage it, with Lennox's help, was an attempt to salvage something else altogether. No! She buried her face in her pillow. She was going back. She had come back only to confirm that she must go back there. Life waited there with Drew.

Drew, delicate, highly strung, sweeping canvases with his special shade of black. In love, he said, and almost with a vengeance, she felt, against his mother's wishes – to work out his own rebellion through Nisha. Lawyer, doctor, *moi?* he screamed while cashing his weekly two-thousand-dollar cheque from his mother. She can take a hike, he said. To his mother, calling three times a week from her Beacon Hill apartment: You don't understand. And neither did Nisha understand why the relationship seemed so out of control, frighteningly obsessive, that she couldn't pass the day without – She snatched the grant money and ran. Lennox, a trick of fate? No!

She ran all the way here to find that river. Why, she couldn't fathom. But the moment Drew pointed at a diamond ring in a shop window, her grandmother's voice echoed in her ears and Dakhin surfaced with its terrible waves and secret island and crocodiles. —I must finish my dissertation now with this scholarship, then I'm going to look for a good teaching position, she had convinced Drew. Let's plan, Lennox had said, ecstatically. This is the real thing, you're on to something, you're getting ready to define this thing, explore and capture this territory of myth and destiny and belief. But she wasn't quite sure why she was trying to define her dissertation then, all of a sudden, after three years of procrastination. She could bloody well forget about this shit and just marry Drew. Green card, no more immigration hassles, go to Gstaad for skiing trips, to Australian beaches, to Hawaiian sunsets. Want to live in New York City or Boston, Drew said. A studio in the Village. We belong there, Nisha. You belong there. Here, with me. And she had felt it, through Drew, the crisp pleasure of being there.

Life moved in two directions in Drew's world, and she was certainly on the up-escalator, smooth and straight. Drew's world didn't spin and lurch, cyclone-like. There were always warnings, and very few surprises. Cable TV took care of that. And darkness was not this agonising river-scent of tuberoses and gardenias trampled against copper mud. Darkness was only the absence of electric lights. No dark goddesses: America had banished them all. No Hecate, no Fata Morgana, no Kali. Just the Statue of Liberty. No destiny to worry about, but opportunity. No karma there, just problems, solvable problems. No *dharma*, only alternative lifestyles. You have rights in America: the right to vote and the right to buy, and you could even kid yourself that the universe is really

218

like a Sears catalogue or the remote control of a television. It's peaceful and prosperous, with an occasional mass-murder to relieve the stasis; and it is the standard of living that the rest of the world envies and covets. Shouldn't that do? Nisha rubbed her eyes. Yes, of course. No island of Manasha to contend with, no mad river to drown all her clear ideas.

Who needs crocodiles and blood and muddy rivers and an epic that is a battle-song of universal destruction?

But instead of seeing studios, Caribbean cruises, chic split-level apartments or Sylvia Lennox's narrowing eyes, she saw herself, her chin on a window ledge, looking down at the black van that took her grandmother away, a frail body strewn with tuberoses.

That rainsmell of tuberoses hung in the night air all around her now, the nightsmell of Binjhar.

Everyone used to be terrified of her grandmother, a tiny woman who had cropped her hair at the age of fifty. Silver curls framing a resolute and exquisite face. Her husband, they said, had died of shock. But she carried on like the mad rain-wind. She carried on redecorating her rooms every year, singing while she pickled mangoes, revealing incredible secrets about magic places and people while she cooked, and in the lazy warmth of winter afternoons created a terrible river and showed Nisha its secret island. A temple, shattered, stones tumbled all around, crawling with king cobras, *kraits*, Manasha's legion, ready to strike any intruders. You float lamps towards the island, say Bless me Manasha, and go back to your homes. Leave a bowl of milk outside for the snake that crosses your yard, and say 'String' at night, or 'Creeper,' never . . . Take me there, please – I want to float lamps! Only when the wind blows, shh . . . it's talking to you, can you hear?

Dakhin, that was also the mad south wind which swept in like a forest fire and set the earth ablaze with spring. And then it

219

brought the rain, the first rain to this hard red ground. Mud-pools like frothing blood.

Cars followed a black van. Ashes were thrown into the river, she heard her father say. But not that river, she knew. They didn't know where that river was. She would find it one day and hear what it had to say to her.

But she had flown over to quite another world and moved that river aside. There was nothing here to hold her, absolutely nothing. Parents constantly nagging, Don't talk so much, don't laugh so loud, what will people say, time for you to get married . . . She had gritted her teeth for twenty years and then got away. She had taken charge of her life, given it a definite shape, goals to move towards. But why then had she run away, and why this desperate need *now* to run again? Had she not felt free for five glorious years? But what now?

Now, through this night pierced with the heady fragrance of gardenia and tuberose, Dakhin was rising, leaping recklessly, wrestling with the moonlight to drown it, rob it of its silver, merge with it. The night brought no peace or silence to Binjhar. You lay awake and shivered as the river laughed its wicked laugh out there till exhaustion took over and closed your eyes. Laughing, the river was laughing, and whispering, telling you – everything, if you knew how to listen.

The river rose and rose and rose, and the moonlight kept vanishing into its waves. Then all the waters swirled like a column of light and spread out enormous wings before her. So enormous, you couldn't decide what it was. What is that? she asked the darkness surrounding her and it. It was blocking everything before her, keeping her in that one dark spot, barring her way.

She tried to move but her feet held her to that dark spot. Suddenly, the shining spinning form swayed to the left, then to

220

the right. A whispery rush of wind wrapped around her. Voices! Whose voice was that? She couldn't make out the words. Whispers blew her hair about her face, stroked her eyes, her throat. A sharp gust slapped her face. She reeled from the impact. The swaying tower of light was swooping down. Nisha ran back, her feet obeying at last. The whispering wind caught her in a surging buoyancy. She was running, her feet barely touching the ground.

The river of light raced behind her. Nisha gasped as she felt the light on her back cold and hot. It was all over her, filling her mouth and nose, chilling her lungs, burning her eyes. Then it passed. The swirling shining mass was racing ahead, and she was stretching out her arms to catch that flame-tail. Must catch, must hold. That buoyancy all around gave her feet a breathtaking tailwind rush. She could almost touch the whirling column of light. So warm, so cool. She was wrapped in its blazing spiral heart. Then she was propelled forward, shooting out of it, a stray flame. And with a circling sweep the light chased after her.

The light rose up like a tidal wave behind her. A hushed roar of falling water. Nisha covered her head and fell to her knees. The flooding light swept over her. She saw rice fields, huts, cattle, people float away on shining waves.

Then she was falling through a blinding waterfall of light, tossing, rolling. Thrashing around wildly, feeling for something to hold, to brake this descent. But there was nothing but yourself to touch, to hold on to. Your fingers slipped through shadowy forms. The silver torrent passed through your flesh as if you were all glass, like water through fine gauze, and you, you too, filtered through its dazzling mass the very same way. What a strange sensation – the mind had ceased to think Oh, what a marvel, had become still, in the midst of this roaring, blazing cascade. What a feeling, this lighting up like a match almost, my word, just staying luminous, yes, illuminated, what a trick, indeed what an illusion!

Silly girl, growled the light, and lifted suddenly. Grandmother! That voice! She knew at last.

Look! Look carefully. Nisha shaded her eyes and searched for the source of that whisper. A river of coiling, twisting snakes glowing silver, and the silver shadow of a shattered temple. Are you there? she asked. Grandmother? Only a torrent of silver snakes circling around her, churning, thrashing, shooting up with a wicked hiss, then swooping down to resume their spinning again. Grandmother? Nisha reached out to touch the coils of light. She felt something sharp scratch her forehead.

Where was the river of snakes? Thundering wings beat around her. A million feathers of flashing light flew about. It was flying away, this cloud of light. The tip of its spread wing had grazed her face.

There. A fading thunder. *Remember that. And remember that for everything there is always an explanation, logical, illogical, and that is why you choose — to believe, and not to believe. To every why, there is always an answer, but you may not know it.*

Another scratch. Grandmother – ? Her voice cracked.

You were there, and I.

'Ouch.' Nisha touched her forehead. She was in bed. Her pillow was under her head, the sheets pulled up to her chin. Her forehead was itching slightly, burning. She jumped out, nearly ripping off the mosquito net, and ran across to the square mirror on the wall. The sunlight reflecting off the mirror made her blink. She moved her hair back and saw two tiny red lines on her forehead, which had a few itchy red mosquito-bite spots on it from before. Two of those spots had been scratched.

After breakfast, she reorganised her notes and arranged her

papers neatly in folders, labelling them and stacking them alphabetically. She wrote a letter to her mother, telling her she was not going to marry their selected specimen. They should give up these idiotic notions. She tore a fresh sheet from her notebook and wrote *Dear Drew*, then scratched it out, tore up the sheet and threw it away. Ramu took the letter for her mother and solemnly promised to post it that very day, that he would run to the next village, 'but later, not now, because now we must all go to the river – the goats, *didi*, come!'

Shailen was standing some distance away from the bank. He turned, hearing Ramu's excited voice. 'Here for the slaughter? You too? Ah, but of course – your dissertation. Had a good night's sleep, I hope?' Nisha looked at him, surprised. 'Just wondering,' Shailen added with a grin. 'I find it difficult to sleep sometimes. So much excitement all around, so many questions to keep you awake.'

'Really?' Nisha raised an eyebrow. 'Why don't you just pop in a sleeping pill or two on such nights?'

'Ah, but then all my torments would cease. I'd have nothing to live for.'

'Oh, what a pity.' Nisha turned away to watch the people gathered at the water's edge.

'Go closer,' he said, 'if you want to. I don't have the stomach for these things.'

'I can deal with it. After all, I must remember all these little details for future reference.' She looked at the three goats being dragged to the river, the chanting crowd moving as if drunk. She closed her eyes tightly when the shining curved blade flashed upwards. The arm was swinging down. Faint bleating sounds, three thuds.

'It's over.' She opened her eyes. Shailen was looking at her, one eyebrow raised. She flushed and turned to look at the river. What

223

looked like three black sacks floated away, trailing red froth. The river began to churn all of a sudden, as if a flood was coming. The black forms were being tossed around, pulled, tugged, the waters violent, thrashing, foaming white and red. People were running away now, from the river. Nisha's head swam. Their faces were wet, shining red, their hands, their clothes. 'Ashirbad,' someone whispered almost on her face, 'the blessing.' A finger touched her with its glistening red stain.

'Are you –' Shailen caught her shoulders and sat her down under the tree. 'Put your head between your knees, down, lower your head.' He wiped her forehead with his handkerchief. 'Tch, you've been scratching your mosquito bites. You should put some Dettol cream on them.'

'One husband and three goats,' someone yelled, 'Manasha should be happy this year.' Laughter on red faces.

Sitting with a cup of tea in the dispensary, Nisha watched Shailen inspect tonsils, palpate abdomens, listen to heartbeats, give a few injections. 'You were looking a bit peaked when you got there,' he said to her over the heads of bawling children, scolding mothers and groans of pain and discomfort. 'Sure you slept well? Or did you dream something frightful – the Binjhar dream?'

She looked at him, stunned. 'You did – aha!' The doctor smiled and winked. 'Ramu gets carried away with the cooking sometimes. A handful of poppy seeds now and then, you know. What was it – monstrous creatures or falling from the sky?' The grin was malicious.

'I have to go.'

'But of course, and write your dissertation, give destiny a talking-to, tell the world nothing is inevitable.'

He's a jerk, Nisha thought, walking towards the school house. An annoying jerk betraying his education, a man of science –

damn him. How could he be a doctor and condone such things? A handful of poppy seeds now and then! Did Ramu tell him about dinner last night, her dinner, if he had thrown in – the nerve! To tell her now – when he should have come running and given her something to control the effects. To laugh instead. After one had had to go through the hideous – so that's what it was, phew. She felt relieved. It was all Ramu's fault. First the nonsensical talk during dinner and then the adulterated dinner itself. Adulterated – doctored, more like. How could she not have suspected anything till Shailen brought it up? How could she have allowed herself to be so manipulated? Was Shailen in on it all along? Perhaps it was his idea. He wanted to scare her. You ask too many questions, he said. Maybe he has reason to be wary. Maybe, just maybe, he was telling the truth on the riverbank last evening. Then it was he – no! That's why he told Ramu to put poppy seeds in her food . . . to confuse her . . . to drug her . . . No wonder he looked surprised when she turned up for the goat sacrifice. She was supposed to be fast asleep, or – She closed her eyes for a few seconds and rubbed her temples. This was getting out of control. *There is always an explanation*. Her ears were ringing suddenly. She was imagining scenarios, accusing, just like Nirmala, like all of them. Her purpose was to reverse their ways of thinking, confuse them, not start – A tidal wave seemed to be crashing against her ears, and behind her closed eyelids a river of light leapt up viciously. She shook her head. A massage, that's it, that's what I need. Ramu must fetch Nirmala – oh, but! She had told Ramu to tell Nirmala not to come for the massages in the afternoons.

Lachmi was sitting on the school steps. 'Where's Ramu?' Nisha asked, a little taken aback. Lachmi shrugged. She hadn't seen Lachmi since that day. She hadn't made her appearance plate in hand – how could she, Nisha had bitten her lips and thought, after such incidents? – and now what to say to her? What does one say to a woman whose husband has vanished? If she were in America she could say – but then husbands, even wives, vanish casually, frequently, back there. But here, in the tiny village of Binjhar? In a small town you could say, well – in Calcutta or Delhi or Bombay, these things happened, were annoyances these days.

'Asleep under a tree, probably,' Lachmi said. 'That's where he usually is. I heard you told Nirmala not to come in the afternoons. I thought, Well, I can go, I'm good too.'

She heated mustard oil in a shallow aluminium bowl and brought it to Nisha's room and closed the door. Nisha lay down on the mat that served as a rug and closed her eyes. Lachmi's hands were softer than Nirmala's. Her fingers pressing in and circling smoothly over her back and shoulders got rid of the ringing in her ears. 'How are things?' she asked Lachmi.

'*Cholche*,' Lachmi said softly, 'going on.'

'Ramu talks about you.'

'Mad,' she said. 'Mad. Doesn't understand. Keeps on saying, You and me, not him, taken care of by fate. Mad. I do like him. But he can be difficult, you know. And there's no telling what he might do and when. No sense in his head. He used to sell bangles. Ever since Shailen-doctor arrived, he's worked for him. Forgot about the bangles. I was happy he was working for the doctor. He was learning things. Shailen-doctor was teaching him – a good man, the doctor –' Lachmi stopped and massaged Nisha's back quietly.

'What about the doctor?' Nisha asked. She saw them again, standing silently face to face.

'He's not like the last one,' she said. 'That one didn't care who lived, who died, who ate what. I asked Shailen-doctor, Doctor, how will you leave when you have to go? He just smiled and looked down. I used to take him dinner too. But now I don't.'

'Why not?'

Lachmi shook her head. 'He asked me not to. Sometimes things are best this way. I'm glad Ramu works for him.'

'Doesn't he sell bangles any more? Not at all?'

'If he has any more after that night! Mad, I said, let me tell you how mad. Three weeks back he saw my husband buy bangles from the bazaar for me. That night – if you only heard the noise! Broke all his old bangles one by one against my door. What can I say? Kanu could only put up with so much. "Come down, Lachmi," Ramu was screaming, "if you don't wear my bangles, I'll break them." I stopped Kanu – God! – rushing out of the house with a stick. I caught his feet. He had to hit someone he was so angry – eyes bloodshot. And Ramu was going on and on and on, "I'm breaking my bangles." What to say, *didi*, I can still hear the glass cracking and tinkling and shattering. The next morning I stepped out and cut my feet on the broken glass. What a mess.'

'I can't imagine Ramu doing something like that. He's so quiet, except when he chatters, but I've never seen him violent.'

'Quiet, yes. But there's an odd streak in him. Oh, I don't know! He and Kanu never liked each other, and Nirmala would play one against the other, she's another one. Kanu would say Ramu's a kind of monster that should be destroyed. You see, many believe he died and then came back – you've heard, I'm sure. Kanu would say Ramu was supposed to be dead. It wasn't right for him to live. People say all kinds of things. And now Kanu is no – nowhere to be found. Nirmala hasn't stopped screaming yet. She's there at the bazaar even today.'

'Nobody's going to believe her, Lachmi.'

'Ah, but then people like to believe the worst of me, except Shailen-doctor. I am the rich man's daughter whose brothers terrorise the village. And Nirmala is now a sister without a beloved brother who was trapped into marriage. Well.' Lachmi let out a short, fierce sigh. 'Have they forgotten Nirmala throwing her only son into the river – a child of three? He called another woman ma because he wanted the sweet she had in her hand. "What?" that Nirmala shrieked, "called her your mother? The river take you, the crocodiles eat you, you ungrateful, unloving son of a pig!" And one swing and then the child screaming in fear, choking, gasping, swallowing water, till the dhobi left the dirty clothes and jumped in and saved the child.' Lachmi eased Nisha's tautening neck muscles. 'Such a mother – will they believe?'

Nisha sat up, took the towel from Lachmi and wrapped it around herself. 'Maybe they won't believe. But tell me, didn't you say anything to Ramu after he broke the bangles?'

'Yes, I did. He didn't even remember. I caught him at the bazaar. "*Sala*," I said, "what do you think you were doing last night smashing your bangles?" He looked at me like I was mad. He didn't remember. Maybe he was drunk, who knows? What goes on inside Ramu's head, only Ramu knows. Manasha will take care of me – that's his line. Anyone who hurts me, Manasha will hurt. Such ideas!'

'Do you have any ideas – what do you think happened to Kanu?'

'I don't know what to believe. No body was found, not even a finger or a tooth or a hair. What should I believe? They say all kinds of things about me, *didi*. I don't know what you think. Maybe I shouldn't have married him, I don't know. What's done is done. It was necessary. But to blame – without knowing exactly what has happened – how to? Who to blame? Somebody did something maybe. Yes, my brothers were angry. Kanu had hit me. Yes, my brothers are thugs like they say. So what? Do you think any brother would make his sister a widow? What about the brothers and father and uncles of that woman who drowned herself, the woman Kanu was supposed to marry? What about them? What about that Ratna's husband, who Kanu had beaten

228

up after luring his sister into the bamboo groves? How about the dhobi's sons, who had lost their four cows gambling with Kanu? Ah, Kanu, everyone always smiled when he appeared. But what did they feel inside? Who was going to say anything to his face? He was stronger than everyone. Who to believe, what to believe . . . are they all what they say they are . . . ? Sometimes I think our hearts are like those bamboo groves – who knows what lurks in there?'

Nisha watched Lachmi rearrange her sari. In the mirror on the wall, Nisha could see her own reflection. With every move, every twist and turn and sway, Lachmi eclipsed Nisha's small-boned self. A whole forest of ancient banyan trees walked with Lachmi. Bamboo groves swayed in her wake. The darkest of rainclouds were shadows of her long thick hair. Nisha's thin, pale shoulders shivered in the mirror. This woman who walked the way she did, looked the way she did, who hardly spoke much when she used to bring in that plate of food, was now talking to her, the completely alien being in Binjhar, who had none of Lachmi's awe-inspiring stature or bearing. There was something truly stunning about Lachmi when she looked at you with those veiled eyes and half-smile, something marvellous and fatal. Lachmi loosened her long hair, let it down, twisted it and coiled it on top of her head again.

'Nirmala,' she said, 'has been like a mother to Ramu. But Ramu always followed me around. Nirmala used to tell Kanu, oh, Ramu did this and Ramu did that, that Ramu was a monster, yes, she used to say that too, and Kanu would thrash Ramu every time she caught Ramu with me. She thought Kanu was her property. Kanu married *me*.'

'Look – don't jump to all kinds of conclusions, OK,' Nisha said to Lachmi's reflection in the mirror. 'We really don't know for sure.'

'But somebody must know something, somebody must.' Lachmi turned around.

'Do you think –' Nisha stopped and swallowed. 'Do you think Shailen-doctor might, er –'

Lachmi placed her hand on Nisha's mouth and cut her short.

'Don't say that.' Nisha moved back, stunned by the look on Lachmi's face. Pain, sorrow – no: when your whole world lies in ashes around you.

'Maybe Kanu will turn up,' Nisha said. 'Maybe we're all letting our imaginations run wild.' She held Lachmi's hand against her cheek.

'Yes. Maybe he'll come back, maybe. I'll pay what I have to pay.'

'You're being silly, really, morbid, that's no way to talk.'

'I'll do something, I will, I won't just sit and do nothing and listen to silly talk.' Lachmi drew her hand back. 'Fate they say, fate, I'll drag it back and forward by the hair, if I have to, but I'll do something. I won't live here any longer and listen to their hateful words like I have for so long.' Lachmi stood up with the empty bowl, her chin raised, her jaw set, her eyelids partly veiling her eyes.

Nisha's notebook stared at her from the desk. The pen lay sandwiched between its pages. Her head began to throb, and a faint nausea began to course its way up to her throat. '*Chalo na*,' Ramu pleaded after dinner.

'*Accha, chalo*.' So Nisha followed Ramu to the dispensary for the TV-watching ritual. She didn't want to meet the doctor again that day, but neither did she want to sit in that sparse, dull room all evening.

'My my, for the first time, missing civilisation at last?' Shailen had brought the TV out on to the steps of the dispensary, and almost the entire village sat outside smoking and munching, hypnotised by the twenty-five-inch colour screen. Nirmala was there with her three children, two daughters and one boy, all of whom were leaning forwards towards the movement of colour and sound, sucking their thumbs loudly. Nirmala glared at Lachmi from time to time, and whispered occasionally to the two women sitting with her. Lachmi stood under the *neem* tree, aloof, her face a dark mask. Ramu sat down with the children two feet away from the screen. Most of the women sat around Nirmala on the right. The men were grouped on the left and in the middle.

'Seat of honour.' Shailen dragged a chair to Nisha.

'I can sit on the grass.'

'She says through gritted teeth. Come, come, I'm getting a chair for myself too.' Nisha refused to sit on the chair. She sat down on the grass. Shailen took one chair, and the other the dhobi claimed with, 'Don't mind, Shailen-doctor, no one else using it, so –'

'The death toll has risen to three hundred and twenty,' they heard, 'forty more dead in Hyderabad,' ten-hour curfew, riots, tear-gas, buses set on fire. 'Why not build a temple next to that mosque?' some of the men asked. 'Killing each other, and for so many days.' 'Prime Minister calls a cabinet meeting'; 'Chief Minister of West Bengal struck on the head with a rotten tomato during a speech'; 'The Nagas have been shooting several rounds again'; 'More riots in Kashmir.' Dal Lake came on the screen. No tourists on houseboats or *shikaras*. Srinagar streets strewn with broken bottles, stones, shoes, torn clothing. 'The Army seized thirty-two Kalashnikovs today . . .' A boy, fifteen maybe, raised his black Kalashnikov to the camera. 'Those Kashmiri rugs have been rolled away, together with the shawls, the silver jewellery, crates of cherries, apples, pears. The only trade for Kashmiris now is to bargain for Kalashnikovs at the border. They seem to be coming in like a flooding river from Pakistan and Afghanistan . . .' 'This government is useless,' someone said. 'Either really crack down on the problem or forget about Kashmir, let Pakistan have it.' 'How can you say that?' another voice challenged. 'No Kashmir, no tourists, no dollars – why don't you think? And why should we give anything to Pakistan?'

Nisha blinked. They had decapitated three goats that morning and smeared their faces with blessed blood.

The film that evening, much to everyone's delight, was an old black-and-white, one of those mythological movies made in the '30s. After the goat sacrifices earlier that day it seemed an appropriate affirmation. Clasped hands on knees, chins cupped in hands, bodies leaning forward, eyes growing larger. Nisha glanced a few times at Lachmi leaning against the tree. The actress reminded her of Lachmi. That same resolute face. Yes, that could be Lachmi singing as she walked through a dark forest. Before her rode Yama on a black horse carrying her husband's corpse. Go away, he said to her, covering his black face, do not follow me, your husband is mine now, his time had been fixed and cannot be altered. But she followed, singing of a love that death cannot destroy.

The forest, in the yellowed old black-and-white print, glistened eerily, a swaying river of light, Dakhin swirling and snarling under a full moon, silver and gold. Nisha closed and opened her eyes. Not a forest – a shining river, and the woman floating on the waves in search of her lost husband. The rustling trees carried that rushing sound of the river. And that woman – Nisha looked at Lachmi again. A hand at her throat, her eyes narrowed, Lachmi was leaning forward. Her face was not a mask any more. She was following that woman's footsteps as if the silver screen had vanished, as if that forest had leapt out and engulfed them in its silvery gold light.

Nisha rubbed her eyes. The film was almost over. Finally, Yama gave up, annoyed, irritated, frowning, helpless before the woman's calm face and relentless footsteps. All right, here's your husband back, all healthy again, his rotting flesh pure again, the light back in his lotus eyes, go and live your lives now, you'll die together at some later date when you decide to seek detachment and enter a forest to sit under a tree and wait for me. I give up, your faith is terrifying, your determination almost invalidating me.

'See,' the people of Binjhar said to each other, to their children, 'see how that works.' 'When the heart is pure, anything is possible.' 'If the wife is pure,' said Nirmala, 'then such things are possible. If her hands are not stained with blood.'

'Come, come,' the dhobi said sleepily, 'enough purity for one night. You'll die anyway, pure or impure.' Yawns started, arms and legs began to stretch.

'I have to go to Cuttack tomorrow,' Shailen told everyone. 'Back in two days. Watch for the air show, planes will be zipping overhead from Cuttack.'

'Don't run off,' he said to Nisha, touching her elbow. 'Can't you even take a joke sometimes?'

'A joke! To hear from a *doctor* – a handful of poppy seeds –'

'What on earth can a handful of poppy seeds do, for heaven's sake? A few nightmares. I can't control Ramu. He's done it to me, too. Now come on. I have two bottles of beer. They've kept the vaccines company for three months in the refrigerator.'

They sat on the steps, each holding a 750-ml bottle of Golden Eagle. Nisha didn't want to chat and laugh. After all, he could be a – he could have, really. Maybe he was just trying to con her right now. Sit down, relax, have a beer. And when her mind was slack enough, he might go to that refrigerator again, take her arm so very casually, and – 'So serious. What on earth are you thinking, plotting, planning? That's just a bottle of beer, not a Molotov cocktail.' He gave her arm a shake. 'Something wrong with the beer?'

'No. I'd forgotten the size of the bottles,' Nisha said, shaking her head as if to shake off her misgivings, 'but then, I'd never had beer until I went to the States.' She laughed, thinking of her first beer, Coors Light, in a campus bar.

'Good to hear you laugh – I feel queasy about those sort of sacrifices, you know, but it was funny when you rolled your eyes and went limp.'

'I didn't think I would –'

'Nobody does.'

'I've always believed that I'm a pretty strong – emotionally a strong person, that I have a certain intellectual hardness, detachment –'

'Have you ever witnessed heads being chopped off, blood spurting up, the red stain spreading, the headless body quivering, shaking uncontrollably –'

'Stop!' Nisha covered her ears.

'Dissecting a cadaver is one thing; operating on a kid hit by a car – torn spleen, four broken ribs, punctured lungs, a leg practically torn off at the knee – well, how do you steel yourself for the unexpected?'

'I don't want to hear this.'

'And you don't want your mother to nag you about marriage either. Well, come on then, drink up, bottoms up.'

'Just amazing,' Nisha said, lowering the bottle and wiping her mouth with the back of her hand, 'just amazing. They know what's what. Riots, border disputes. Yet something was made clear on a very different level for them by the movie. I don't understand.'

'Is it necessary to understand, always?'

'Yes. I must at least try to understand.'

'I think you do understand, but you're denying it, because the understanding is not taking place in an area over which you can exert complete control.'

'I control everything about me.' She held the bottle tightly. 'Except that – when that boy, his face taut with hate, pointed that Kalashnikov,' she said, 'I couldn't move, as if he were right here before me, and that bullet was going to shatter my head.'

'Yes,' he said, 'it's that sense of helplessness. But if you were holding that Kalashnikov, you would feel quite different.'

'I wonder. I might have just pulled the trigger out of sheer helpless desperation. The look on that boy's face – it wasn't hate, was it?'

'He believes desperately, that's all.'

'So does everyone else out here. I'm not going to let that happen. I'm not going to be caught here, and get all torn up between media-hype and myth. I got out, and I'll stay out.'

'You make it sound like a place.'

'It is a place – this place,' she struck the ground, 'and all that it contains, all the crippling ideas.'

Shailen shook his head slowly. 'Yes, perhaps it is a place. But I don't think it's under our feet. It moves around with you, that's the problem.'

'No, it's not a problem. I've kicked it loose.'

'What if that restless river twists around you, reclaims you?'

'Is there such a power? I'd like to harness it then, scan it, know its circuits, use it.'

'And you would control it if you knew what it was all about?'

'Naturally. Knowledge is –'

'Don't even say it,' Shailen cut in. 'That's what I used to think when I was fresh out of medical school.'

'You *know* that. You can figure out in seconds what's killing a person. Day by day, you learn, know more and more.'

'Yes, and day by day, I walk with my head bowed lower and lower, with each new drug, with each unique death.'

'God, you're morbid.'

235

'Have you ever looked into Lachmi's eyes?'

'At her eyes?' Nisha smiled a wry, one-sided smile. 'So what *is* going on, Shailen-doctor, that you look at Lachmi but can't say a word?'

He turned and looked at her. 'Must you know everything?'

Nisha bit her lips, startled by the contempt in his voice. So there was one spot you could not touch. She cleared her throat.

'Sorry,' he said, touching her hand lightly, 'there's nothing to tell.'

'Well, she had things to tell.'

'Oh? Like what?'

'And do I have to tell *you* everything?' She couldn't stop the malice creeping into her smile.

'Want to play games, do you?' he asked very softly, looking squarely at her.

'All good things, doctor,' Nisha said, 'don't you worry. How wonderful and noble you are. You are wrapped in the glorious myths of others.'

He laughed, his face relaxing. 'Is that what we're wrapped in?'

'What else? Myths of others creating us, reinventing us day after day.'

'And do we live up to them?'

'I hope not. God, I hope not.'

'But when you start believing –'

'But that's where you come in,' Nisha cut in. 'You should set them right. The goat sacrifices, for instance. Who ever heard of sacrifices to Manasha? Why don't you set them straight?'

'I can't get rid of the crocodiles and the floods, so how can I set anything straight, how can I explain? I've stopped beating my head against a wall. They're happy this way, and I have interfered enough. Now I just want to get to Puri after my replacement arrives.'

'Why?'

'Vacation, really. And future work, too. A friend has opened a clinic. I've saved some money, need some more, lots more actually, to buy a partnership, but I'm planning to do so, somehow.'

Nisha laughed. 'I have almost five thousand dollars.'

'Really? But you're not the charitable kind, are you?' He laughed too. 'What would you live on if you gave that to me, now?'

'On nights like these I can allow myself to feel I could give everything and live on just the sound of that river out there.'

'Allow yourself –' He stopped. 'I thought you had got out, that you were planning on staying out.'

The night roared around them with the restless thrashing of the river. The darkness lit up in spots, bursts of tiny green flames circling the soft trunks of banana trees, the dark tops of hibiscus bushes. And when the wind swirled into Binjhar from Dakhin, it rushed the darkness with that rainsmell of gardenia and tuberose and the tiny, white, star-like *juin*, a smell made particular to Binjhar as that laden wind collected in its path the mud-and-blood smell of the red earth that lay beneath their feet and under the river. 'These nights make me think of Lachmi,' Nisha said, 'and tempt me to go to the riverbank and ask for something. Genuflect on the red mud, I want to whisper: Manasha, they say you never refuse, grant my wish then, tell me what to believe.'

'On nights like these, with the river so loud, I wouldn't tempt anything with words like that,' Shailen said. 'Would you really allow a god or goddess that much power? I never would. I would rather my gods failed to deliver, then I could wipe away their tears, and forgive them, love them, continue to pray to them, and not expect anything in return except that precious uncertainty, never really knowing why or how, but always believing, in spite of all the horrors, that happiness is perhaps inevitable, if someday we learn to recognise it.'

'I can't believe you're a doctor,' she said.

'I can't believe you're doing what you're doing out here. Beware, though, because Binjhar has seduced you.'

Mosquitoes had formed buzzing clouds above their heads. They clapped their hands to drive away the insects, stood up and smiled. 'You're in way over your head,' he said to her. 'I hope you know that.'

'Am I to believe you don't give a damn?'

'I am . . . just the doctor.'

'There's no need to cover a hurt and tired child with a blanket and put him to bed on your operating table because he's sprained his ankle, is there?'

'I'm just doing my job.'

'Yes, so you are, Shailen-doctor, and good-night.'

Nisha turned and looked back at the dispensary from the cluster of banyan trees at the end of the narrow lane that lay between the dispensary steps and the red dirt road. Under the dim light of the veranda, Shailen stood looking down at the empty beer bottle in his hand. He looked up slowly, but not towards the banyan trees under which Nisha stood, but to the left of the dispensary. Nisha moved behind one of the trees, drawing in her breath sharply. Lachmi entered the dim circle of light. Shailen was moving back as if startled. Lachmi said something, but from where she was Nisha couldn't hear. Shailen shook his head. Was he refusing something or denying something? Lachmi moved closer to him and reached out to touch his face. Shailen stepped back. He sat down heavily on the steps, covering his face with his hands. Lachmi knelt before him. She touched his hair, his hands, his feet. Then she rose, and with that slow, deliberate walk disappeared round the side of the dispensary. Shailen sat there, face in his hands, his slender body convulsing, bending lower and lower, until his head came slowly to rest on his knees.

Nisha walked backwards slowly. Well, well, Shailen-doctor, I wonder if you have anything on your shelves for such fractures?

From her window, Nisha saw the jeep drive off, trailing clouds of rosy dust. What happened – she bit her lips. No, she was not going to think anything at all. What if – No, he certainly was not. But what if it was his photograph that her mother had seen and chosen? Nonsense. Why on earth should she even think something like that? And about him, too? Especially after what she had witnessed last night. But what did Lachmi say? Did she ask him, accuse him? Oh, no. Nisha pressed her fingers against her temples. Why did she ask Lachmi about Shailen? Why did she have to bloody interfere? Her words may have made Lachmi suspect the doctor. Shailen sitting there shaking, face in his hands. Nisha stared at the glowing road with clenched fists. She had actually smiled then, even felt a twinge of glee to see his pain. She unclenched her hands. Won't do this to myself. She tossed her hair out of her eyes.

The bright sunlight had cleared the dawn mist and the morning air was fresh with the odour of dung cakes being slapped on walls, of guavas and cooking rice. Ramu brought the bicycle around, the chain fixed, cleaned, oiled. She rode to the bazaar and all the way along the river, following the red path out of the village. She paused before the bamboo groves, hearing a high-pitched whine above. For a fraction of a second, she saw six silver streaks, MIG-29s, possibly, or Mirages. She looked at the green-gold forest of bamboo before her.

Glittering eyes flashed in her head, and a viciously leaping cobra's head. The wind whistling through the groves brought the tangy fresh odour of bamboo with it. Nisha felt Lachmi's hand against her cheek. A dark heavy wave coursed through her. On the ground her shadow was split in two by the shadow of a slender bamboo. One half of her shadow appeared larger than the other half, as if someone was standing by her side. Nisha turned to look. Of course there wasn't anyone, although she could swear she felt Lachmi right next to her, almost a part of her. She turned the bicycle around quickly.

On the way back, she slowed down near Lachmi's house. Two men in *lungis*, their muscles straining, sweat pouring down their backs, were unscrewing the hinges of Lachmi's teak door. Two boys stood ten yards from the house. 'What are they doing?' she asked them.

'Lachmi told her brothers to remove the door,' they said.

'Why?' They shook their heads, turned the palms of their hands upwards. Nisha watched them for a few seconds. So these were Lachmi's brothers. Yes, they were thuggish all right. Strips of red cloth tied round their shaved heads, burly bodies, curling moustaches. Odd, removing the door. Maybe they wanted to sell the wood. They would get a good price for that door.

On the steps of the school Ramu stood arguing with an old man in a dhoti and a brown shawl. She could see the holy string across his chest and back. His head was shaved except for a rat's tail of hair that hung from the crown of his head. On his forehead were three vertical sandalwood stripes. The priest from the Shiv temple! 'Right now,' he said to Ramu, shaking his fist, 'right now!'

'Something wrong?' she asked.

'Oh – you are the – no, no, nothing wrong. Lachmi is being foolish. She came for the *puja* this morning and said some silly things, so I come here, tell Ramu go and get Lachmi. I want to talk some sense, because when I went to her house her brothers threw me out and said they would do as they were told and began to take down the door. What to say – no education, no common sense. *Puja* is one thing: put some flowers on the altar, light a lamp, a few sticks of incense, say a few prayers, some sandalwood paste on your head, few drops of the water in your mouth – and go home and forget. But then to have idiotic notions of what can happen if – tch tch, what to say? Nobody listens to me, what can I say? Old man, be quiet, go ring your bell and cook your rice.' He shook his head and tugged at his holy string. 'I'll go back. I'm an old man. I'll come and talk to Shailen-doctor tomorrow.'

'What's going on?' she asked Ramu as the priest walked away, muttering to himself. Ramu shook his head and shrugged. 'I'm going to the bazaar,' he said, and ran off. Nisha sat down on the steps and breathed in deeply the warm air.

Winter had vanished. A short sharp exhalation. The long deep breath of this spring-summer, the regular rhythm of the year, had settled in, as regular as the continual unrest of the river that was leaping its way relentlessly towards the sea. Even thinking about Dakhin dragged you along with it. How terrifying, she thought, how marvellous and how odd, taking down that gorgeous teak door.

She sat there and ate her lunch, dozed, sat up startled as parrots, dazzling green, fought among mango leaves with harsh grating shrieks. Then the rhythmic chant-like call of those tiny birds faded in, up and down in cadence. They were the birds her grandmother used to tell her about, who continually urged, Wife-talk-to-me, and that's what they were called, *bow-kotha-kow*, a name formed from the sound of their call. The call was so insistent suddenly, drowing out the parrots and crows and sparrows, as if these brown birds really wanted to hear someone talk. Bow-kotha-kow-kow-kow-kow. The afternoon was loud with voices and wings and feet and hoofs.

She watched the sun glaze the banyan trees copper and vanish, felt the night touch her with its cool river breeze and close her eyes with its heady scent. Smoke of sandalwood incense came from somewhere, together with the smoke of wood fires. Something was happening around her, she felt, but she couldn't put her finger on it. What if Shailen was – what lunacy, not again! What did Lachmi say to Shailen? Had they been – were they still – ? He must have done something, something terrible. Or was it Ramu after all? Was Shailen protecting Ramu? If he knew Kanu was dead, had been killed, why didn't he make out a death certificate when the DM asked for one? But had Shailen got rid of Kanu in his own careful way, sliding the needle in gently under Kanu's skin? He had covered that boy in his surgery so gently. Pulled the blanket up to his chin, moved his hair out of his eyes. Yet when he had caught her shoulders, pushed her against the tree, that eerie flicker of a smile moving from his mouth to his eyes – Stop. Hypothesise, Lennox would say, analyse. Shailen's body shaking, his face in his hands. Lachmi had reached out to touch his face.

Nisha touched her burning face. Lachmi's hand against her face. The warm smell of bamboo brought by the wind. 'Lachmi,' Nisha said softly, 'Lachmi.' She closed her eyes. She saw her reflection in the mirror merging, vanishing into Lachmi's shadow-dark form. For a fraction of a second, her body felt heavier, as if she was breathing in another's shadow. If only she knew for sure – but this heady darkness was swirling around and re-creating, reviving, lost forgotten worlds.

Something marvellous and terrifying, can't explain, don't know how to express, perhaps it's just illogical and not quite within my grasp, but I'm trying to: why that damned door, why that agitated brahmin, why this sandalwood smoke takes you to dark temple altars, to riverbanks where corpses are set aflame, to sandalwood pyres into which desperate women fling themselves, but what exactly, find out tomorrow, definitely, verbalise, give it utterance, frame it in the necessary language, but now the night compels silence and thought is, really, if you can believe, quite, almost absolutely, irrelevant, as eyes are closing and the mind lapsing –

'Wake up! Wake up!' Ramu was shaking her. Nisha sat up in shock. 'I can't stop her!' he said. 'I can't stop her, nobody can, maybe you can.'

She ran with him to the river. Not only the people of Binjhar, but many people from the next village, were gathered on the bank. Many carried plates of marigolds, hibiscus, garlands, smoking sandalwood sticks, clay lamps. The old priest was standing under a *neem* tree and shaking his fists at the crowd. '*Imbeciles! Idiots! Murderers!* Look,' he said to Nisha, seeing her, 'just imagine. On that door, look, she's insane, and they are here with flowers, look.' Nisha ran down to the bank.

Lachmi stood there in a white cotton sari which had a red border. On her wrists were bangles made from white conch shells. Her long black hair was wet and hung below her hips. 'Lachmi,' Nisha whispered. Lachmi turned with blank eyes. 'My husband will come back,' she said. Her two brothers, their eyes red and streaming, carried the heavy door right to the edge of the water. They touched Lachmi's feet, and moved back crying loudly. Men, women, children, old men, old women, all bowed and touched Lachmi's feet. There was silent awe on their faces. Nirmala stood with her children a few yards away, a sullen, confused look on her face. Ramu clasped Nisha's hand and began to cry into her palm. 'Stop,' said Nisha, 'stop,' her voice faltering. 'What are you –' They pushed her away, told her to be quiet, not to disturb such a holy moment.

Lachmi walked slowly to the water and stepped on the door. She raised her folded hands, looked up, then at the river, and closed her eyes. She sat down in the centre of the door, folding her legs under her. Her two brothers, crying, wiping their faces, pushed the door on to the river's surface. The waves lifted the door and pulled it out. '*Jai ma, jai ma, jai ma . . .*' Flowers were thrown in, lamps floated. People stretched out on the bank and touched the earth and the waters with their foreheads. '*Jai ma, jai ma, jai ma.*'

Nisha's knees touched the soft red mud. Her hand was wet with Ramu's tears. The brahmin under the *neem* tree was shaking his fists still, but now screaming out a string of arcane abuse: '*Scoundrels! Cads! A race of pigs! Children of whores! Diseased offspring of diseased whores! Ignorant asses with worms in your heads! May Shiv strike you down!*'

Nisha tried to call out but her voice had disappeared. Her mouth seemed filled with ashes, and she coughed to clear her throat, but only a choking sound came out, much like the gurgling sound wetting her hand. Shailen, she was screaming inside, God, if only he would hold her hand. Shailen, come and stop this. Why aren't you back? Lachmi sitting erect on the bouncing teak door. Nisha couldn't see her any more. The currents pulled the door round the river-bend and Lachmi disappeared among the waves and dark rocks of Dakhin. 'Phone –' she gasped, 'Ramu, must phone DM.'

Dragging Ramu, she ran to the dispensary. It was locked. Ramu, crying hysterically, ran round to the back and brought a hammer. She began to strike at the lock and the bolt. The lock broke. They flung the doors back and rushed in. Nisha picked up the phone and listened to the receiver intently, then replaced it. Dead. There was no jeep either, to drive to the next village, to the post office, to the hospital. They could walk or Ramu could take the bicycle. But where was Lachmi now?

Ramu pulled her back to the river. No one was there. Flowers had been washed back, garlands of marigold, hibiscus. The air was still scented with sandalwood and myrrh. Nisha sat down and leant her head against the *neem* tree. That limey bitter smell. Ramu's head was buried against her side, his body convulsing with sobs. The river breeze felt like a slap. Tears rolled down her face. She couldn't stop crying. She bent forward, bringing her head over her knees, and covered her face.

She hadn't been able to do a thing. It had happened, just like that. Without even a hint. Is that how it always happened, just like that? Is that how it works? Where was Shailen, damn it, where was he? Lachmi, proud, beautiful and, oh God, young, was torn to pieces by now. Nisha gasped through her sobs and hugged herself. She felt skin lacerate, burn, tear, arms rip off, legs, ears, mouth, fingers. A thrashing river, thrashing with its merciless creatures, Dakhin, a mad wind gone insane with blood and myth. Why did she have to be witness to this?

What was happening? She didn't have a clue. Two days ago they were arguing about Kashmir, about the government. Today, they had aided and abetted – What was the psychology of riots, Hindus and Muslims killing each other day after day over a decision to build a temple where a mosque stood? A Kalashnikov in the hands of a fifteen-year-old boy. A TV screen red with a bloodstained street, a river red with blood and red silt. And they were standing in between, unable to move.

She had frozen, hadn't been able to stop them or Lachmi. She had taken notes, written everything down diligently, asked her clever questions, to some extent even got them to question what they believed. It'll be an exciting dissertation, Lennox had said. She would write it, and then go back and defend it. She hadn't been able to – she hadn't paid attention, hadn't listened carefully enough, hadn't observed – hadn't learnt to – Look, the voice in the dream had whispered, look carefully – the door, the brahmin – She had sat and relaxed and let it happen, hadn't, yes, analysed what was happening before her eyes, on this red earth, hadn't even looked! Failed so utterly that there were no words to, no emotion devastating enough – Lachmi had floated away like a feather drops and floats away from a bird's wing in flight. Lachmi lying on the ground, beating it, crying like her heart was breaking.

Two boys and three girls wandered near the bank. They looked at the two huddled forms, tilting their heads, listening to the gasping, choking sounds coming from there. When the sound of a backfiring jeep cut in, they turned their heads.

Running footsteps came to a halt. Nisha moved, only to fall sideways, burying her face in her hands. She felt Ramu slide with her. 'Get up, stop this. Pick him up, bring him along.' Nisha felt hands lift her up. She was flung over a shoulder. Blue cotton, a faint odour of diesel and dust. 'Stop,' she heard again, and began to scream, 'No, no, no.' They were moving. She was lowered and pushed into the back of the jeep. Ramu was pushed in after her. The priest got in, and began to smooth her hair, whispering Tch, tch, tch, *shanti shanti shanti*, with each bump on the way, every jolt, every slap of the red dust that rose and obliterated vision. Then she was pulled out, flung over the shoulder again, pushed into a chair.

'Oh, Shailen-doctor, oh, Shailen-doctor –' A woman's worried, anxious voice.

'*Ki?*' Shailen turned towards the door.

'Tulu ate poisoned berries – now vomiting blood.'

'Now? This, now?' He pressed his temples with his fingertips. 'Bring him in.'

'The phone's dead, dead,' Nisha heard herself mutter, her voice cracked, hoarse.

'I know. It was that damned airshow, the MIG-29s, flying low to show off and scare the Cuttack crowd, flew into the phone lines and tore them off. I'll drive back and – don't struggle, I don't have time – shut up – I'm going to give you both sedatives. Won't hurt much.'

'Ouch.'

'There. Put her in there, Ramu in the other one. Where's the boy?'

Nisha felt drops of water on her mouth. She opened her eyes and saw a dropper above her face and a hand holding a glass. 'Here, drink, you asked for water, and sedatives can make you thirsty.' She raised herself and drank from the glass. 'The DM's assistant's come and gone. They're going to search the river. Now I'd like you to get up slowly, splash some water on your face, and go to my office and sit there. I have to stitch someone's finger before it falls off.'

'Don't you know what's happened – don't you care – ?'

'I need this room and table for an emergency, now, and there is nothing physically wrong with you, or me, so please –'

Ramu was asleep under Shailen's table, one fist under his chin, the other under his head. Outside, people were sitting in rows, groaning, coughing, sneezing, calling on God, destiny and Shailen-doctor. Nisha stood up, straightened her clothes and walked out slowly.

The door of the schoolhouse had been left open, but everything was still there. She went to the room that functioned as a kitchen and found Nirmala cutting vegetables. 'What –'

'*Didi-didi* –' Nirmala threw herself on the floor and caught Nisha's feet.

'What the – stop –'

'*Didi* – don't send me away – no one wants – they turn away – turn their faces away – Shailen-doctor, assistant DM, they gave everyone such a talking-to – now everyone looks at me like –'

'Could you just make me some tea or something?'

247

'Yes.'

Nisha went back to her room. She rearranged and relabelled her files. Nirmala brought tea spiced with cloves and basil. Nisha sat looking at her notes, crossing out words, adding commas, semi-colons, dashes. What had she written? Page after page after page filled with what they said about the doctor. She documented his daily routine, his likes and dislikes, what he had said to the dhobi, to Ramu, the barber's wife, what they said he had said to them; then she had written Ramu's version of it all; and Nirmala's; everyone's except Lachmi's. Lachmi's words never entered her journal. Why not?

She stared down at the words. The doctor this, the doctor that, Shailen, Shailen, Shailen . . . When did she write all this? She couldn't remember. Had someone altered her entries? Did she really write all this? Why? She reached forward and pressed PLAY on the tape recorder. Nirmala's high-pitched voice – yes, she remembered that story. The dhobi's voice came next, then Ramu's, then the barber's wife's. All talking about the doctor! And about Lachmi. Three-quarters of her material was centred on Shailen. What possessed her –

What would Sylvia Lennox say? My dear, who gets to tell whose story, and why? And was there yet another narrative that she had missed completely, hadn't a clue about, a narrative containing all – ? Nisha covered her face with her hands.

'Shailen-doctor *aiche*.' Nirmala entered quietly and ushered him in.

'A letter for you. The dhobi went to the post office in the next village to collect the mail.'

'Why?' she asked. 'Why did they let – how could she – ?'

'How should I know?'

'You must know! What did she say to you? What did you do?'

She couldn't understand why he stood there with his fists

clenched, his face drained of colour, his eyes so haunted, as if his world had burnt to ashes. 'Just go away,' she said, her voice breaking, 'I would like to be alone.'

'You sent him away like that, *didi*,' Nirmala whispered. 'Did you not see his eyes? Don't cry, *didi*, don't.' She wiped Nisha's face with the corner of her sari. 'Not what I wanted, God,' Nirmala said. 'What could I do, or you, or anyone? Don't cry, *didi*, I will have to live with this, and tears don't help.'

The next morning, loud voices, running feet and whirring engines woke her. She dressed quickly and ran out. Everyone was running towards the river again. A helicopter had landed. Policemen were moving people away from the river. Shailen was almost in the water, examining something. A policeman stopped her with his club. 'Please, miss.'

'Don't come here,' Shailen turned and said, hearing the policeman. A large canvas sheet was thrown over whatever the doctor was bending over and then carried to the helicopter. The corner of a white and red sari leaked out from the bundle. People touched their foreheads and then their chests. '*Shanti ano ma, shanti*.' Shailen was removing blood-smeared latex gloves from his hands. He came up to her. 'Come, let's go.' Ramu was whimpering under the *neem* tree, rubbing his head against its trunk. 'It's all over. Come,' Shailen said. His eyes were blank.

Within the hour, the temple became the stage. Bells rang constantly, and mountains of flowers surrounded not only the Shiv *linga*, but the altar and temple courtyard as well. The smoke from burning incense, oil and wood stung the eyes as one reached the stone steps. The brahmin's assistants were handing out rice with ghee, together with chopped dates, and sugar candy in banana leaves sprinkled with holy water. And being a Shiv temple, *bhang* was poured generously into every glass, cup,

249

mug or vessel held out. So for three days Binjhar swayed, heady with *bhang*, and its natural accompaniment *ganja*. Even Ramu loudly sucked the clay pipes offered and, after draining a glass of the milky, saffron-scented fluid, poured a glass on his head. Nirmala was drinking glass after glass of *bhang*, and even feeding her children the same, saying, 'Drink, drink, and hope there is forgiveness.'

'Who killed Kanu?' the dhobi asked, slurring, hiccupping, stretching out an arm towards the altar. 'You up there, tell me.'

'Lachmi for certain,' another slurring voice assured him.

'Manasha called Lachmi,' the barber's wife said, rolling from one end of the temple courtyard to the other. 'Manasha called her, yes, called her,' she chanted as she rolled back and forth across the flagstones, her eyes turning up, showing their whites, white foam dribbling from the corners of her mouth. 'She'll call us, too, call us, call us, call us, call us . . .'

Nisha clutched Shailen's arm. 'Have they gone mad?'

'Drink,' Shailen said, grabbing a glass, 'drink up. What are we resisting anyway? Do we know any more than them, really? Don't we want to forget?' Then she was laughing, like everybody else, crying sometimes, giggling, crying again, as Lennox's voice kept echoing in her head, Analyse, hypothesise. Giftwrapping reality for Syliva's three chapters – If she could have dragged her to the river when that door had bounced away, made her feel jagged teeth on flesh, water filling your mouth and nose and lungs, made her smell this red silt with goat blood frothing on it –

They rolled on the temple courtyard, laughing, crying, singing, stumbling to the river, rolled on the mud, crying for Manasha and Shiv, rubbing the mud on themselves as if its redness might cover the other deeper red that now held them captive. Caked with red mud they fell asleep wherever they were, woke up, went to the temple, ate kilos of rice and fruit, and the *bhang* again, and *ganja*.

250

On the fourth day the rice ran out, the *bhang*, the fruit, the flowers, except the *ganja*, and their *nasha*. But now they had entered a different stage of intoxication. Every sound was magnified by a hundred decibels, every colour turned blinding bright and every movement slower, heavier. When out of the hot white sky a silver helicopter descended, the people of Binjhar ran out of the temple courtyard in slow motion, covering their ears and eyes, and with impossibly stiff jaws and lips called out to Manasha to save them from the claws of the bird of death, from destiny.

Nisha and Shailen walked a little swifter then the others, were a little less muddy. The whirr of the engine stopped. The door opened, six men jumped out, holding between them what looked to all like – a madman. Trussed up with ropes, bare to the waist, a bloody bandage around his head, the man was screaming hoarsely, as if he had been screaming for days. The district magistrate came forward. With him was a woman in a blue sari, her greying hair braided loosely at the back. 'Shailen-doctor, my goodness, what on earth, you look – here, take mine, clean and starched . . . oh, well, yes, now I can see your face somewhat, but what – never mind, look here, missing person, out of the blue –'

'What are you doing here?' Shailen asked the woman next to the spluttering DM.

'Why, you wrote that you were waiting for a replacement so that you could leave,' she said to him.

'Yes, yes, they informed me she, Dr Sanyal here, needed a lift to get here, so I said come along, since I have to –' the DM added.

'I wasn't expecting you so soon,' Shailen said, wiping dry mud off his hair.

'Why, you're – you're –' Nisha stammered and stopped. It was Dr Sanyal, from Delhi, an old friend of her mother's who had left Delhi when Nisha was three or four. What was she doing here?

She recalled her mother writing about Dr Sanyal recently, that she had come back to Delhi, to work there. But here she was, standing two feet away, smiling enquiringly as if expecting Nisha to explain what it was that Nisha was doing here. And why was Shailen talking to Dr Sanyal as if he had known her almost all his life?

'I have to show you the place,' Shailen said to Dr Sanyal. 'Things are a bit of a mess.'

'But – but –' cut in the DM, 'you are not looking. I have come to deposit the missing person and make an arrest, and the missing person, doctor, look.'

The people of Binjhar stood in a semicircle, red clay statues melting slowly as if they had run into a blast furnace, and regarded the madman with mouths hanging open. 'Kanu.' A hoarse whisper rushed like the river breeze.

'Hit on the head last night, you see, three villages down west, drunken fight, then went running to the police station with "I remember, I remember." This business with the dead woman – the recent suicide I've entered it as – the Manasha business – but when you called me first, remember when you wouldn't make out the death certificate – before that, he says he was hit on the head, so the doctor there said he forgot; second hit, he remembers. Now we must arrest.'

Ramu had crept up to Nisha, his whole body shaking. 'Not possible,' he whispered.

'Him, him!' The madman stamped his feet and screamed hoarsely.

'Handcuffs,' the DM ordered. Two policemen stepped forward.

'He was there!' The hoarse scream again. 'When the branch hit me on the head.'

'Wait a minute.' Shailen stepped in between the policemen

and Ramu. 'You have no bloody proof except for that oaf's screams. So just wait a minute. You want to say something, Ramu?'

'Shailen-doctor, if Manasha took him how can he be standing there?'

'What did you do?' Shailen asked.

'We'll question him at the station, come, come.'

'No.' Shailen pulled Ramu to the side. 'What did you do?'

'For one last time I thought I'd try to kill him!' the madman screamed, struggling with the ropes, tearing at them. 'My wife's been eaten by crocodiles because of him.'

'I was sleeping under the tree near the water,' Ramu said. 'It was dark, and suddenly I woke up because somebody was strangling me. Kanu was trying to kill me. I struggled but couldn't free myself, and I was going to die, but then –' Ramu's eyes became glazed.

'A branch fell on my head –' Nisha stared at the madman pulling at the ropes and screaming. His enviable face was streaked with mud and blood, and so was his body. He looked strong enough to wrench a bull's head off.

'Yes –' Ramu stammered – 'fell on his head from above, and he fell down. Then as I looked at Kanu lying at my feet, the river –'

'What?'

'The river swelled up and grew so loud. Manasha was calling, telling me to give Kanu to her, since he had tried to kill me – so –' Ramu tugged at his lower lip and moved back towards Nisha.

'He dragged me down the slope and rolled me into the water. Let me get my hands on you – ohh, I was stunned by the blow, couldn't move, otherwise –'

'Picked up shortly, you see,' the DM cut in, 'by a launch, but they didn't know, he had memory loss, you see, so dropped him off three villages down, so –'

'You little –' Shailen shook Ramu. 'Why didn't you tell me?'

'I forgot. I was afraid.'

The people of Binjhar opened and closed their mouths. 'The husband brought back. The wife goes to Manasha, and the husband comes back.' Another whisper like a wave, and thick red mud dripping from bodies with every movement. Nisha closed her eyes for a second. It was the smell of that mud, the same smell as on the red finger that had touched her face with its wetness on an afternoon when everyone had turned shining wet red.

'Here, here, just a minute,' the district magistrate tapped Shailen on the shoulder. 'I am thoroughly confused. I don't like this business at all. Ruffians, liars. I shall leave. I have important things to take care of.' He waved his hands at his men. 'Untie the wretch. Let's go.'

'But you can't leave Kanu here,' Shailen said agitatedly. 'He'll kill Ramu.'

'Oh, really? Untie him.' The DM clapped his hands. The policemen untied Kanu. Kanu shook himself like a bull shaking off water and mud. Slowly, with heavy steps, he walked towards Ramu, who was hiding behind Nisha. The DM marched swiftly and pulled Ramu out to face Kanu. Ramu fell to his knees, rolling his eyes. 'Stand up,' the DM said, pulling Ramu up. Kanu stood before the DM, shoulders hunched, fists at his waist. He opened and closed his eyes rapidly, breathing noisily through his mouth. 'You –' the DM poked Kanu's chest with a forefinger. Kanu took a step backwards. 'You listen. And you –' he gave Ramu a shake. 'If he,' the DM pointed at Ramu, 'dies, then you –' he poked Kanu again – 'you hang.' Then he pointed at Kanu, faced Ramu and declared, 'If he dies, then, Ramu, you hang. Manasha's blessings on you. Goodbye. Dr Sanyal,' he said to the woman, touching his head with two fingers, 'enjoy your stay. Shailen-doctor, you can have the jeep, duty calls. See, all settled. I know how to deal with these criminal types.'

People backed away slowly. Ramu and Kanu stood facing each

other, one rolling his eyes and shaking like a leaf, the other breathing heavily and glaring with bloodshot eyes. They didn't move an inch to either reduce or increase the yard of red earth between them. Nirmala crawled on her hands and knees towards them. She reached out to touch Kanu's leg, then withdrew her hand, crouching between them, whimpering.

The helicopter, blinding silver in the afternoon sun, rose with that same thousand-decibel whirr like a shining creature of light spreading spinning wings.

Nisha and Shailen listened to Dr Sanyal chatter on about the New Delhi hospital while they walked to the schoolhouse. Nisha eyed Shailen warily. He was quiet, nodding occasionally, almost sullen. 'Ah, I must take a good look inside,' Dr Sanyal said, poking her head in through the door. 'Come, Nisha, we've a lot to talk about too,' she added before disappearing inside.

Nisha swallowed and looked at Shailen and then at herself. Dry red mud clung to their clothes, skin, hair. 'She was one of my professors, and she kind of adopted me, I guess, after my mother died.' Shailen paused and touched the mud on his shirt. 'I wrote to her last year,' he started again, without any prompting, words tumbling out, 'and then, just a few weeks back, telling her my plans, though I wasn't expecting her to turn up so suddenly, without a word, to be the replacement, not her. Anyway, I have to pack my things, show her the stuff. You'll have company – she's going to stay in the schoolhouse and you can talk about old times, I'm sure. Her things are on their way.' They looked at each other blankly. Shailen rubbed his temples. 'I have to show her around a little bit.' Nisha swallowed again.

'Mud,' she said.

'Yes. Must change.' Shailen backed away a few steps, then turned and ran towards his dispensary.

Nisha entered the schoolhouse slowly. She heard the barber's wife talking to Dr Sanyal. 'Poor Nirmala, one feels sorry for her now,' the barber's wife was saying to the doctor. 'The woman crawled on hands and knees to her house, crawled through the bazaar, all the way down the road. Crawled to her bed, and under it. She's lying there now. Won't come out.' Nisha closed her eyes. Nirmala whimpering at Kanu's feet, then crawling, as if dragging a half-torn body across an alien battlefield. No one reached out to help her to her feet. The villagers just stood and stared at Nirmala's rolling, writhing form twisting its way through the deserted bazaar, up the red dirt road to the cluster of huts where her children stood with their thumbs in their mouths and the blankest eyes Nisha had ever seen.

Nisha slipped into her room, unnoticed by Dr Sanyal or the barber's wife talking in the next room. She picked up her journal and, holding it tightly against her chest, went into the bathroom and closed the door. Three iron buckets of water and a wooden stool stood on the unfinished cement floor. She sat down on the stool and stared at a tin can half-submerged in one of the buckets. The can quivered slightly from time to time, glinting viciously in the sunlight streaming through the open window. Nisha reached for the can with one hand, while keeping the notebook pressed against her with the other. Slowly, she began to pour water over herself.

The mud liquefied and streamed down her face. The sunlight was red and shining wet before her eyes. A red pool widened under her feet. Was all her blood leaving her? That eerie sweet smell again. The first rains on a scorched red earth. The hard mud collapsed at its touch, melted, swirled into a mad river. This river-scented mud flowing swiftly down her skin, along her throat, shoulder, arm, collecting at her wrist – Nisha held her wrist against her nose and mouth. A burning sandalwood taste. A scorching smell. Her body convulsed, bringing her head down sharply on her knees. Her notebook slipped from her hand into the muddy water at her feet. She straightened up at the sound of the soft splash. Blue ink blending with bright copper. She picked up a bucket and overturned it clumsily above her head. A silver torrent of light washed the red out of her eyes.

An hour later, Dr Sanyal knocked on Nisha's door. 'Ah,' she said, 'Shailen has managed marvellously. I hope I shall do half as well.' Nisha combed her wet hair before the mirror on the wall. The mud was finally gone. Her head felt a little heavy. Dr Sanyal took the cup of tea from the barber's wife, who had now taken charge of the kitchen.

Nisha sat quietly for a while on her bed. 'Is your work coming along well?' Dr Sanyal asked her. She nodded. 'What on earth I arrived in the middle of –' Dr Sanyal touched her head. 'But how have you been, working here in this village? Your mother's quite worried, you know, ever since you went abroad. She wants you to get married, settle down, or so she's been telling me for the past year, since I went back to Delhi from the Medical College in Calcutta where Shailen was a resident – under me, you know, such a bright boy.' Nisha went to the table and picked up her mother's letter that Shailen had handed her a few days back. *If you don't come home right away, we are sending your brothers to bring you back. You are getting married this summer.* When would this nonsense end? Nisha dropped the letter into the tin can under the table.

'I'm sure Shailen will have a wonderful vacation in Puri,' Dr Sanyal said. 'He needs it. He said he's going to stay there for at least a month, maybe even work there. He decided to leave right away, started packing, doesn't want to linger. Well, you can't blame him considering everything,' she carried on. Nisha heard only the rush of the river all around.

Shailen was going to vanish, then. Nisha shifted on the bed.

The afternoon felt warm and wet and sticky against her skin, as if hands had slapped that damp red mud all over her again. A red clay figure to be thrown into the river, when the south wind crossed the land, for some inexplicable blessing. A warm rosy splash, and then you were lost – those are pearls that were your eyes, of your bones are coral made – blood on latex gloves, the soil turning perfect for rice this year. Dakhin – The south wind piercing my heart, her grandmother used to sing.

She had wanted to find a river, that's all. But it was as if the river had dragged her there to devour her, body and mind. She stifled a gasp. Body and mind – the river had crashed through the dam between. She had come here to write it down, neatly, write that river down; but Dakhin had rewritten her. Does text define context or context define . . . ? Sylvia Lennox, leaning back, crossing her legs, twisting a lock of her hair. Your life in your own hands, child. Her grandmother running her forefinger over Nisha's palm. Look here. In your own hands. All written in your hands.

Nisha looked down at her palms, then slowly clenched her hands. She must get away from Dakhin's warm red waves. Lachmi – pulled away into that redness – and now she was drowning in it as well, just like that. She must get away from that blood-and-mud smell, and from this roaring afternoon crashing against her ears, from this river that rushed through your head sweeping everything out, this river that wanted to take everything away.

She went to the window. The river sounded like one long scream. Nisha held the bars. Had Lachmi heard it too? The river wanted to wash away this sticky red feeling. To walk into its warmth, submerge in it, to let Dakhin take you away to that secret island. Dakhin was calling, spreading its tide out for you, rising up for you. Tell me what to believe, she had asked. Dakhin would tell you everything, make you understand fear, doubt, belief, curse, chaos. So Dakhin was beckoning now, Manasha's spirit rising through it, offering that incomprehensible answer.

Outside, the red dust rose up in the wind, twisted, coiled, swept forward in a rush, pulled back, scattered. A glittering copper glaze, rising and falling, circling, engulfing.

Shailen would drive away, drive all the way down the banks, and then away, far away. She turned from the window sharply. Dr Sanyal was still sipping tea and smiling benignly at the trees outside.

'Barber's wife, help me,' Nisha called. The barber's wife came running. 'Pack.' Into two suitcases she threw her clothes, shoes, books, towels, soap, shampoo, haphazardly stuffing them in, two three four items at a time and what didn't fit she told the barber's wife to take. Dr Sanyal's eyes widened. 'Are you – ?' Nisha slung her leather bag over her shoulder, picked up her suitcases and ran out.

She ran to the middle of the red dirt road as the jeep drove up. She would be miles away from it all soon, she felt almost sure. How long could this river follow you? Shailen braked, looking puzzled. Nisha ran to the back of the jeep and threw her suitcases in. 'What –

'You've got to take me –'

'I'm going to –'

'Me too.' She climbed in beside him. She would outrun it. They would be driving away.

'The Cuttack airport, I guess. You can get a plane to Calcutta, and from there –'

'I don't want to go to an airport. Please, just drive.'

'But what do you intend to – I mean, what will you –'

'Please, just drive. I need a month, just to rethink some things, that's all.'

'How much money do you have?'

'Five thousand dollars – almost; I told you that before.'

'One *lakh* rupees, hmm, well, that'll last for a year at least –'

'A partnership, didn't you say? A cut for me. We can talk about it.'

Shailen's eyes shone with a wicked light. 'Well – OK, get in, but let me make one thing clear, your family had better not come chasing after me with a gun and expect me to marry you.'

'Nobody's going to make me marry anybody.'

'A month of rethinking, hmm,' Shailen rubbed his chin. 'Anything can happen in a month, in a week, in a day.'

'Just drive, damn it.' But what if – if it was Shailen, and she had jumped into this jeep, but this was getting away, but what if he was, what was she getting away from – Nisha shook inside. Who are you, she wanted to scream, why were you here? Running from or running after – what am I doing? Tell me what to believe, she had laughed and asked that restless night. What had she received – curse or blessing? And how to know one from the other, when Dakhin with its stormy thrashing was sweeping away the hardness under her feet, when Dakhin was raging through her viens?

'Are you going to drive or what?' she asked, her voice high-pitched, cracking.

'Before something overtakes – yes, I'd better.'

'Stop,' she said, as they passed Lachmi's doorless house. 'Why won't you say anything?' The brick house gaped at them, its interior so dark that the darkness almost seemed like a drawn curtain. 'I don't know what to think, what you think, feel, what she said, how can you be so –'

'Don't ever –' He braked gently, avoiding even the most natural jerk on that bumpy road. 'It's over,' he said, his eyes an opaque black, 'so let it rest. You can't possibly know everything,

260

even think you can know everything. Just let it rest. You have no idea –'

'No,' she said, 'I have no idea.' She heard the stormy hiss of the rising tide in the distance, Dakhin climbing over the bank, pulling the land in with one shining swoop.

'You and I can only run away, and hope to give that something the slip,' he said, changing gear.

Red dust followed them out of the village, together with running children, Ta-ta Shailen-doctor, come back soon. Nisha closed her eyes as they passed the spot where the helicopter had landed. Ramu and Kanu had stood there, hunched, shaking, staring at each other, desperate with rage and fear. Ramu and Kanu, sentenced to live, holding the secret of their life and death in their frozen hands.

Dakhin roared under the bridge ten miles east, louder, the waters churning violently. The bridge rocked from side to side, up and down under the speeding jeep. The south wind was piling the waves higher and higher till Dakhin rose and swept across the bridge. In the rear-view mirror, Nisha and Shailen saw a gigantic copper and silver wing of water leap up and shatter into a million glittering eyes.